THREE PLOTS *for* ASEY MAYO

THREE PLOTS
for ASEY MAYO

Phoebe Atwood Taylor

New York
W · W · NORTON & COMPANY · INC ·

Copyright, 1939, 1941, 1942, by
PHOEBE ATWOOD TAYLOR

FOR

HILDUR

CONTENTS

THE HEADACRE PLOT——11

THE WANDER BIRD PLOT——105

THE SWAN BOAT PLOT——209

THE HEADACRE PLOT

THE
HEADACRE PLOT

O VERHEAD, a hot sun beat down on the high
September tide creeping in from Cape Cod
Bay to cover the marshes at the foot of Asey
Mayo's orchard. It beat down, too, on the bare head
of the man in the crumpled green cotton suit, creeping his stealthy, persistent way through the orchard
toward the driveway where Asey Mayo stood.

For ten minutes the man had been edging toward
Asey, and for seven of those minutes Asey had been
watching him, covertly following his movements as
they were reflected in the side and rearview mirrors
and against the brightly burnished chromium body
of the sleek Porter roadster he was pretending so
earnestly to clean.

At his first half-glimpse of the figure sneaking into
his orchard, Asey grinned and took for granted that
Sam Howe, the editor of the local paper, was about
to indulge in his favorite pastime of popping out like

a jack-in-the-box from behind a bush and yelling at
the top of his lungs, "How's the Homespun Sleuth
today? How's the old Codfish Sherlock? Didn't even
spot me creeping up on you, did you, Eagle-eye?"
Like some others who had known Asey over a period
of years, Sam found it both amazing and amusing
that Asey, the Porter family's former handy man and
yacht captain, should turn out to be a well-known
detective and a director of Porter Motors to boot.

When a second glimpse revealed that the figure belonged, not to Sam, but to a tall, black-haired stranger, Asey shrugged and dismissed him as another
tourist camera fan snatching distance shots of him. If
the fellow ran true to form, he would presently march
up and ask him to put on his yachting cap and old
canvas duck coat, grip his old-fashioned Army Colt,
and assume a typical gravure pose beside the Porter
Sixteen.

It was his third view of the stranger which caused
Asey to whistle softly and, while he continued to dust
away at the roadster, to watch closely the man's reflected movements. He might be a tourist, Asey
thought, but he wasn't any camera fan, for his hands
were empty and his shoulders bare of camera straps.

Asey stifled his impulse to call out. Better to wait
and see what was on this fellow's mind, he thought,

than to shout out and perhaps scare him into dashing away. The fact of his being stalked didn't disturb him unduly, as long as the stalker was as unarmed as this one appeared to be. On the other hand, Asey admitted to himself that there was something faintly sinister about all this sneaking and slinking from tree to tree. He didn't like it.

A blurred flash of the man's face on the car hood showed that he was near, now. In another minute he would have crept up by the old quince tree. At that point Asey intended to whirl around, collar him, and demand some explanations.

Giving a final whisk to a door handle, Asey regarded it while he mentally counted sixty, and then he swung around. "You—"

He stopped short. The fellow wasn't lurking behind the quince tree, or anywhere near it. He was nowhere to be seen.

"Want to play hide an' seek, huh?" Asey squared his shoulders and started down the orchard path. "Okay, I'll humor you! An' I'll also teach you to slink around my orchard!"

He was frowning when he returned, some fifteen minutes later, from his unsuccessful search. The fellow wasn't hiding in the grass, he wasn't perched up on any branches, he wasn't lying low down on the shore. If someone had draped him with a magic cloak he couldn't have vanished more completely. Why in time, Asey asked himself, had the fellow spent ten minutes sneaking up toward him, only to melt away into thin air?

A muttered exclamation escaped his lips as he reached the driveway. Parked beside his roadster was a tan convertible coupé. And beyond, on his own back doorstep, sat the fellow in the green cotton suit!

He was taller and huskier than Asey had thought at first, and younger, not more than twenty-three or four. Asey's inquiring glance took in such details as his expensive white buckskin sports shoes and a chronograph wrist watch as the fellow took off his dark glasses and walked across the lawn toward him.

"Asey Mayo?" The smile that showed his even, white teeth was tense and forced. "I thought I recognized you from your pictures. Mr. Mayo, I need your help. A most peculiar thing's just happened to me."

"You don't say, now!" Asey's Cape Cod drawl had a purring note which would have warned anyone who knew him that Asey was in no mood to be trifled with. "A peculiar thing just happened to me, too!"

"I—I've lost my wife!" The young man folded his dark glasses, and then nervously unfolded them and put them on. "She's disappeared!"

"Which?" Asey inquired quizzically. "You mean, you put her somewheres an' now you can't find her, like a collar button, or did she dissolve in a puff of smoke?"

"This isn't any joke!" The young man flushed. "My name's David Arlington. I've got to find Lora, and I don't know how to go about it myself—God knows what that crazy fool might have done. I told Lora his letter had all the earmarks of a plot, for all it sounded so friendly and forgiving! I begged her not to go, but she did, and now she's disappeared, and if that crazy fool—"

"Who is this crazy fool you keep referrin' to?" Asey interrupted.

"Lora's uncle, Colonel Tiberius Head," Arlington told him. "Of Headacre House, over in Weesit—d'you know him?"

"I've heard of him," Asey saw no reason to add that he had spent the previous day sailing with the Colonel. "I know he has a brother, Jules. Is your wife his daughter?"

"That brat Penny? Thank God, no! Lora's mother was a sister of the Colonel and that fat fool, Jules, and they were her guardians. They wanted her to marry one of the clique that runs their damned factory, and so, when she married me, they cut her off without a cent. Lora hasn't seen any of the Heads or had a thing to do with 'em for two years, till today. And now she's disap—"

"Why today?" Asey inquired.

"Because before we started on our vacation Lora got a letter from Colonel Ty, asking her to come see him some time this month, and today she chose to go. And if that crazy nut—"

"Why do you keep callin' him crazy?" Asey wanted to know. It was his own impression that Colonel Head, the retired president of the Head Lathe & Grinding Company, was a pleasant, intelligent man whose only fault was a tendency to talk your ear off.

"Why, he *is* crazy!" Arlington said. "Didn't you ever see Headacre House, littered with all that crazy stuff of his? I ask you, would a sane person collect flying horses and wooden Indians, and wooden figure-heads and wooden statues and then stick 'em by the hundreds all over his lawn and grounds? The man's mad. Mad as a hatter. And so was I, to let Lora go there. . . . Mr. Mayo, instead of asking me any more questions, will you take my word that my wife's disappeared, and help me find her?"

"I can't very well help you," Asey said, "till I understand what's gone on. An' there's a point I'd like explained, Mr. Arlington, before—"

"Look here," Arlington said impatiently, "this morning I drove Lora to Headacre House to see the Colonel, and left her there. Half an hour later I went to get her, as we'd agreed. When she didn't come out I drove around some more. Then I went back and blew the horn. Still she didn't come. Then I went to the village and phoned the house, but nobody answered!"

Asey asked, "Why were you so elaborate about things? Whyn't you just ring the front door bell in the first place?"

"I'm not welcome at the Colonel's," Arlington said shortly. "Anyway, I finally did go back and ring the bell, but nobody came! Nobody's there, but the garage is full of cars!"

"So?" Asey said, remembering the Colonel's crew of servants. "Wa-ell, don't you s'pose, Mr. Arlington, that your wife just drove off with the Colonel in someone else's car? I think you'll most likely find her across the fields at Jules's place. Now, I'd like to know why you—"

"She isn't at Jules's!" Arlington gave Asey no chance to mention the orchard stalking. "I phoned there, and no one knows a thing about her! If Lora'd changed her mind about leaving at ten-thirty, she'd have come out to the car and said so. And there's something else. Come here! I'll show you!" With the air of a man about to play the ace of trumps, he strode over toward his car.

Asey, as he strolled after him, tried to figure out what in the world this husky lad was up to. He was nervous and tense, but, as far as sentiment or anguish was concerned, Arlington might as well have lost an old necktie instead of his wife. Only the drawing of Colonel Head into the picture made Asey feel that someone was not trying to play an involved and not very funny practical joke.

He tried to focus his thoughts on the day before. In the course of their sail the Colonel had touched on practically every subject under the sun. But there was one special thing he'd mentioned that had to do with all this. Asey tilted his yachting cap back on his head and tried to recall what it was.

Then Arlington stepped on the running board and leaned over the coupé's door, and the swift movement revealed something that brought Asey back from his consideration of the Colonel's sailing monologue with what amounted to a thud. Protruding from Arlington's trouser pocket, previously concealed by his coat, was the handle of a revolver!

"Here!" Arlington turned around and held out

a small, damp bundle of blue linen. "Look! It's Lora's skirt, the skirt she was wearing! All stained purple and green. I found it on the Headacre House lawn! Now d'you see why I need your help?"

Asey fingered the linen reflectively, glanced at the blotched stains, and wondered why the skirt hadn't been displayed to him at once as Exhibit A.

"I don't know what's happened," Arlington went on, "but I can't find Lora where she ought to be, and something *has* happened over at Headacre House! You've got to admit it!"

"S'pose," Asey said with crispness, "we take my car an' look into things there!"

Asey swung the Porter Sixteen past the gates of Headacre House a few minutes later.

"What're you going to do first?" Arlington asked. "Search the house?"

"Blow the horn." Asey put his thumb on it.

"I told you," Arlington said impatiently, after Asey finally removed his thumb, "the place is deserted! Except for those crazy flying horses and the rest of the Head collection of woodiana. *Now* what?"

"Did you walk through the rose garden," Asey pointed, "over that hill to the swimming pool? Did you look for 'em there? Then come along," he added, as Arlington shook his head. "I think that's where we'll get a few explanations, an' I think that's where you'll find your wife an' Colonel Ty."

But it was Asey, hurrying on ahead, who found the Colonel on the rose garden path, with a bullet between his eyes.

Asey looked down at the still, crumpled figure, and bit his lip.

Automatically he noted the absence of a weapon, and the presence of marks in the path which indicated that the body had been dragged there from some other spot.

In something less than a split second, Asey told himself, Mr. David Arlington was going to be relieved of his gun. Mr. Arlington was going to come clean on his part in this hideous, brutal business.

Asey turned around slowly, poised to jump. Then he relaxed.

Young Mr. Arlington was not coming along the path directly behind him. Either he had stopped by the way, or once again the fellow had put on one of his quick-exit acts.

Asey walked swiftly to the path's first turn, and then he paused.

Arlington was standing by an arbor, waving reassuringly to someone in the woods on the hill. Then his arm was flung out in a warning gesture that said, as plainly as any words, "Keep away!"

Asey jumped up on a bench just in time to see the figure of a girl, swathed in what appeared to be an oversized robe of vivid crimson, as she disappeared among the pines.

"Bird in hand!" Asey muttered to himself, and was making for Arlington as footsteps sounded on the gravel, and the stocky form of Jules Head appeared.

At the sight of David Arlington, the smile vanished from Jules's face as if it had been wiped off, and his fists clenched stiffly against the pockets of his blue flannel coat. "You!" Jules's little mustache almost bristled as he spat the word out. "What're you doing here?"

"I brought him," Asey said before Arlington could answer. "Mr. Head, do you really know this fellow? Is he your niece Lora's husband?"

"Yes," Jules was breathing heavily. "I can only assume you don't know, Mayo, that he's not welcome here. And the sooner you take him away, the better. If you'll come back later, alone, I'll be glad to explain. . . . Arlington, get out before Ty sees you!"

"I won't!" Arlington retorted. "I shan't leave till I find Lora! Where is she? What've you people done with her?"

"Lora?" Jules sounded incredulous. "I haven't seen her!"

"You have, too!" Arlington took a step forward. "What kind of a plot have you and the Colonel been cooking up, anyway?"

"Just a minute," Asey interposed, "before either of you goes any farther. Come along down the path, please. Here."

The tears ran down Jules's cheeks as he knelt beside his brother. Arlington, after an almost perfunctory glance at the still figure, involuntarily jerked his head in the direction of the pine woods. When he looked back a mask seemed to have settled over his face.

"Mayo," Jules said brokenly, "is—is there any use, any hope in my calling a doctor?"

" 'Fraid not," Asey said. "I don't think a doctor could've helped much if he'd been here when that shot was fired. But I wish you'd phone Doc Cummings, anyway. He's medical examiner. An' call Lieutenant Hanson, of the state police. Or ask Cummings to get him."

"I know Hanson. And when he comes I'll tell him

a few things about you, Arlington! *You* killed Ty!"
Jules turned on his heel and started back to the house
before Arlington could reply.

"Now," Asey said casually, "face around an' look
at that sundial."

"What for? Hey, what're you doing?"

"Friskin' you," Asey told him. "Where's that gun?
What you done with your gun?"

"What gun? What're you talking about? I haven't
any gun! See here, Mayo," Arlington said irately,
"I'm not going to stand here and let you frisk me,
and let Jules accuse me of murder! Who's Jules to do
any accusing? What was *he* doing, walking down this
path, anyway? Where was *he* going? What was *he*
after? I didn't hear any car drive up to the house!
Was he *in* the house when we came? Why not frisk
Jules instead of—"

"See that bench?" Asey interrupted. "Go sit on
it. Shush! I want to think!"

"But—"

In a sharper voice Asey repeated the order, and
Arlington sullenly obeyed.

Asey watched him thoughtfully for a moment, then
he turned and looked down once again at the Colonel. The bullet which had killed him had not come
from a small-caliber weapon, like a twenty-two. That

was obvious. And the shape of the gun in Arlington's pocket didn't indicate that it was any small-caliber weapon, either. And there *had* been a gun in the fellow's pocket.

Out of the corner of his eye Asey watched Arlington squirm around on the marble bench, trying to peer through the bushes. The fellow was crazy to get to the girl in red, who would turn out to be Lora, Asey thought, unless he was vastly mistaken. Asey wanted to get to her, himself, before she had any chance to talk with Arlington. But there was no sense in his letting on that he knew of her presence, and, besides, the girl was stuck there. She couldn't get away. So, for the time being, she would keep.

There was no question in Asey's mind but what the body had been moved. In addition to the marks in the gravel, there were grass stains on the Colonel's gray flannels and small shreds of clover adhering to his gray tweed coat.

Carefully, Asey walked around and squinted at the grass. He had been killed, Asey tentatively decided, about twenty feet from the path in a little alcovelike semicircle formed by a tall privet hedge. That almost had to be the place where the murder was committed, because the gravel marks proved that the body had been dragged from that direction, and it wasn't likely that the body had been dragged through that hedge. So, somewhere inside that semi-circle, the Colonel had met his death.

There were no bird baths or sundials or arbors in the little enclosure, and the only reason for the hedge, as far as Asey could see, was its value as a backdrop in displaying some of what Arlington had called the Colonel's collection of woodiana. Crammed into the space were two old flying horses, old merry-go-round horses, mounted on wheeled pedestals, and beside them stood a life-size wooden man with a derby hat and Dundreary whiskers, and a dozen cigars gripped stiffly in his wooden fist. Next to him was a small, sedate wooden pony with a raised forepaw, a flowing mane of real horsehair, and a worn and cracked leather saddle. Asey grinned as he looked at it, remembering the almost identical pony that had stood for years outside the old Weesit Hardware and Harness store.

Beyond the pony was a huge wooden eagle whose smooth, upraised wings towered over Asey's head. Lacking a stand, the eagle was braced with soapboxes and stakes. And on the grass before it lay an open kit of tools and an assortment of cleats and wire and pulleys.

"I wonder!" Asey murmured.

Suppose that the Colonel had been alone here in the enclosure, tinkering around to make a stand for the eagle. Suppose he'd heard a noise, and looked up, only to get that bullet between the eyes. The hedge would make a fine screen for someone to hide behind. Standing on the other side of that hedge, someone could have called out, and fired as the Colonel lifted his head.

Something like that must have happened, Asey felt. The Colonel was quick and alert. He never would've given someone like Arlington, or anyone else he didn't like or trust, any chance to take careful aim and shoot him squarely between the eyes. The Colonel must have been shot before he had the slightest inkling of any danger.

But there was, of course, always the alternative, the horrid possibility that someone well known to and trusted by the Colonel had suddenly whipped out a gun and fired point-blank at him.

"I wish," Asey said to the figure with the derby, "you could talk! I wish one of you hosses could point a paw at someone!" He sighed.

Asey walked back to the path as he heard Jules return.

"I got Doc Cummings," Jules said. "And Hanson, too. They were both at the doctor's office, and they're on their way here now. . . . Arlington, I know Lora isn't here! She's visiting the Slades in Falmouth!"

"She is not! She—say, how d'you happen to know anything about the Slades?" Arlington demanded.

"Do you suppose"—the ends of Jules's mustache turned up in a bitter smile—"that we haven't kept an eye on you both for the last two years? Do you think we'd let Lora go out of our lives and never think of her again? Certainly not!"

"So you've spied on us!" Arlington said angrily. "Well, your Pinkertons are all wet! The Slade plans fell through! I brought Lora here this morning. Ty wrote and asked her to come!"

"He never told me so!" Jules said.

"I've got his letter to prove it. Now, where—?"

"Will you two"—Asey stepped between them— "stop glarin' an' go sit on that bench? I don't think this's the time or the place for any in-law battlin'. Save it for Hanson!"

He made another circuit of the alcovelike enclosure and was starting around to the other side of the hedge when Jules walked over to him.

"I can't sit here another minute! Mayo, I phoned for Ty's servants to come back. My daughter Penny borrowed 'em for this Bundles for Britain bazaar over in Tonset. She took Ty's because we were having a dinner party tonight at my house. That's why I walked over here just now. Penny'd commandeered all our cars, and I intended to drive Ty to the bazaar in one of his. Mayo"— Jules's voice broke— "You've no idea what this means to me! I—I can't seem to think! I can't seem to grasp it! I almost feel I don't know what I'm doing or saying!"

Asey nodded.

"Mayo," Jules went on, "if Lora really *is* here, I know she didn't have anything to do with this. I wouldn't believe a word Dave Arlington said, though. Not a word! The fellow's a wastrel. He married Lora for her money. We were all against the marriage, and we frankly did all we could to stop it, and I wish we had!"

"You think the Colonel wrote her to come here?" Asey asked.

Jules pursed his lips and nodded. "Possibly. You see, we withheld her money, after her marriage, hoping she'd realize her error as soon as possible. But lately Ty changed his mind about Arlington, because he was apparently doing well at the brokerage house where he works. Ty may have wanted to talk with Lora before consulting me about her money. I don't know. Only, if she was here, where is she now?"

"A car's stopped at the house," Arlington said

as he came up behind them. "Did you hear it?"

As he finished speaking, Dr. Cummings, carrying his inevitable little black bag, bustled down the path. He was followed by Lieutenant Hanson, of the state police. Asey took them aside, succinctly summed up what had happened, and added his own theories about where the shooting had taken place.

"So, there's your story," he concluded. "Now, have you got some of your men comin', Hanson? . . . Good. Have 'em watch Arlington. If his wife turns up, don't give 'em a chance to talk alone. An' don't leave him an' Jules Head together. They'll most likely black each other's eyes if they get goin'. I'll be back in a few minutes."

Hanson hooked his thumbs into the leather belt of his blue uniform coat. "Where are you going? I want you here, Asey! There's lots of things I don't get!"

"You know all I know," Asey told him. "I won't be long. I got a little errand." A few minutes later, his roadster flashed out from the driveway and along the shore road.

About a mile and a half beyond Headacre House, Asey swung the car onto a narrow, rutted lane, and started to circle back in the direction from which he'd come. When the chimneys of Headacre House were at last visible, he parked the car by a clump of bayberry bushes, got out, and continued on foot along the sandy lane. Then he left the lane, skirted a swamp hollow, and walked through the scrub pines until he reached the hill directly across from the Colonel's.

From one point, where the trees had been thinned and the underbrush cleaned out, he caught a clear view of the rose garden and the terrace, and he stood and watched while Hanson and some of his men carried a stretcher up to the house. He could see Dr. Cummings, looking shorter and fatter than ever as he bustled along the path beside Arlington, who towered over him.

Things, Asey thought, seemed to be proceeding as they should. And he was glad, now that he had an opportunity of surveying the landscape from this angle, that he'd chosen such a circuitous route to locate the girl in red. No matter what pains he might have taken to sneak to these woods directly from the house, someone standing on the hill would have seen him coming, and acted accordingly.

Quietly, Asey set out over the thick carpet of pine needles.

Within a hundred yards he found her, a slim, dark-haired girl swathed in a crimson flannel robe, stretched out flat on her face beside the stump of an old pine tree.

Asey looked down at her. "All right," he said. "That's a becomin' pose. Make a nice magazine cover if only your face was showin'. Get up, if you please!"

The girl didn't move.

"Come, come!" Asey said wearily. "I know this routine. I met up with it before. Pretty soon you'll wiggle one foot, an' then the other, an' then you'll blink, an' scream, an' say, 'Where *am* I?' an' 'How long have I *been* here?' Let's skip it. Get up!"

The girl still didn't move.

"Get up!" Asey spoke in his quarter-deck voice. "Or—"

He bent over her for a moment, and then slowly straightened up. The startling, unbelievable truth of this situation was that the girl actually had been knocked out! There was a large lump on her temple to prove it!

Asey leaned back against a tree and tilted his yachting cap back on his head. He would wait a bit and hope that the girl would come to.

Her left foot, encased in a blue sandal, gave a little wiggle just as he was on the point of walking over and picking her up. Then the other foot moved, and a shudder ran through the girl's body. She sat up suddenly, blinked, and, with a thoroughly feminine gesture, clutched the voluminous red robe and drew it around her as she became aware of Asey. "Where," she demanded in a shaky voice, *"am* I?"

"In Colonel Head's pines." Asey couldn't keep a note of suspicion out of his voice. "Where'd you think?"

The girl sat up a little straighter and propped herself on one hand. Her eyes were red-rimmed and her cheeks a little swollen from crying, and she was clearly making a tremendous effort to hold back more tears. "How long have I been here, Mr. Mayo? You see, I recognize you!"

Asey shook his head. "I wouldn't know. Mrs. Arlington, the plan had its points, but it didn't work." He threw out the last sentence as a feeler, and its results rather surprised him.

"It was Dave's idea, not mine. And I should think, myself"—Lora looked at him appraisingly—"that Dave would've guessed he couldn't get away with it, when he made his preliminary survey of you. Didn't he get any chance to look you over before he spoke with you? He intended to."

Asey sat down beside her and drew out his pipe.

"So!" he said. "So that's what that orchard stalkin' was. A preliminary survey of *me*. Huh! Mrs. Arlington, will you tell me just what's gone on, anyway?"

She smiled a wan little smile. "I wanted to make a clean breast at the start. Only, Dave thought— Did Dave tell you about Uncle Ty's letter? Then you know why I came. Dave brought me, and I rang the bell, and Ty opened the door— D'you know about Dave and Ty?"

"Some. Not all."

Lora drew a long breath. "They just didn't get along," she said. "Uncle Ty claimed Dave was no good because his father was no good and said he was a no-account wastrel. And Dave did have trouble getting started. I admit that. Only—well, to make a long story short, it was one of those misunderstandings that never would have existed if people had said or done things a little differently. Because—" She paused, and Asey could see the tips of her nails digging into the palms of her hands. "Because I loved them both very much," Lora went on, "it—it was hard for me. It was hard this morning. I knew Dave didn't want me to come here. But I wanted so to see Ty again. I've missed him terribly."

"Here." Asey held out a handkerchief as she groped in the pockets of the red robe.

"Thanks. I thought"—Lora wiped her eyes—"that I'd finally managed to pull myself together. It's been a hideous morning, Mr. Mayo! I was so fond of Ty!"

"I liked him myself," Asey told her, "though I only knew him this summer."

"If I'd known that"—Lora looked at him steadily —"I'd never have let Dave carry out this plan of his. Now I'm sure you'll understand and believe me."

"I'll try," Asey told her. "Now, tell me about things. What're you wearin' this red rig for? What happened to your skirt?"

Lora lighted a cigarette. "After Ty let me in he took my hands and said, 'Lora, I've done you and Dave a great wrong. I want to admit it right away. I want a long talk with you.' I can't remember his exact words from then on—I was so excited and glad to see him! I'd dreamed for two years that something like that would happen! We went into the library, both of us talking a streak at once—and then that ink!"

"What ink?"

"Oh, three beastly bottles of it!" Lora said. "Black and green and purple. You see, Ty'd been working on his catalogue of wooden figures, and so the ink was there, uncapped, on his desk. When I reached out for a cigarette as I went by, my bracelet caught in the purple, and over the bottle went! And Ty grabbed the catalogue to save it, and he knocked over the green. And then, when I tried to right the bottles, the desk blotter and everything on it slid onto my lap. You never saw such a mess! There wasn't anything for me to do but retire to the bathroom and wash out my skirt and get to work on my hands with pumice soap. See"—she showed him her hands— "I didn't begin to get my nails clean!"

"Uh-huh," Asey said. " I see. But what happened? What did the Colonel do while you was tidyin' up?"

"He asked if he could help, and I said I didn't see how, and then he asked if I'd be very long, and I said, 'Probably hours. Fifteen minutes, anyway.' He laughed and said if I didn't mind being left alone with my labors for a couple of minutes, he was going to pop out to the garden and bring in some papers before they blew away. Well—" Lora paused. "Well, when I finally found Ty out in the garden, about twenty minutes later, he was dead."

"An' you didn't hear the shot?"

Lora shook her head. "No. The water was running, and I was scrambling around so to get cleaned up. Dave says I was mad to do what I did next, and I suppose I was. But my only reaction, my only impulse was to take Ty into the house at once."

"You mean, it was you who moved him?" Asey asked. "Why?"

"I don't know why!" Lora said helplessly. "I just had this overpowering feeling that I should—I wonder if I can make you understand how I felt? It's silly to say it was a shock to me. It was more than a shock. I couldn't feel—I didn't even cry till later. I couldn't. I couldn't think. I'm sure I didn't grasp the fact that he was really dead! When I got him as far as the path, it occurred to me that the shot'd been fired from here in the woods—"

"What made you think so?" Asey interrupted. "An' tell me, how was he lyin'?"

"On his back. I'll show you how, and the place, too, when we get back. Anyway, I looked toward the woods, and I thought I saw someone. So I rushed over, with this robe of Ty's nearly tripping me at every step, and then someone hit me. That's what happened. That's all I know!"

"Who was it?" Asey asked.

"Who biffed me? I don't know. I remember seeing a face peering down at me afterward. A blurred face, without any features. And wavy blond hair."

"You're sure," Asey said quizzically, "it was wavy?"

"I know it was. And, even if I didn't see the face, I'd know that hair again if I met it ten years from now in a black-out."

"Huh." Unlike her husband, Asey thought, this

girl wasn't putting on any act. "Huh. How long do
you figger you was unconscious?"

"I haven't any idea. When I did come to, I heard
a car horn blowing and recognized it as ours. Somehow, I staggered over to the house, but, by the time
I got there, Dave was gone."

"Then what?"

"All of a sudden," Lora said, "my knees just gave
way. For the first time, I began to be frightened. I
was terrified! I heard the phone ring in the house
while I was sitting there, and I yearned to rush in
and answer and beg someone to come quickly and
bring Dave. But I was so weak and trembly that
my feet wouldn't budge. I just sat and shivered till
Dave finally came back."

"I see," Asey said thoughtfully. "Then, figgerin'
you was in a kind of tough spot, or anyways that
you most likely would be when the cops got goin',
Dave thought out this plan of easin' me into this
situation by a different route, as you might say."

"I suggested Dave's going for you after he pointed
out the position I was in," Lora said. "I hadn't
thought of you, or it, before. Then Dave wondered
if he couldn't wangle you here on the pretext of
locating me. He planned to try and size you up first,
and then show you my skirt. He thought if he could

get you worked up about finding me, maybe your
first impression of the case would be more sympa-
thetic toward me. You know, enlisting your aid in
finding a lost wife is lots different from telling you
that the same wife was present at Colonel Head's
murder, but knows nothing about it."

"Uh-huh. I s'pose," Asey said, "after allowin' me
to find the Colonel, we was to have a brisk hunt
for you, an' finally find you stretched out in the
woods, your mind being a blank. I see. Wasn't you
pretty brave to wait here all alone, after bein'
knocked out?"

"I didn't want to, much," Lora said, "but Dave
thought it was the best thing to do. I waited over
by the clearing, and, to tell you the truth, I was
scared stiff! Then I saw you, and Dave waved, and
then I started back to get into position to be found.
I was going to lie down and pretend I'd been out
all this time. Then," she added, "to show you how
things work out, I stumbled over this robe and
really *did* knock myself out. My head hit this stump.
See the mark? The other lump on my temple is
where the blond biffed me. It still throbs like fury,
too."

"Why," Asey asked with disarming casualness,
"does your husband carry a gun?"

"Carry a gun? He doesn't!"

"Oh, but he does. He was carryin' a large one in his hip pocket when he came to get me. I seen it. An'—"

"Wait!" Lora said. "Did it have a black handle? . . . Well, that wasn't a real gun! It came from the dime store! It's one of those that makes a crackling noise when you press the trigger. You see, Dave's been away on selling trips, and I hated staying alone in the apartment and Dave bought me that gun as a joke, so I'd feel protected. And I stuck it in the car when we started our vacation. It's just one of those silly items that's hilariously funny to us, and stupid to anyone else."

"So," Asey said, and wondered, if the gun were a toy, why Arlington should have got rid of it, and denied having it.

"Mr. Mayo, you don't really believe all I've told you, do you?"

"Wa-ell," Asey drawled. "Wa-ell—"

"I know you don't! I can tell you don't! It's just what Dave predicted," Lora said. "He told me, no matter how fair anyone tried to be, it was a whale of a story to ask anyone to swallow in one piece. But every word I've told you is true!"

"Uh-huh," Asey said. "Only, there's a couple of

little flaws, Mrs. Arlington, that kind of bother me.
Tell me again, now. What did the Colonel say he
was goin' to do while you washed up your skirt an'
cleaned off the ink spots?"

"He said he was going to pop out to the garden
and get some important papers he'd left there. He
was afraid they'd blow away in the wind."

"That's what I thought you said. But did it occur to you," Asey asked gently, "that there wasn't
a whiff of wind this mornin' around ten an' ten-
thirty?"

Lora looked at him with wide-open eyes. "Why,
that's right!" she said slowly. "And—why, there
wasn't a single paper near him, or anywhere else
I looked before I found him! Why, that means someone—"

"Lower your voice a mite," Asey said, "an' keep
on talkin', an' don't turn around. Say anythin' that
comes to your head, but keep talkin'. An' don't
yell out when I say that I hear someone sneakin'
up on us from the road yonder."

Lora moistened her lips, and the fingers of the
hand she was leaning on dug deep down into the
pine needles. "All those wooden horses of Ty's—"
Her voice quavered a little. "Look; I simply can't
prattle on! Who is it? Can you see?"

"Not yet," Asey said, "but someone's gettin'

nearer. The instant I get a glimpse, I'll go after him."

"You mean, you're going to *shoot* him?"

Asey grinned. "I haven't a gun, an', besides, you can't go pottin' away reckless at people. They might turn out to be some innocent soul that's lost his way, or even some neighbor takin' a short cut. I'll just make a dash for him."

Lora seemed appalled by his nonchalance. "But suppose," she protested, "he shoots *you?*"

"A body'd be mighty dumb to shoot me," Asey said, "because the sound of a shot'd bring out Hanson an' his boys— Hey, he's retreatin'!"

Before Lora realized what was happening, Asey had leaped up and disappeared out of sight beyond the trees. But, quick as he had been, the person retreating was even quicker. No matter how Asey lengthened his stride or how fast he ran, those fleet footsteps remained always ahead of him.

Then, suddenly, the footsteps stopped. Asey slowed down. It was just possible that the person had taken cover and was waiting for him. Laying for him, perhaps.

Asey stopped. Considering the amazing accuracy of the shot which had killed Colonel Head, caution was indicated.

Gliding over the pine needles, Asey made for the

tallest tree in his immediate vicinity, and shinnied up it with the catlike agility of a sailor going aloft. Several minutes passed before his ear again picked up the faint scrunch of footsteps, and then, through the bushes ahead and to his left, he saw the person approaching.

It was a girl. A girl, furthermore, with a shock of blond hair!

Asey leaned forward precariously and strained his eyes to see her face, but she turned suddenly and crouched down beside a clump of low scrub-oak bushes.

Asey slid down the tree. A few moments later he was behind her, and his right hand was gripping both her wrists in an iron grip.

The girl screamed as she turned around, and Asey drew in his breath sharply. He recognized her. She was Jules Head's daughter, Penny, the one Arlington had referred to as a brat. And, if Asey was any judge of expressions, she had made up her mind to act like a brat right now.

"Let me go!"

"Uh-huh." Asey's left hand burrowed into the dirt and leaves, and groped at the object that the girl had been so industriously burying.

"I—I'll scream!"

"Scream away," Asey told her calmly, and brought to light a pearl-handled, silver-plated forty-five Colt revolver.

Still maintaining his rigid grip on her wrists, Asey held up the revolver and read the words engraved on the backstrap: " 'Presented to Jules Head by the Southfield Pistol Club.' Huh!" Asey let go of the girl's wrists. "Now, I wonder just why would you be interrin' this, Miss Penny Head? I wonder if maybe perhaps—"

Pulling back the catch, Asey swung out the cylinder of the revolver, tipped the muzzle of the gun up, and ejected the cartridges into his hand. Five were loaded, and one had been fired. Recently, too, Asey guessed, as he sniffed at the empty case.

"Miss Head"—he spoke sharply—"you can start explainin', right now!"

The girl's lips clamped shut.

"P'raps you didn't understand," Asey said. "I never asked you to imitate a baby refusin' his gruel. I said, *explain!*"

Penny continued to pout defiantly at a bayberry bush.

"Very well!" Taking her by the elbow of her soft white polo coat, Asey turned her around so she faced in the direction of Headacre House. "If you

prefer bein' given a third-degree grillin' by Lieutenant Hanson, march along an' get it!"

Her only retort to his threat was a shrug that
seemed to dismiss all police, including Hanson, as
something beneath her notice.

" 'Course," Asey said, "I really know why you're
up to such silly business. When your father phoned
you to send the Colonel's servants back to Headacre House, he told you the Colonel'd been shot,
an' ordered you to get his own gun an' bury it quick.
That's the story, ain't it?"

Penny just looked bored and pretended not to
hear him.

"Okay," Asey said. "Suit yourself. . . . Nope, we
won't cut over to the house here. We'll pick up
your cousin Lora first."

"Lora?" Penny turned to him quickly. "Is she
here? Where? Is—? Oh, I see her! . . . Lora! Lora!"

The two girls dashed toward each other, flung
themselves into each other's arms, and simultaneously
burst into tears.

After patiently waiting until they gave some indication of returning to normal, Asey spoke to Lora:
"Mrs. Arlington, maybe I ought to take back my
harsh thoughts about that wavy blond hair you
spoke of seein'."

"What? Oh, you don't think for a second it was Penny I saw!" Lora said.

"Wasn't it?" Asey asked innocently, in a voice that purred.

"Don't be dull! It was a *man* I saw. And, besides, Penny's hair isn't wavy. It's curly."

"Uh-huh," Asey said. "But she seems to have been the person who was sneakin' up on us just now, an' when I found her, she was occupyin' herself in a way I can only sort of charitably call suspicious. She was buryin' a gun."

"Oh, Penny, you weren't!" Lora said.

"She was." Asey watched Penny's face out of the corner of his eye. "An', furthermore, the gun belonged to her father, an' it'd been fired once, not so very long ago."

"Penny, how awful! I never," Lora said hysterically, "dreamed there could be such a hideous, ghastly day!"

She was referring, Asey felt sure, to the day as a whole. But Penny was taking her commentary as a deadly personal insult. She was already beginning to pout.

"Horrible!" Lora continued. "And did you know, Penny, *I* was actually in the house while Ty was being shot, and I don't know how it happened, or who did it?"

"Oh, don't you?" Penny pushed her blond curls back from her forehead and glared at Lora. "Was Dave there with you, not knowing about it, too?"

"Penny, are you insinuating—?"

"If trying to get rid of Dad's gun is hideous, I certainly think your actually being in the house when Ty was shot is a whole lot worse!" Penny told her angrily. "And what were you doing there, anyway?"

"I came to see Ty!" Lora said. "He—"

"The *last* time you came to see Ty," Penny interrupted, "Dave *almost* practically killed him! And, this time, I suppose Dave *really*—"

Penny took a step forward, and Asey grabbed her hand just a split second before the palm struck against Lora's mouth. "Before you two start any hair-pullin'," Asey said, "we'll chat with Hanson. Come on!"

Hanson, whom they met in the hall outside the library, instantly pointed to the gun in Asey's hand, and demanded to know whose it was and where Asey had found it.

Asey handed it to him. "An' here"—he fumbled in his pocket—"is the cartridges that was in it. For further information, ask Miss Head. This's Mrs. Arlington, Hanson, an' this's Miss—"

"I know Miss Head," Hanson said briefly, and whistled as he scanned the engraving on the gun's backstrap. "Asey, you sure manage to get to the root of things! This was all I needed to nab Jules Head."

"Don't be utterly idiotic!" Penny told him. "Dad never had a thing to do with Ty's being shot. I can prove it!"

"Yeah?" Hanson looked at her. "Same way you proved you weren't going eighty-nine miles an hour last week, huh?"

Hanson turned to Asey. "I got to wondering about Jules Head right away," he said, with pride. "Right off the bat, he buttonholed me—see?—and started giving me all this information I never asked for, and didn't care a whoop for, anyway. Then he tossed in a lot about how Arlington nearly murdered the Colonel once, and what a crook Arlington was, and stuff like that. I knew right then he was lying his head off!"

"How so?" Asey inquired.

"Why, say, I *know* Arlington! That is," Hanson amended, "I never met him till now, but I know all about him. He coaches our main barracks football team. Used to be an All-American end, you know. Arlington's okay!"

"I see." Knowing Hanson, Asey refrained from pointing out that a man could play end and still be capable of pulling a trigger. "I see. An' I suppose you got some evidence that Jules Head was here around ten-ten, say, or ten-fifteen this mornin'?"

Hanson nodded. "He left his own house on foot before ten, and came back around eleven-thirty. *He* claims he was taking a walk through the woods over to the shore, but no one saw him. He can't prove he wasn't here, or where he was."

"An' I suppose," Asey said, "you found some good motive for his possibly shootin' his brother, huh?"

"You bet!" Hanson sounded very pleased with himself. "This man Sewall got talking. He told me the motive. You can't find fault with me this trip and say I haven't got a motive! Sewall just tossed it in my lap!"

Asey wanted to know who Sewall was.

"He means Charles Sewall!" Penny answered before Hanson had a chance. "He's treasurer of the Head Company, and an old friend of Dad's and Ty's, and I *know* he never gave this idiot cop any motive for Dad's killing Ty! It's ridiculous!"

"I'll bring him in"—Hanson continued to ignore Penny—"and let him tell you, himself!"

"Charley Sewall," Penny informed Asey angrily, as Hanson left, "is spending the week end with us, and he's practically one of the family, and he *never* said anything against Dad, ever! That foul cop!"

Asey broke off as Hanson returned with a tall, scholarly looking man in tweeds.

"Mr. Sewall, this's Asey Mayo," Hanson said. "Now, tell him what you told me about Jules Head getting kicked out of the presidency of the Head Company, and the Colonel going back in his place."

"I wish"—Sewall sounded like a schoolteacher, Asey decided—"that I hadn't mentioned the matter, Lieutenant!"

"Why?" Hanson demanded. "Isn't it the truth?"

"In one sense, yes. But I want Mr. Mayo to have a complete picture of the situation. Jules, Ty, and I discussed the business last night, Mr. Mayo, and we came to the conclusion that the directors reached some time ago—namely, that with the tremendous increase in our output, Ty should return and take charge. Jules and I wanted him to when it became apparent that the country was going to re-arm in earnest. I don't know if you know what the Head Company—"

"They're machine tool makers," Asey said. "I know."

"Yes. The doctors first advised against Ty's return, but this week they reversed their decision. Now"— Sewall leaned forward—"I want to emphasize these points. Jules wanted Ty back. Jules had handled the company well. But he knows, as we all know, that he could never hope to match Ty's executive genius. Jules was not kicked out, as the lieutenant phrased it."

Hanson made a little exclamation of impatience. "When you boil that down," he said, "it's what *I* said! Jules is out; the Colonel's in! Whether he's kicked out or just stepping aside, he's out, just the same! *You* claim Jules likes it that way. *I* say, that's not human nature!"

"I cannot alter any conclusions you may choose to draw," Sewall said in his precise manner. "I wish only to make this clear: When I mentioned to you the fact that Ty's loss to the company at this critical time could only be considered a serious blow to us all, I meant just that!"

"Hanson," Asey spoke with sudden briskness as he got up from his chair, "will you check with Doc Cummings on the caliber of that bullet? Phone him. An' see if *you* can succeed where I failed"—he opened thc library door—"an' get Miss Head to tell you why she was buryin' that gun."

"Oh!" Hanson said. "So she was burying it for her father, was she? Come along, Miss Head!"

"I'll join you"—Asey stopped just short of shoving Hanson and Penny out of the library—"soon's I ask Mr. Sewall a couple of things."

The instant the door closed behind the pair, Asey darted across to the wide bay window that overlooked both the main road and a portion of the pine woods.

"What was it?" he asked Sewall. "What did Penny see? I been watchin' her in the fireplace mirror. All the time you was talkin', she was edgin' over here an' takin' little peeks outside—what was she lookin' an' waitin' for?"

"I rather think," Sewall said, "it was that scarlet automobile."

"Scarlet auto? You mean that red roadster that went whizzin' by?"

Sewall nodded. "That's Penny's new car, you know."

"Hers? Who was drivin' it, did you see?"

"No," Sewall said, "but I think I know who was at the wheel, and I think he is the man who shot Ty."

Asey stared at him. "Whyn't you tell Hanson if you thought you knew who killed the Colonel?"

"I didn't wish to tell the lieutenant in front of Jules. In fact," Sewall said, "after the totally erroneous conclusion he drew from my mentioning Ty's return to business, I didn't wish to confide in the lieutenant at all. I preferred to wait and tell some less impetuous and more reasonable individual, like yourself. I *do* think I know who killed Ty. I'm very sure that Penny knows, also."

Asey leaned back against a mahogany desk and tilted his yachting cap back on his head. "Huh!" he said. "It dawned on me just about the time I come into this room that maybe that young lady had been foxin' me with all her poutin'. It wasn't her that was sneakin' around in the woods, but somebody else, an' she deliberately let me catch sight of her so's the other person could get away. Golly, I'm an ole fool! Mr. Sewall, does this fellow have wavy blond hair?"

"How," Sewall asked in complete amazement, "did you deduce that?"

"Because," Asey said, with a grin, "Mrs. Arlington was so sure that someone with wavy blond hair knocked her out. Seems like it ought to've been the murderer who knocked her out, an' you said this feller was the murderer. 'Fraid it ain't even very spectacular guessin'. Mr. Sewall, who is this feller? What's the story on him?"

Sewall toyed with the little scarab that hung on his heavy gold watch chain. "I infer," he said, "that you know of Ty's dislike for David Arlington and for all the other young men who flocked about Lora. Ty was very fond of Lora, and he wanted her to have a husband he considered perfect. Jules, I regret to say, is the same way about Penny."

"I get it," Asey said. "The blond boy's one of Penny's beaux—but why should he kill the Colonel?"

Sewall sighed. "I hired this young man, myself. He's a brilliant engineer with broad experience in other countries, and just what we needed in the plant. In time, he met Penny, and at once Jules began to find fault with him. When we started to work on government orders Jules promptly dismissed Fritz."

"Fritz?" Asey raised his eyebrows.

"Fritz von Harburg. And he's as American as you or I, but he's spent most of his life abroad, which accounts for his slight accent. When we started in on government orders everyone in the company was thoroughly investigated. Not unnaturally, I think, in view of the type of work and the necessity for secrecy. The officials asked specifically about Fritz, and Jules used that as an excuse to dismiss him."

"Brought up the Fifth Column angle, huh?" Asey asked.

"Jules defended his action on those grounds, saying he couldn't afford to take chances. Which is, of course, true. But Jules also forbade Penny's seeing Fritz again. Er—I assume you know what happens when one crosses young love?"

"I can guess," Asey said dryly, "with an obstinate girl like Penny."

"Exactly," Sewall said. "Fritz spent this past summer as a counselor in a camp near Pochet. Jules didn't know, but Penny confided the fact to me in July. Fritz expected to get a new position this fall, and Penny said he'd given Ty's name as a reference instead of Jules's."

"With the Colonel's consent?" Asey asked.

"I assumed so. Now, I don't know whether Ty recommended him favorably or not, but I do know Fritz didn't get the new position. Quite by accident, I overheard Penny's phone conversation with him shortly after I arrived yesterday. I know she planned to leave this Bundles for Britain bazaar to meet Fritz in the woods between here and Jules's house this morning."

"So," Asey said. "D'you know when?"

"Penny said around eleven. Knowing Penny," Sewall said, "I'm sure she'd never arrive before half past. Knowing Fritz, I think he probably came early. Now, all this is conjecture, Mr. Mayo, but Fritz feels he's been badly treated by the Heads. If he missed getting this new position because Ty wouldn't recommend him—well, there's motive there. I can't say I'm positive Fritz shot Ty with that gun Penny had, but I'm positive Penny never used a gun in her life, and I'm positive that Jules would never do anything so foolish as to ask Penny to bury his gun."

"Huh," Asey said. "Now, I wonder if the reason Jules presented Hanson with so much miscellaneous information isn't maybe because Jules has this uneasy feelin' that maybe Fritz's involved. Maybe he's tryin' to shield an' protect Penny. An', for all we know, maybe Penny's tryin' to protect her father. Anyways, I think we'll look into this feller Fritz."

Walking over to the library table, he picked up the telephone. "That you, Annie?" he inquired of the operator. . . . "This's Asey. Say, you know the red roadster of the Head girl's? . . . Well, yell out to whoever's on duty at the Four Corners light to stop it an' hold the driver if they see it, will you? Pass the word along as far's the bridges, too. . . . What? Oh, have 'em bring the fellow to me at Headacre House. Thanks, Annie."

"Is that," Sewall asked curiously, as Asey replaced the receiver, "your customary method of picking up suspects?"

Asey grinned. "Wa-ell," he drawled, "Hanson prefers to send license an' motor numbers out over the teletype, all legal an' proper. But my way kind of gets goin' quicker, because Annie talks to everyone an' tells 'em, while only the cops see the teletype. I think I'm safe in sayin' that if Fritz's within a radius of fifty miles, I'll know it within ten minutes."

"Do you feel sure he was in the woods just now?" Sewall asked.

"Seems so. I think he was the one creepin' up on me an' Mrs. Arlington that I chased, an' I think he's the one that biffed her. Seems odd she didn't recognize him."

Sewall pointed out that Fritz appeared on the scene only after Lora married Dave. "Indeed," he added, "I doubt if Lora knows of Fritz's existence."

"I see," Asey said. "Well, I think while Fritz was runnin' away from Mrs. Arlington an' me, he run into Penny, an' they arranged in a hurry for Penny to distract me while Fritz eased himself out of the picture. I think he laid low in the woods till he was sure I was here in the house an' off his trail, an' then he got Penny's car from wherever she left it, an' departed."

"Wouldn't it help you a great deal to find out just what Penny was doing with that gun?" Sewall asked.

"Uh-huh," Asey said, "an' I suppose I could always ask her. Only, I don't think, right now, that I'd find out the truth. She'll probably stick her chin up in the air an' tell me not to be utterly idiotic—she shot a skunk an' was buryin' the gun instead of the skunk."

Hanson strode into the library and slammed the door behind him viciously. "Damn that brat!" He tossed his visored cap down on the couch. "She's lied her way out of tickets all summer, and now you know what she says? Says she shot a skunk this morning with that gun, and, if I want to prove it, I can send troopers out and they'll find the skunk! What'll I do, Asey?"

Asey told him to cheer up. "If Penny won't fit her part of the puzzle into place, we'll fox her an' fit in the parts around her."

"Yeah? Like," Hanson demanded, "what parts?"

"Wa-ell"—Asey paused in the doorway—"I'd say one of 'em was Jules, an' one's got wavy blond hair an' is named Fritz. Mr. Sewall'll tell you about him. An', by the way, if someone brings Fritz here, hang on to him, an' don't let him talk with Penny. Don't let her guess you know about him, either, just for fun. Now, I'm goin' to take another look around this place, an' then I'll pick up my car, an'—"

"See here, Asey; I wish you wouldn't go rushing

off!" Hanson said. "I've got to tackle Jules Head when he gets back with the doc, and I want you here with me. I need you! These people that're cousins to all the judges and call the governor by his first name, they throw me! I wish you'd stay!"

"I'm just goin' to get my car an' drive it back," Asey assured him. "An' don't let the upper classes thwart you. Especially Penny. She thinks it's stylish to be rude. Tell the doc to wait for me."

On his way through the garden he paused by the alcovelike enclosure, and then, after declining a trooper's offer of assistance, he walked twice around the semicircle, finally stopping beside the wooden man with the derby and the Dundreary whiskers.

This was where the Colonel had been. Who else had come? Where were the papers the Colonel had mentioned to Lora? And, what to Asey was the most puzzling question of all, how had a man like Colonel Head allowed anyone to shoot him point-blank?

Asey was still standing there beside the wooden man fifteen minutes later, when Sewall tiptoed down the path. At the sight of Asey he came to an embarrassed stop, his feet awkwardly embedded in the gravel.

"Who," Asey asked curiously, "are you stalkin'?"

Sewall cleared his throat. "Oh, I didn't know *you*

were still here, Mr. Mayo! I thought you'd gone. I won't intrude on your meditations!"

"Wait a minute," Asey said, as Sewall started to turn away. "Good Lord, Mr. Sewall, you look like a kid caught robbin' a jam jar! What was you bein' so stealthy about?"

The scholarly, precise Mr. Sewall turned very red and stammered something about wings.

"Wings? Man," Asey said, "stop floundering around! If Hanson saw you actin' so guilty, he'd cart you off to headquarters on principle! What wings?"

Sewall pointed to the wooden eagle. "I brought that to Ty yesterday," he said, "and I wanted to see if he'd braced the wings. I didn't want to mention it —after all, it is a paltry issue! But I would like to make sure it didn't topple over. Perhaps a trooper could help me brace it properly? I'd really resent having it broken, after all the trouble I had getting it here, and the scratches on my car and all the splinters in my fingers. Ty took one out of my thumb this morning."

"*This* mornin'?" Somewhere, out of the back of his memory, Asey recalled suddenly a Porter Motors directors' meeting, and someone's voice saying that Charley Sewall might resemble an absent-minded professor, but he was one of the shrewdest men in

New England. "So, Mr. Sewall, you was here this mornin'?"

"Why, yes. I drove over on Penny's orders," Sewall said, "and picked up Ty's contributions to the bazaar —a spinning wheel he was tired of and a wooden cock weathervane and a wooden pig. It was a very fine early-American pig, and I bought it myself. Its tail—"

"What time was this?" Asey interrupted.

"A few minutes to ten, I'd say," Sewall told him.

"'N'en," Asey said, "you went on to this bazaar?"

"Yes. I was posted at a driveway gate with Raymond, Ty's butler, and given tickets to sell— Poor Raymond! He's terribly broken up about Ty," Sewall added. "He and the maids cried all the way back from the bazaar, and kept comparing the trip over, when we were quite gay and pleasure bent."

"On the trip *over?*" Asey couldn't keep a tinge of disappointment out of his voice. "You mean that Raymond an' the maids was with you goin' *to* this bazaar?"

Sewall nodded. "I picked them up with the spinning wheel and the weathervane and the pig. We were really quite crowded."

"Huh," Asey said. "I see."

"I'm quite sure," Sewall went on, "that any of the servants would be only too glad to—er—corroborate that fact, Mr. Mayo, in case there is any doubt in your mind."

"I wasn't feelin' dubious about you," Asey said. "I was thinkin' of these horses. Tell me, Mr. Sewall, why in time did the Colonel collect all this stuff, anyway?"

"I'm afraid," Sewall said, "that it's my fault. Ty called me into his office, the day the doctors told him that he absolutely must retire if he wanted to live, and asked me what in the world he could take up as a hobby. The doctors had suggested that he take one up. Quite on impulse—there was a circus poster on a billboard opposite the office—I asked why he didn't devote himself to collecting old circus items, like flying horses, and he did."

"Honest?" Asey said. "All these horses an' stuff come from that?"

"Yes. That's a rare item"—Sewall pointed to the flying horse behind Asey—"with Barnum's name carved on it. I helped Ty track it down. The little pony there must be the saddler's store figure he wrote me about."

"I noticed this little fellow with the upraised paw." Asey stroked it. "That sort of took me back to when I was a boy."

"This was where he kept his choicest pieces,"

Sewall said. "They show well against the hedge. Will it be all right if I brace the eagle?"

"Brace away," Asey said. "Call a trooper if you want help. I'm goin' on an' get my car."

Halfway to the woods Asey stopped abruptly, about-faced, and marched back to the house.

Ten minutes later he strode back toward the woods. The Colonel's butler and three assorted maids had assured him, individually and collectively, that Sewall had been in their company from before ten that morning until their return to Headacre House. At least, Asey thought as he walked along, Sewall could account for his movements, which was more than could be said of any of the others.

Asey sighed and tried to sort things out. There were the Arlingtons. Dave hated the Colonel and resented the Head family's treatment of Lora. After leaving her at Headacre House, Dave might have sneaked back and shot the Colonel without Lora's knowing anything about it. Perhaps Lora knew, and was lying about everything, including her ink-stained skirt. Perhaps Lora, herself, had shot the Colonel with the gun she claimed was a toy. There was only her word to prove that the Colonel had become reconciled to Dave and that all was forgiven. And certainly Jules hadn't been aware of any forgiving gestures.

Then, Asey thought, there was Jules, the expert

pistol shot, who said he was taking a walk during the time of the murder. Jules's tears had seemed genuine enough when he first saw Ty's body on the path, but Hanson was right in pointing out that nobody liked to play second fiddle after leading the band. And, on the other hand, Sewall was right that the Colonel's death only increased Jules's problems at the plant.

At the thought of the part played by Penny, Asey shook his head. The trouble with a spoiled youngster like her was that you really couldn't begin to hazard any guesses about her actions or her motives. And, as for Fritz, the trouble with him was a temptation to guess too much.

Suppose, Asey thought, after the fellow was kicked out of the Head Company and forbidden to see Penny, that the Colonel had refused to recommend him for this new job Sewall mentioned. Suppose the Colonel even intimated that he'd expose Fritz's carrying on with Penny. There was a setup that might goad anyone to the point of committing a murder.

And, Asey decided, there was another angle on Fritz, one that Sewall apparently hadn't considered. But it wasn't beyond the realm of possibility that Jules had been justified in dismissing Fritz. Perhaps the official investigation of the Head employees had uncovered details about the fellow which not even

Sewall knew about. Suppose that Fritz was using Penny, suppose that Penny unwittingly was aiding him in sabotaging the Head Company or stealing its secrets. That angle would at least explain the absence of the papers Lora said the Colonel had gone out to get.

Asey continued to turn over in his mind the problem of Penny and Fritz as he strode on through the woods toward the place where he had left his car.

Where would the fellow have gone in Penny's red roadster, anyway? If he knew Penny as well as it appeared, certainly he should have known that hers was a marked car. Why had he chosen to drive past Headacre House when he could have driven, undetected, through wooded lanes? If Fritz was in the habit of meeting the girl in these woods, he ought to have known all about its highways and byways.

"I wonder," Asey murmured, "if he drove past the house on purpose? If it was me, I think I'd drive by an' give the impression I was goin' somewheres else in a hurry, an' then, I wonder if I maybe wouldn't creep back here where nobody'd expect to find me, an' wait till night to slip away."

He paused beside the Porter Sixteen, looked around, and then walked toward a rise beyond to his left.

He had hardly settled himself down on the pine needles, before the red roadster slid quietly into view on the lane below him, and a tall, blond fellow jumped out and looked cautiously around.

It was sheer fate that he should spot Asey just as Asey got to his feet. At once he sped away through the woods like a deer, with Asey racing after him.

They were rushing away from Headacre House, toward the ocean, and Asey caught jerky glimpses of blue water sparkling through the trees. On and on they tore, and still Fritz seemed as fresh and full of speed as he had been at the first bound. Then, by inches, Asey began to gain. Little by little the gap between them narrowed, until Asey could begin to make out the plaid pattern of Fritz's coat.

Suddenly, as though the whole precipitous pursuit were only a casual warming up, Fritz forged ahead out of sight, and the sound of his footsteps was only a faint thudding somewhere in the foreground.

Asey wanted more than anything else in the world to stop and rest and give his lungs a chance to breathe, but he kept doggedly on, across the road below Headacre House and back to those infernal pine woods. He had been outrun, all right, but this was only the first heat.

The hum of a car motor starting up sent Asey dashing forward with the last ounce of speed he could muster, and he reached the spot where his Porter had been parked just in time to see it shooting away down the lane, with Fritz at the wheel.

Asey grinned as he bolted for Penny's red roadster. Fritz had the advantages of the better car and of a head start, but there was in Asey's mind no doubt as to who would win an auto race. Not on these roads, which he knew like the palm of his own hand!

With a bland disregard for Penny's fenders, Asey hurled the red roadster through bushes and ferns and tangles of berry patches, and made his own short cut to the tarred road. His grin widened to a smile as he caught sight of the Porter's chromium body flashing over the hill toward the village.

As he sped on in pursuit, Asey had a sudden horrid suspicion of what might happen when he came to the Four Corners.

And it did.

The town policeman on traffic duty switched the lights to green to let Asey's familiar Porter roar past, and promptly switched them back to red at the sight of Penny's equally familiar red roadster. Coolly, he walked out into the path of the onrushing car and held up his hand.

A moment or two later Asey crawled out of the

crumpled roadster that seemed to be embracing the center blinker light, and smiled at the speechless officer.

"Okay," he said. "You was told to stop it, an', by gum, you did!"

"But, Asey, I thought you was in *your* car, and—"

"Never mind," Asey said. "It's all in a good cause, an' I guess it's all for the best, considerin' the state of what Penny Head laughin'ly thought of as brakes. Huh! While I go over to the phone office an' tell Annie to get my roadster stopped, now, have someone clear this mess out of the way. Oh, an' see if you can scare up some kind of vehicle for me to get on with, will you?"

Half an hour later Asey was bouncing along over the shore road back toward Headacre House in a borrowed dump truck, and his ears were still burning from the ribbing he'd taken when the cop and the rest of the Four Corners onlookers realized that his own roadster had been snatched away from under his own nose. Fritz, Asey thought with a touch of bitter, had also won the second heat!

As he rattled around a curve, he saw the flash of his windshield reflected for a moment against a chromium-plated car parked by the tiny Weesit Yacht Club. Asey blinked, and swung the truck down the club driveway in a cloud of tan dust. That was his own Porter parked there!

It took only a moment to learn that Fritz, whom the wharf boy knew only as one of the counselors from Winnigook Camp, had taken out the camp's motorboat some fifteen minutes ago, and that the boat had headed up the south channel.

"Whose"—Asey pointed to a trim speedboat moored at the wharf—"is this?"

"Gladding's. But you can't—you won't—"

"I'll fix it up with 'em." Asey jumped nimbly into the speedboat and beckoned to the boy. "Come along. I may need you. Cast off, an'—"

"But you haven't—"

"Shush!" Asey said. "Hustle!"

The wharf boy was still trying to protest, even after the speedboat had cut out across the bay. "Mr. Mayo, I know you, but—"

"Hush up!" Asey said. "I'll explain to the Gladdings! Now, are you dead sure he was headin' for the south channel? That'd mean he was makin' for Pochet Inlet."

"Yes, but I'm afraid you'll—"

"An' there he is, by gum!" Asey said. "I know that broad-beamed camp craft! Huh! We'll see who wins the third heat, my hearty! You'll find— Hey!"

The speedboat's engine spluttered, and then stopped completely.

"That's what I was trying to tell you, Mr. Mayo, if you'd only let me!" the wharf boy said. "It wasn't your taking the boat I cared about! I was afraid you'd run out of gas before you got very far! The Gladdings were out in this all morning, and I didn't think they'd filled the tank when they got back! And now we're right smack in the channel with the tide going out, and we'll go out with it!"

"Uh-huh," Asey said slowly. He was staring down at his right hand as it rested on the wheel. "Seems as if."

"Don't you," the boy inquired curiously, *"care* about not catching that camp boat, after getting this far?"

Asey grinned as he opened the knife. "I got a new vista to brood about, feller!" . . .

It was seven in the evening when Asey returned at last to Headacre House.

Dr. Cummings, seated out on the terrace, waved his cigar at him as he walked along the flagstone path. "Asey Mayo, where the hell have you *been?* Hanson's inside tearing his hair out in bunches because you aren't here. . . . Whew! I smell fish!"

"Mayo comes to you this evenin'," Asey informed

him, with a chuckle, "through the courtesy of the 'Jennie J.' An' if all you can smell is her fish, you ought to be powerful thankful. Don't ask me for any details of my voyage. I want to forget 'em."

"But, Asey, what have you been *doing?*"

"Wa-ell," Asey drawled as he sat down, "for the most part, I been bein' foiled. I been foiled on foot, an' by car, an' by boat. Let it go at that. What did you find out about things?"

Cummings lighted a fresh cigar. "Hanson's having a field day with alibis," he said. "For nearly an hour he felt Sewall must be guilty, because four servants swore he wasn't out of their sight from before ten till nearly noon. Hanson thought that was altogether too watertight."

Asey grinned. "I thought he would."

"Then," Cummings said, "he had an interval of suspecting Dave Arlington. Two people swore he was in the drugstore drinking a chocolate malted from a few minutes past ten till ten-thirty. Hanson thought a chocolate malted was an awfully sissy drink for an ex-All-American end."

Asey laughed.

"Then," Cummings said, "he brooded about Penny, because practically all the best people insisted that she worked like a beaver all morning at that bazaar. Hanson's been brooding about motives, too. He thinks Sewall ought to have a peachy motive, considering he's in the Head Company—"

"Like what?" Asey interrupted.

"Oh, Hanson doesn't know what; he just thinks there ought to be one. And he thinks Arlington's got a fine revenge motive, and he thinks—"

"Doc," Asey said, "I don't honestly care much what Hanson thinks. Not if that's a sample of his mental gymnastics. What did *you* find out?"

Cummings shrugged. "Not much, really. Here's the bullet that killed the Colonel—can you see it all right in this light? It's a forty-four Russian. Not a forty-five that would match Jules Head's gun that his daughter had. That virtually broke Hanson's heart."

Asey looked thoughtfully at the little blob of lead.

"It certainly seems to put an end to any conjecturin' about Jules or Penny. Huh! Did you find out which of 'em shot the forty-five this morning?"

"Jules told a vivid and rather gruesome story of shooting a skunk with it on his walk through the woods. I believe him. I think he really did. But Hanson was still asking him questions in the library a while ago."

"How'd Jules account for Penny's havin' the gun an' tryin' to bury it?" Asey inquired. "Or didn't he?"

"He didn't, because he couldn't," Cummings said. "He told us he left the gun at his house before starting over here to take Ty to that bazaar, and when Hanson broke the news about Penny's having it, Jules was fit to be tied."

"You mean, Doc, nobody's found out *yet* what the girl was doin' with that gun?"

"No," Cummings said. "The interview culminated in Penny's having violent hysterics, and I advised taking her out of circulation for a while till she calmed down. At the moment, she's stretched out on a couch in a guestroom yonder, moaning. What the girl needs," the doctor added, "is the hell of a good spanking."

"She inspires me that way, too," Asey said. "What become of the Arlingtons? Where are they?"

"Playing Chinese checkers in the living-room. Grimly, I might add. Dave Arlington presented Hanson with a toy gun a while ago and said he was sorry he hid it. I don't begin to understand why, and I'm sure Hanson doesn't. Do you?"

"Sort of," Asey said. "Lora probably told him I'd spotted it. What else's gone on? Had any reporter trouble?"

"Things are being momentarily hushed up because of the Head Company," Cummings said. "Jules convinced the powers that be that notoriety now would be injurious. Nothin's really happened, Asey. Sewall spent most of the afternoon setting a wooden eagle on a stand, and the rest of it bothering me."

"Did he get more splinters?" Asey asked.

"No, he kept telling me what a remarkable man you are. It got very tiresome. In short," Cummings wound up, "nothing's happened. We've all been waiting for you to show up with something spectacular. What about this elusive Fritz? He fascinates Hanson."

"Wa-ell," Asey said, "I can assure you he's elusive! . . . Doc, what d'you really think went on here this mornin'?"

"To tell you God's truth, I can't understand things," Cummings said. "Carter, over at the laboratory, and I, we're frankly stuck! Carter came here, and he and Hanson and I spent a long time looking things over in that alcove place where he was shot. And we can only figure it out one way. . . . Asey, do you believe what Lora Arlington says, that the Colonel went out into the garden to fetch some important papers?"

"Do you?" Asey countered.

"If his papers were so important," Cummings said, "then why'd he leave 'em out there in the first place?

Why didn't he bring 'em in when he came? Apparently he *was* indoors when Lora rang the bell. *I* should think he'd have carried any important papers in with him, wouldn't you?"

"Seems so."

"Jules says," Cummings went on, "he can't tell what private notes the Colonel might have jotted down, in view of his returning to business, but he doesn't know of any papers that specifically related to important company business, at all! Half a dozen times I've come to the conclusion the girl's lying! What do you think?"

"Wa-ell," Asey said, "I done some broodin' myself over them papers an' the wind that wasn't strong enough to carry 'em away anyhows, an'—"

"But, damn it all, the only way Hanson and Carter and I can figure," Cummings interrupted testily, "is that the Colonel *did* go out for his damn' papers and found someone there in the process of swiping 'em. Get the picture? Fellow pulls a gun and tells the Colonel not to make any fuss. But the Colonel calls his bluff, and so the fellow shoots him. That's the way it's got to be, Asey, because the fellow couldn't have been more than three feet away when he fired that shot. Carter is positive of that. And he—Asey!"

"Uh-huh?"

"Look down toward the garden, quick! See where that shaft of light from the house slants down to the pool? See the horse there? Well, look at the figure next to the horse, quick! Is that a wooden statue that's moving?"

"It's Fritz!" Asey said softly. "He just can't keep away! Huh! Doc, wait till after I sneak up on him a bit, an' then pop inside an' call out everybody to help me get him!"

Just as the doctor started toward the door leading from the terrace to the living-room, a shot rang out in the garden.

It was a long time later, long after the unsuccessful dash for Fritz was over and done with that Asey found Jules Head in the garden, lying in the same little alcovelike enclosure where the Colonel had been shot, with a bullet through his forehead. . . .

Hanson slammed into the library and walked over to the couch where Asey and Dr. Cummings were seated. That his entrance put an abrupt end to their conversation and left it dangling in mid-air was a fact which escaped Hanson, in his distracted frame of mind. He missed, too, the significant contrast of Cummings's puzzled expression and Asey's air of firm determination.

"Listen, Asey; let's clear up the business of this

shot! *I* thought *you* fired it!" Hanson thumped the
couch arm to emphasize his words. "Because, just a
second after I heard it, the doc rushed into the living-
room and said Fritz was in the garden and you were
catching him, and for us to hurry and help you! Naturally, I thought you'd taken a pot shot at the fellow!
Who'd *you* think fired that shot, I'd like to know?"

"Why," Cummings said, "bring that up again? And
don't," he added, as Hanson opened his mouth to
protest, "tell Asey again that he must have seen Fritz
fire that shot! He didn't!"

"He should have!" Hanson grumbled. "He was
there!"

"Fritz wasn't far from me," Asey said, "but he was
out of my view. It was hard tryin' to follow him, with
all those horses an' figures in the way."

"*One* thing's certain!" Hanson sat down heavily in
a leather chair and loosened his belt. "Nobody in the
house fired that shot! Sewall and the Arlingtons were
in the living-room. I'd just gone there from here, and
Jules'd left here—oh, eight or ten minutes before. He
said he was going out for a breath of air. I thought he
meant out on the terrace, but he must've gone straight
through that side door from the hall into the garden,
instead. A maid was with Penny, and the other serv-

ants were in the kitchen. So that lets out everyone in the house."

"Seems so," Asey said. "Who do you think shot him, Hanson?"

"After what's just happened, you can ask me who?" Hanson sounded incredulous as he sat up in his chair. "Why, this Fritz von What's-his-name; who else?"

"Why him?" Asey inquired.

"Why? Listen! Jules Head's shot the same way and in the same place and apparently with the same caliber gun as his brother, isn't he? Yes! So you can guess it's the same person killed 'em both, can't you?"

"Why?" Cummings asked, responding to a prod from Asey that Hanson didn't see.

"Carter thinks so," Hanson said. "And I think so! I'll be pretty surprised if Carter doesn't prove that the same gun fired both bullets! Now, we got some suspects who might've shot the Colonel, but we know none of 'em shot Jules, don't we? Yes! And if they're cleared of this murder, they're cleared of the first, aren't they? Yes! Who does that leave you with? Fritz!"

"Uh-huh," Asey said when Hanson finished, "but when you come right down to brass tacks, what proof or evidence have you really got against him? You

haven't got the weapon that was used, or even circum-
stantial evidence to prove he was here when the Colonel was killed, even if you know he was in the woods
later. You—"

"Listen! The Colonel went to the garden to get
some papers. Fritz got 'em first, shot the Colonel, and
beat it!"

"But if it was me that shot the Colonel for his important papers," Asey said, "I'd stay away from here
afterwards. I wouldn't keep poppin' back, Hanson."

"Don't you see *why* he came back? He wanted a
chance to get Jules! And he did!"

"Meanin'," Asey said, "you think Jules was killed
for some important papers, too?"

"Of course! That is," Hanson amended, "it probably was for some kind of business secret, even if we
couldn't tell from looking at his pockets if anything
was missing. It's all Fifth Column stuff. You can't
deny it!"

"I ain't an expert on Fifth Columny," Asey said,
"but I know if I'd killed Colonel Head for papers, I'd
take 'em an' beat it an' not come back!"

"Well, maybe he passed the papers over to someone else, then!" Hanson said impatiently. "Maybe
he's not the only Fifth Column around!"

"That's just the point I'm aimin' at," Asey said. "If

what you call a Fifth Columnist killed the Colonel, I
don't think you'd ever set eye on that same fellow
again. An' consider. If you wanted to swipe business
papers or secrets from Jules, would you expect to find
'em at the house of his brother? Would you linger
here with all the cops around, when you could go
across the fields to Jules's own house, an' rob it to
your heart's content, while everyone's attention's focused here? Nope, the more I think about Fritz, the
less he sounds like any Fifth Column to me."

"Yeah?" Hanson was beginning to get mad. "Well,
what *does* he sound like to you?"

"Like a boy," Asey said gently, "tryin' to meet a
girl."

Hanson got up from his chair and glared at them.
"I get it!" he said. "You two're trying to get me off
the track of this fellow, so you can get him yourselves!
Well, nothing's going to keep me from nabbing
him!"

"I wish you luck," Asey said, with a smile. "He's
plenty elusive."

Hanson slammed out of the library, and then
rather belligerently returned, picked up his cap off
the floor, and slammed out again.

"My, he's mad!" Cummings said, turning to Asey.
"Why were you baiting him?"

"Baitin'?" Asey asked innocently.

"Oh, what you pointed out to him was true enough, but you were baiting him, just the same! He meant to go after Fritz anyway, but you've worked him into a state where his getting Fritz is practically a holy crusade! Asey, while I wait for the ambulance, tell me where you were, all the time we thought you were chasing Fritz! What happened?"

"I chased," Asey said, "hither an' yon an' yon an' hither."

"If you want me to believe you were fluttering around chasing fireflies for an hour, you're crazy! What's your belt doing in your coat pocket?"

"Wa-ell," Asey said, "I thought I might need it for other than the usual uses, an' I didn't, as it turned out. Doc, I'm goin' to do an errand, an' then I'm comin' back for you. We got a little job to do later, you an' me."

"What?" Cummings asked suspiciously. "I won't— Say, what're you doing in my bag?"

"Gettin' iodine for a minor abrasion I suffered on the boat this afternoon," Asey said.

"Know what I think?" Cummings chewed on his unlighted cigar. "I think you've already got Fritz! I ought to have guessed, you looked so bland and purring when you came back! You used that belt to tie

him up! You've got him, and you don't want anyone
to know!"

"Now, what," Asey said, "makes you think if I had
him I wouldn't turn him over to Hanson?"

"Because you apparently want Hanson and his
men away, chasing like fury, while you *do* things,
that's what! Who are you trying to fool, anyway?"

"Doc"—Asey was suddenly serious—"this is a crazy
idea I got, but I don't know any other way to go about
it! I had kind of an inklin' this afternoon, but I
couldn't begin to figger it out. Even if I'd got back
here sooner, even if I'd known a hundred times
more'n I'm guessin' now, I don't think I could've
kept Jules from bein' killed. But you an' I got to see
if my guess is right. No matter how it works out, we're
bound to learn somethin'. I'll be back for you in an
hour, an', in case anyone should ask you, remember
we're goin' to help Hanson hunt Fritz!"

Shortly after two that morning, the last light went
out in Headacre House, and Asey, standing with
Cummings on the edge of the woods, squared his
shoulders. "I'm goin' to start circlin' back to the
house now. You can see everythin' from here with
them night glasses. You know what to do if there's
any trouble." He disappeared into the woods.

Minutes later, Cummings finally came to the con-

clusion that the figure by the rose garden hedge was
Asey, although how the man had got there so unobtrusively, the doctor couldn't understand. More than
once in the next quarter-hour Cummings lost sight
of him, despite his concentrated watching, for in the
dim starlight Asey's tan coat and corduroys made him
almost indistinguishable from the wooden figures all
about.

At last Asey halted opposite the alcovelike enclosure, and stood there as motionless as the wooden
horses on either side of him.

It was nearly daybreak when he rejoined the doctor. "Did you see?" he asked briefly.

"I saw," Cummings said. "And take that look off
your face, man! It makes me feel colder than I am
already! You guessed right, but, Asey, how are you
going to play it out?" . . .

The sun was shining brightly on the terrace the
next noon when Dr. Cummings appeared and was
greeted by the Arlingtons, Sewall, and Penny with a
single question: "Where's Asey?"

"Did he really go away in the Porters' plane?"
Penny asked quickly, and Cummings marveled at the
change which had come in her overnight. Except for
her dark dress, she looked the same, but the petulance
had gone from her voice and the sulky pout had dis-

appeared from her lips. "Cook said the grocery boy told her someone saw him taking the plane! Did he? Is he still hunting Fritz? And where's Hanson? What's happened since last night? No one's told us a thing!"

"I've just got back"—Cummings parried her questions with a simple statement of extraneous fact— "from the hospital, myself. It's another boy for the Whitlocks, by the way. I don't know where Asey and Hanson are at the moment, but Asey is supposed to meet me in my office at one."

"Then," Penny said, "will you give him these?"

Cummings looked curiously at the sheaf of folded papers she thrust out to him. "What's all this?"

Penny's lips began to quiver, and Lora came to her aid: "Oh, in effect, Doctor, it's her part in things yesterday. What she did, and wouldn't explain, and so on."

"All these pages?"

"It turned out to be awfully long when she wrote it out," Lora said, "but it really isn't— Want me to tell him, Pen, so he can sum it up for Asey?"

Penny nodded as she wiped her eyes.

"Well," Lora said, "it seems, when Jules called Penny at the bazaar, he also told her to cancel all their week-end plans and particularly their week-end guests. So Penny went back to their house to phone, and while she was phoning she saw that gun of her father's on the hall table."

Cummings nodded. Jules had said he'd left it there when he told about his skunk-shooting the day before.

"And, about the time she noticed the gun, she also saw a trooper striding across the lawn toward the front door. She was naturally overwrought and the sight of him scared her, and in a moment of panic she grabbed the gun and put it in her coat pocket. Without ever once thinking," Lora said, "how hard it would be to dispose of afterward. Well, before coming over here, she went to the woods to see Fritz. She was already hours late for a date she'd made with him —that's the part that took her so long to write."

"Why?" Cummings wanted to know.

"Because while she was trying to tell Fritz what had happened to Ty, and how he must leave at once, Fritz was shushing her and telling her to be quiet, because the strangest things were happening, and he was being followed. How they ever got each other's points and made up their minds so quickly," Lora said, "*I* can't understand. But they did. Penny told him to hurry away and hide, and when it was safe to take her car and get away. Penny listened, and didn't hear anyone, so she started to bury the gun. It seemed an awfully bright thought at the time, and, besides, it was beginning to haunt her. And then Asey came, and—"

"And I acted that way with him," Penny interrupted, "to keep him from going on and finding Fritz! And it *wasn't* Fritz who knocked Lora out!"

"Who was it?" Cummings puffed at his cigar and tried hard to seem as interested as if he really didn't know.

"It was a tree branch!" Lora told him. "At first, I didn't think it was possible. But I went out and found the place this morning, and changed my mind. You see, Fritz saw me staggering toward the woods, yelling —it was just after I'd found Ty, and I was sort of out of my mind. Fritz was starting toward me, when he saw me rush headlong against this low branch. Really, it's a wonder I didn't break my neck, with that flannel robe of Ty's practically dripping around my feet! Anyway, Fritz told Penny he came and looked at me, and then he went away."

"Why?" Sewall asked. "What a very strange thing for him to do!"

"I don't think so!" Penny said. "He didn't know Lora! And, if you were in Fritz's position, you'd probably think, as he did, that it would be best if he wasn't involved in any way on property belonging to the Head family with a strange woman in a man's dressing gown who was madly screaming, and would probably accuse him of assault when she came to! I couldn't understand that, either, when he told me about her, and that was another reason why I told him to hide and then take my car! I was worried to death about him till I saw the roadster go by the house. I'd told him to drive by, and I was so afraid I wouldn't see him when he did. I—oh!"

Penny gave an anguished little cry, and pointed toward the front of the house.

Asey's roadster had just drawn up, and Hanson was getting out, closely followed by a tall, blond boy to whom he was obviously handcuffed, and then by Asey.

"Fritz!" Penny said. "Oh, Fritz!"

"Sorry, Miss Head," Hanson said perfunctorily, as he thrust her away from Fritz with his free hand. "We got him. All but his gun, and my men're dragging for that in the pond where I saw him throw it away. Come into the library, Miss Head. You, too." He nodded toward the Arlingtons. "And you, Doc. I want to get some loose ends cleared up."

"Fritz!" Penny said.

Dave Arlington put his arm around her. "Don't, Penny! Don't cry! We'll see you through, Lora and I! We'll get lawyers, and maybe—"

"They won't help! . . . Asey," Hanson said brusquely, "you go down to the garden and dig up what you spotted there yesterday!"

"Okay," Asey said. He paused for a moment on the terrace and watched with Sewall as the others filed into the house.

"That's too bad," Sewall said. "I'm sorry for him. For Penny, too. I had no idea she really cared so deeply for the boy." He cleared his throat. "What did you find in the garden, Mr. Mayo, a clue?"

Asey nodded. "Come along, if you want, an' I'll show it to you."

"I won't be in your way?"

"Nope; come along."

With Sewall following, Asey started down the garden path, and at the alcovelike enclosure he stopped and got down on his knees.

"I think it was right about here. You know"—Asey looked up and nodded toward the little wooden pony opposite—"every time I come near this place an' see that critter, it takes me back to my childhood. Let's see; I guess this is the spot."

"It's a charming item," Sewall said. "I was wondering, d'you suppose"—Sewall toyed with the scarab on his watch chain—"this pony might be one of those I've read about? One which lifts its head and opens its mouth when the upraised paw is pushed down?"

"You mean, it *moves?*" Asey asked skeptically. "I never knew that any of 'em could move! How?"

"Probably it has a combination," Sewall said. "Most of these wooden objects, if they do move, have to be started from a certain position, with just the right pressure on certain places. I tried several ways yesterday afternoon when I was here working on the eagle braces, but I didn't have any success. It seemed to me if you pressed down the paw— Oh, I'm sorry!" he said apologetically as Asey got up on his feet. "I didn't mean to distract you from your clue!"

"I ain't in any rush. Hanson'll be an hour," Asey said. "This is real interestin', Mr. Sewall. Show me what you mean about the little horse."

"Well," Sewall said, "it seemed to me that if you pressed down this upraised paw with one hand, and simultaneously pressed against—hm—say, that carved strap button, for example. That should make it work. That was how the one I read about worked. But apparently I'm not strong enough. Perhaps you could be more successful."

"I can always try," Asey said. "Let's see, now!" He

turned and faced the pony, and stooped over, so that his right hand was on the carved strap button below the pony's throat, and his left hand rested on the upraised wooden paw. "That right?" Asey said. "Now, I'll press down the paw!"

As he did so, there was the sound of a sharp click.

And then Asey swung around and smiled at Sewall, whose startled eyes were focused on the big, old-fashioned Army Colt that had amazingly appeared in Asey's right hand.

"It didn't work!" Sewall seemed to be mumbling to himself.

"Nope," Asey said, "it didn't work, because I unloaded your little device on you last night, Mr. Sewall, after you'd reloaded."

"You—you *knew* about the pony? You *unloaded* the gun?"

"Uh-huh. But this Colt I'm pointin' at you," Asey said, "is very much loaded. Hanson"—he spoke over Sewall's shoulder—"d'you see how he worked things? That pressin' down on the wooden strap button don't have a single thing to do with the workin' of the paw mechanism that pulls the trigger on the gun he's got fitted into the pony's head. That was just to make people stoop down, so their head'd come in the right place to get a bullet between the eyes. All Sewall had

to do was to egg Ty an' Jules on to stoopin' a little an'
pressin' that paw down. Sewall didn't have to be
within a million miles of here to kill Ty an' Jules,
with this setup!"

"Watch out for him!" Hanson dived forward and
grabbed Sewall as the latter lunged at Asey.

"Until he gets that mad-dog look out of his eyes"—
Cummings appeared from behind a wide bush—
"watch out for him anyway— Oh, so he's going to
crumple now, is he? I should think he would! Just
the same, don't take chances with him! Asey, how the
hell does all this work?"

"Wait before you show him!" Hanson said, as he
gave Sewall over to two of his troopers. "I want to
see! It's all I could do to keep away from here and my
hands off that pony, but Asey was so afraid I might
gum up his trap— Now, what happens when you
press down the paw?"

"You'll have to take things apart to see just exactly
how it's rigged," Asey said, "but the main thing's
that a wire runs from the paw here to the trigger of a
Russian singleshot Remington that's fitted into the
head. When you press the paw, the head don't move
a mite. That's just more of Sewall's trickery to make
you watch close an' keep your head in the right spot.
The jaws don't move, either. They don't need to, be-

cause there's enough of an openin' there for a bullet. What does happen is that the wire pulls the trigger. Watch."

After groping around in the pony's heavy mane, Asey indicated a small catch on the back of the wooden neck.

"What's that for?" Cummings demanded.

"Undo it," Asey said, "an' see. The whole top of the head lifts up, exposin' your gun. The mane an' the carved trappin's an' the leather strap conceals the hingin'. The slopin' grip of this particular gun makes it fit elegant with the head an' the slope of the neck, an' the way the breech's exposed makes it a matter of seconds to reload. It was kind of a clever setup," Asey concluded, "an' I don't know but what maybe he might of got away with it, if it hadn't been for that splinter of mine." . . .

"How," Lora asked, half an hour later in the living-room at Headacre House, "did you figure this out from a *splinter?*"

"I didn't," Asey said. "But it was a splinter that first set me thinkin' about Sewall. Out on Gladding's boat yesterday I felt a splinter stickin' into my hand, an' I tried to think where I picked it up, considerin' I hadn't had nothin' in my hands but car wheels an' a boat wheel, an' none of 'em wood! 'N'en I remembered before I left here an' chased Fritz, I stroked the little horse, an' kind of run my hand over it. That was where I got the splinter."

Lora said it still didn't make sense to her. "You and Hanson were so busy talking to Penny and Fritz before they went off with that lawyer, I never got any of my questions answered! How could that splinter set you thinking of Charley Sewall?"

Asey smiled. "He told me yesterday he'd got splinters in his hands bringin' that wooden eagle to Ty. He even said Ty took one out of his thumb for him. But, as I remembered 'em, the wings of that eagle was so old an' worn, they was smooth. Smooth as satin. Now, Sewall was so precise-like, he wouldn't have said *eagle* if he'd meant somethin' else, but if he really meant *eagle,* it seemed to me he was lyin'. An' why he wanted me to think his splinters came from that eagle, I couldn't imagine. It stuck in my mind, along with my own splinter from that little horse. An' all the other horses. I planned, after I talked with the doc yesterday evenin', to take another look at that eagle. But Fritz popped up in the garden—"

"Now that he's gone," Cummings interrupted, "will you explain what really happened when you chased him then? He told me last night, but, with his accent, I couldn't understand much more than half he said."

"When he reached the cover of the woods," Asey said, "Fritz stopped short, which kind of confused me. I was all set to grab him an' tie him up with my belt, when he spoke up an' said he was afraid this chasin' was goin' too far, an' would I take him back to Mr. Sewall, who he thought he'd seen at Headacre House. I couldn't understand him very well either, an' asked who he meant, an' he said, 'Sewall, the Head Company treasurer.' His bein' treasurer," Asey added, "was somethin' else that kept stickin' in my mind. Anyway, Fritz said he didn't think he'd get a square deal from the police with just Jules Head around, but he thought Sewall was a fair man who wouldn't make him out to be any deep-dyed villain, an' he was perfectly willin' to talk with the police as long's he had Sewall to vouch for him. I knew Hanson'd grab the boy the instant he saw him, so, after talkin' with Fritz an' hearin' his story, I hid him in the rumble seat of my car, an' come back here to have a little talk with Jules. But Jules'd been shot."

Dave Arlington wrinkled up his forehead. "I'm still stuck with that splinter," he said.

"After findin' Jules in the alcove, I run my hand

over that eagle," Asey said. "You just couldn't pick
up a splinter from it. But you couldn't miss gettin'
'em on the little horse. An', as I stood there, I got
to wonderin' how both Jules an' Ty could be am-
bushed in the same place an' in the same way, an'
so awful accurate. An' seemin'ly never any footprints
or traces of anyone lyin' in wait for 'em. There was
somethin' mighty inhuman an' mechanical an' precise about it. 'N'en I begun to think of possible con-
trivances instead of people, an' there was the little
horse. An' Sewall's lyin' about them splinters! It
begun to make some sense. I didn't dare linger by
the horse or call attention to it then. I got Hanson
to take his men off to hunt Fritz, an' then I come
back to the garden, an' waited."

"I see." Dave nodded slowly. "You cleared the coast
and made the garden seem safe for anyone who might
have some gadget planted in the horse."

"Uh-huh. I thought most likely it'd be the time
someone'd choose to dismantle whatever setup there
was. But Sewall loaded the gun. An' after he slipped
back to the house I unloaded it. An'—"

"Why didn't you grab him right then?" Lora asked.
"I would have!"

"I wanted to," Asey said. "But consider. I couldn't
grab him till I seen what he was up to. An' if I

grabbed him afterwards an' accused him of loadin'
the gun, he'd most likely have claimed he never
touched it!"

"But you *saw* him!" Lora protested. "You saw
him!"

"Even though I was certain sure he did," Asey
told her, "I couldn't have sworn in court I'd *seen*
him load that gun. Not in that light, an' considerin'
how far away I was standin'. He could've claimed
he'd been thinkin' about the possibility of some such
contrivance, an' had come out on a quick inspiration
to take a look. Sewall was too careful an' precise to
have left any incriminatin' loose ends. I'm willin' to
bet nobody'll ever be able to trace his buyin' that
gun, or find out where he got that horse."

"Where did it come from?" Cummings asked. "Did
Sewall bring it?"

"No one seems to know, Doc."

"But someone must! After all, Asey, a wooden horse
isn't anything you hide in your pocket!" Cummings
said acidly. "Someone must have seen him bring it,
if he did!"

"Seems so, but remember that with all the horses
there is here, an' with the Colonel movin' 'em about
every few days, everyone's awful used to horses. They
don't pay much attention to 'em. It's probably safer

to move a dozen wooden horses around here without bein' noticed than to shift just one flowerpot on your front porch, Doc."

"Someone," Cummings insisted, "must have seen Sewall bring that horse here, or helped unload it!"

"Nobody did. But one of the maids told me when Sewall brought the eagle here in his car, day before yesterday, he drove his sedan around the side of the house an' almost up to the alcove, an' he an' Ty unloaded the bird. I think they unloaded the horse, too, even though nobody remembers it. You see how safe Sewall was? If you accused him of bringin' the horse, he'd only to say that what he brought was an eagle."

"This eagle"—Lora lighted a cigarette—"confuses me— Don't look so ashamed of me, Dave! I don't think you understand it, either!"

"The eagle was Sewall's red herrin'," Asey said. "When I mentioned the little horse, Sewall spoke of the eagle he'd brought Ty. When I looked around the alcove yesterday afternoon, Sewall hurried after me an' talked about settin' up that eagle properly. He put on a fine act for me. He even asked for a trooper to help him, just to show me there wasn't nothin' wrong about that eagle he'd brought Ty. He also told me the little horse must be one Ty wrote

him about gettin', but I bet you he can't ever produce
any such letter! He was just tryin' to make it seem
that the horse'd been here some time."

"What was his motive?" Lora asked suddenly. "Not
money. He's got money to burn! Why did he do it?"

"Money," Asey said simply. "Remember, he was
the treasurer of the Head Company! That's why I
took a plane to Boston early this mornin' an' found
out a lot of interestin' facts from some directors of
Porter Motors that's also directors of the Head Company. There's already been a few whispers about
Sewall—"

"I'm dumb!" Dave Arlington said bitterly. "I'm
a dope! It's taken me all this time to catch on! Sewall
was milking the Head Company, and he got away
with it as long as Jules was president, but he knew
he'd never get by Ty, when Ty went back on the
job! Ty had the brains! Asey, how did Sewall work
this horse business with Ty, anyway?"

"All he had to do was to leave the horse here an'
wait for his opportunity. I guess he figgered he'd
never have a better one than yesterday mornin',
when Penny's askin' him to take the servants to that
bazaar not only left Ty here alone, but give Sewall
a watertight alibi as well. Prob'ly, as Sewall left, he

told Ty that if he followed the proper directions of shovin' down the paw an' stoopin' over an' pressin' down on that strap button, he could make the little horse move. Prob'ly he said it was a surprise he'd been savin' for Ty, or somethin' like that. Then he departed, leavin' the rest to Ty's curiosity an' his passion for them horses. An' I think, Mrs. Arlington, that just as Ty was startin' for the garden to play with the horse, you came. An' I think that's why, when you had your accident with the ink bottles, he said that about the important papers."

"By George!" Cummings said. "I never thought of that angle! *She* wasn't making those papers up! The Colonel was! He used 'em as an excuse!"

"An excuse for *what?*" Lora wanted to know.

"I don't think there's any doubt but what the Colonel was overjoyed an' delighted to see you," Asey said, "an' I don't think he'd have left you, in the ordinary course of events, to go play with that little horse. But you know how much he liked those wooden horses, don't you? An' can't you imagine how much he wanted to see that little one work. So, when you told him you'd be years an' years, an' anyway fifteen minutes, cleanin' up that ink, he grabbed his chance to pop out an' work the horse; see? But he *said* he was goin' to get papers, an' you tell me if

I haven't guessed right on the reason why. Didn't
you used to sort of kid him about his horses?"

"Always," Lora said. "Unmercifully. He loved it,
too. Asey, how did Sewall inveigle Jules into it all,
I wonder?"

"Hanson says Jules an' Sewall'd been talkin' together before Jules went out to the garden last night.
We can only guess, but prob'ly Sewall suggested to
him the possibility of such a contraption, an' he put
it forceful enough so Jules went to investigate. Bein'
a pistol expert, he prob'ly felt capable of lookin'
into it by himself, without tellin' Hanson. P'raps Sewall warned him not to. The point is, Sewall persuaded him to go, all right!"

"But why should he have wanted to kill Jules,
too?" Dave asked. "He'd always got by Jules,
hadn't he?"

"Uh-huh. But it worked so fine with the Colonel,"
Asey said. "Me an' Hanson was all off the track, an'
there was Fritz loose, to be the goat! Sewall saw his
chance. With Ty gone, he was safe. But, with Jules
out of the way, then *he* could be head of the Head
Company; see? An' he would have been, accordin'
to those fellers in Boston. As head, himself, no one
would ever know how much money he had stolen
from the company!"

"There's only one thing that puzzles me now," Dave said. "Why did you keep Fritz away, and bring him back in handcuffs, and all that?"

"I didn't want there to be any chance for Sewall to guess I'd guessed. An' I was pretty sure Fritz wasn't much of a Fifth Columnist if he had to depend on a camp launch to make a getaway. Fritz understood, an' agreed to let himself be maligned. An' we fooled Sewall into feelin' safe. I was goin' to lead him to the garden while I pretended to dig up a clue, an' then I was goin' to mention the pony an' see what his reactions was. If he hadn't egged me on to pushin' down that paw, I was goin' to suggest to him that maybe the horse moved, an' see what happened then. But Sewall felt so safe, he couldn't let the chance pass to get me. It was too good. As far as he knew, everyone was in the house out of sight, an' the minute I was shot, he'd only to rush in an' say I'd been killed by some more Fifth Column! He had no gun. He was safe from any kind of suspicion."

"And how he crumpled up afterward!" Cummings said. "Hanson expected a full confession by the time they got to headquarters. . . . Well, I've got to get on with my calls!"

"Mind takin' me along with you?" Asey asked.

"What's the matter with your mighty Porter?"

"Oh, I presented that to Penny as a gift," Asey said, "havin' smashed up hers. She—"

Cummings chuckled so suddenly he almost choked on his cigar. "Asey, I just thought of something! This isn't a case of the Fifth Column, it's—"

"I know," Asey said. "I thought of it, too. Not the Fifth Column, but a Trojan Horse!"

THE WANDER BIRD PLOT

THE
WANDER BIRD PLOT

T O THE bored bellboy on the nearly deserted
sun deck of the Weesit Inn, watching Mrs.
Chatfield was as good as watching a clock.
When she stopped writing letters, that meant it was
just ten, Eastern Daylight-Saving Time. When she
put away her tatting, it was just ten-thirty. Now, after
her usual nap, the old girl was hauling out her binoculars. That meant it was eleven, and time for Lizzie
Chatfield's second regular morning survey.

The bellboy yawned, and wondered how the old
girl could keep it up, day after day, summer after
summer, peering around through those glasses as if
there was really something going on that was worth
looking at. As far as he was concerned, the view from
the sun deck was as dull as the rest of the Cape Cod
scenery, and the less he looked at it the better he
felt. But Lizzie Chatfield, she seemed to think it
was swell.

And Lizzie did. To her, the spread of beach from
the sun deck was a fascinating, provocative, ever-
changing panorama. It was particularly exciting this
glorious August morning, with all of Weesit out after
a nasty week of northeast winds and driving rain.

Directly below her, two loads of Inn guests were
setting out for a fishing trip, and a squad of girls from
Miss Barclay's Camp were giggling and squealing
while they waited for their launch at the dock. Beyond, the Yacht Club crowd were bailing boats and
drying sails. On South Point, the maids at the Latimer
mansion were putting out an enormous wash. Over
at North Point, summer cottagers aired bedding and
blankets. The public beach seethed with children
and dogs, and the private beach was dotted with
children and nursemaids. Near the old oyster wharf,
Mr. Dinwiddie's painting class was starting a new
seascape. A little apart from them sat that surrealist
fellow, Jere Warren, moodily staring at a canvas.

Lizzie clucked her tongue as she adjusted the binoculars to get a better look at him. Of course, Jere
was dear Mrs. Latimer's friend and protégé, and if he
wanted to spend the summer painting moodily at a
picture of a dead skate surrounded by pink gum-
drops and a jag of lightning, he had every right to
do so. On the other hand, the skate picture bothered

Lizzie. It didn't seem healthy for a nice-looking young fellow to keep painting at a dead fish.

It didn't seem to her, either, as if Jere himself were quite happy about it. Sometimes he drew the nicest little sketches, not surrealistic one bit, but normal sketches of the Inn guests, and Lizzie wished he would do more of them. One of the chambermaids had told her that Mr. Warren had lots of nice sketches in the closet of his room, and she'd given it as her opinion that Mr. Warren must have some secret sorrow, like a love affair, that made him paint that awful fish for Mrs. Latimer.

Lizzie paused in her reflections and gave a gurgle of pleasure. There was Mrs. Latimer, dear Nora herself, out in her speedboat in the harbor! It seemed like old times to have Nora out in a boat.

A brand-new boat, too, a beautiful new boat. Lizzie clucked her tongue again. Really, it wasn't right for Nora Latimer to go dashing around the harbor in speedboats so soon after her operation. Dashing around in speedboats was much worse than making trips around the countryside in her car. Lizzie had spoken sharply to Nora about driving, the previous week. Nora ought to give up all that sort of activity until she was really well. People often had relapses. . . . Of course, there was a man at the wheel of the boat. Nora at least wasn't trying to manage it alone.

Lizzie brought the man's face into focus. If it wasn't Asey Mayo, out there with Nora! She would be perfectly safe with Asey. He knew all about boats.

The bellboy raced suddenly in front of her and came to a stop at the deck railing.

"Young man," Lizzie said in annoyance, "I can't see through you!"

"Say, Mrs. Chatfield, Pudge says it's Asey Mayo out in Mrs. Latimer's boat! Asey Mayo, himself, Mrs. Chatfield!"

"I know," Lizzie said. "D'you mind moving aside?"

Like so many of the summer people who had known Asey Mayo over a period of years, Lizzie found it hard to remember that his reputation as a detective had made him a familiar figure in the gravures. She knew him as a jack-of-all-trades, and the Porters' former hired man and yacht captain. It rather amazed Lizzie when people made a fuss over him because he was a detective and a director in the Porter car factory.

"Gee, Mrs. Chatfield"—the bellboy looked longingly at her binoculars—"I wonder if—uh—if you'd tell me what he looks like. I never seen him except in pictures."

"Oh," Lizzie said, "he just looks like any Cape

Codder. He talks like one. No g's on the end of his words. And he sort of drawls—"

"The papers say he always drives a big Porter Sixteen roadster," the bellboy interrupted eagerly. "They call him the Lithe Hayseed Sleuth. They say he's sailed the seven seas in every kind of boat, and he's solved murder cases. . . . Oh, boy, they're heading in to the wharf!"

Lizzie watched the bellboy bound down the gangway to the beach. Then she picked up her glasses and her knitting bag, and scurried after him. She really should speak sharply to Nora about overdoing things, and she would also work in a few words about that couple from Chicago who played those swing records all night long, up the corridor.

The manager had listened politely enough to Lizzie's complaints, but no steps had been taken. Dear Nora would be sure to have it stopped. It was so convenient, Lizzie thought as she hurried out on the wharf, to know Nora. So very convenient, what with dear Nora owning the Inn.

Pushing her way through a cluster of bellboys, all of whom were chattering excitedly about Asey Mayo, Lizzie cupped her hands to her mouth, and piped toward the speedboat: "Nora, oh, Nora dear!"

Mrs. Latimer waved at her, and then unobtrusively

spoke to Asey: "Pretend you're just circling, and cut back to the bay. You can do your tinkering by the breakwater. I feel lots better today, but I haven't the spirit to cope with Lizzie, and she's waiting to pounce on me." She raised her voice: "Yes, Lizzie! I'll see you later! Later, Lizzie!"

Asey Mayo grinned at her as he swung the boat out into the bay. He well knew Lizzie's reputation for volubility.

"She's telling the bellboys all about you," Mrs. Latimer said. "And she'll never rest till she finds out how you happen to be in my boat. You know, I like Lizzie. She's goodhearted. I don't even mind her constant chatter. But sometimes that insatiable curiosity of hers gets on my nerves. She read me a lecture on my driving a car last week, but I think she was more interested in where I went than in my state of health. Is the carburetor all right, Asey?"

"I think so," he said. "Syl hadn't played with it enough. Won't take two shakes to fix it."

Out beyond the breakwater Mrs. Latimer watched with interest as Asey tinkered away. His successes as a sleuth, she thought, had not changed Asey Mayo. His blue eyes still twinkled when he spoke, his chuckle was as infectious as ever, and his Cape accent just as drawly. She wondered how old he was. She, herself, was forty-five, and she'd seen him first at the Porters' house, thirty years before. He must be older than she, but his lean figure and his agility both defied arithmetic.

"Asey," she said, "I appreciate your taking your cousin's place while he's away."

"Syl was worried," Asey said, "that you'd try to take the boat out alone, an' he didn't think you should, so soon after the hospital. You feelin' better now?"

"Better," she said, "but old. I'd forgotten all about my years, and now they're being hurled at me. By my lawyer particularly. The instant he heard I was sick he began clamoring about my will. I never heard such a dither. The Latimers are so realistic about their wills and their trusts. It makes me feel every minute of my age. . . . Asey, how old are you?"

"My age," Asey told her with a smile, "is my only secret. Even Dr. Cummings, over home, he can't guess. That reminds me, the doc said for me to send you his regards, an' he's glad you're better. What was it that took you to the hospital?"

"A horrid little appendix." She made a face. "Such a nuisance. I was alone on the West Coast, and what a time I had!" She told him all about the operation, and never thought till later how blandly she had been sidetracked from the topic of Asey's age. "So," she concluded, "that's what happened. I feel marvelous now, except—Asey, what nerve! What utter gall! Look—over on South Point!"

A black roadster with an aluminum trailer on behind was drawing up by the field below the Latimer house.

"Look at that girl!" Nora said. "Undoing the gate! Asey, can you beat the nerve of some of these tourists? That field is fenced, gated, and sprouting with No Trespass signs. And there are Martha and Gertrude, hanging out sheets, oblivious of— Honestly, with seven trailer camps in town, of which I own two, why must they pick my field? It infuriates me. I'm boiling over!"

She looked it, Asey thought. That was the trouble with these folks who owned everything from trailer camps to fancy hotels. They all got so sensitive about their property.

"Like me to go over to your landin'," he asked, "an' do some evictin' for you? I'm in fine evictin' fettle. I evicted twenty trailers from my own orchard this year. Tourists like orchards." He started up the engine. "So much nice wood handy."

"That girl!" Mrs. Latimer banged her fist against the seat. "Leaving her car and going to bathe, is she?

Oh, make yourself at home—the place is yours! That lovely beach, and the float, and the landing. Oh, those aren't for Mrs. Latimer! Perish the thought! I just fix those up for the tourists. Latimer service! . . . Asey, that looks suspiciously like a Tootsy-Wheetsy outfit!"

Asey stared at her. "A which?"

"One of those contest trailers from the Latimer-West Company's last campaign. Tootsy-Wheetsy, the Nation's Breakfast Food. . . . No, it isn't. There's no insignia on the side. Well, it looks just like the ones we gave away last month as prizes. . . . Asey, I can't get over the nerve of this wretched girl!"

"She's not a bad-lookin' sort—"

"Take the boat hook! Here!"

The girl in the bathing suit smiled pleasantly at them as they drew up to the landing. "Good morning." Her voice, Asey thought, was no ordinary tourist voice. It was a low, well-bred voice, and it came from the vicinity of Boston. "Good morning. Isn't this a glorious day, after that horrible weather?"

Mrs. Latimer swallowed twice. "A superb day," she said acidly. "May I ask who gave you permission to enter the field, and use my beach and float?"

The girl stood up, a slim, straight figure. "Why, I'm sorry if—I mean, I asked in town for the best place to swim where there weren't mobs around, and they directed me here. I—" She stopped, her face pink.

"Without doubt," Mrs. Latimer said, "this *is* the best place to swim without mobs in attendance. But it belongs to me. I erect fences, gates, and signs for the express purpose of keeping it exclusively mine. Do you understand me?"

"Oh. I—I'm sorry," the girl said. "I suppose it's someone's idea of a frightfully good joke, sending me here. Rural humor. I'm terribly sorry. I'll go at once—"

"Help her"—Mrs. Latimer spoke to Asey—"with the gate, please. Snap the padlock, too, if it's not been broken."

The girl bit her lip, started to speak, and then changed her mind. Asey felt sorry for her. She was not the sort who needed any such rubbing in, and Mrs. Latimer should have known it.

"There's a fine beach," he said, as they started off, "over at—oh, I wouldn't cry if I was you. Mrs. Latimer's gettin' over operations, an' she's at that stage of bein' riled easy. Forget it. Are you cruisin' around alone?"

"No, Uncle's with me," the girl said. "I'm sorry to drip so. I don't usually cry at the drop of a hat, but this has been the hell of a morning, briefly speaking. The hell of a week, in fact. Whoever thought up trailers is a sadist. Seven solid days of rain in a trailer—why, my God!" She stopped short, and stared at the trailer.

"What's the matter?" Asey inquired.

"That—that's not our car! That's not our trailer! Ours has insignia on the side!"

Asey looked at her curiously. "You feel all right?" he asked.

"Uncle!" The girl ran to the trailer door and wrenched it open. "Uncle—oh! Oh!"

Asey followed her to the door, and peered over her shoulder at the interior, and at the figure of a man sprawled on the floor. He stepped inside for a moment, then turned and faced the girl. "I s'pose," he said in a voice that purred, "that this unfortunate an' very dead gentleman whose head has been bashed in so nasty an' so thorough, I s'pose he ain't your uncle, either?"

"I tell you, it's not even our trailer!" the girl said blankly. "That's not my uncle in there. I never saw that man before in all my life!" . . .

"This"—Mrs. Latimer found a cigarette and scratched a kitchen match against the side of the rock on which she sat—"is without exception the most ridiculously, impossibly fantastic yarn I ever heard!"

It was not a new thought with her. She had repeated it, in substantially the same words, for the previous twenty minutes, even during two near-fainting spells and an outburst of hysterics.

"And that girl is crazy!" She turned to the white-faced maid. "Gertrude, you may go back to the house, now Asey's returned. I'm perfectly all right. Help Martha find clothes for that girl, and then bring me something to sit on—"

"Why not," Asey suggested hopefully, "go up an' rest on the porch, where it's cool?"

"And bring me a hat with a brim, Gertrude," Nora added indomitably. "Asey, explain. *Why* can't the police come at once? Where's that Weesit cop?"

"He's got some of the Inn crowd out fishing in his boat." Asey filled his pipe. "An' the state cops is all tied up, with senators investigatin' a new cruiser in Provincetown Harbor, an' with strikes near Boston. The detective outfit's knee-deep in the Crane case. Hanson told me to carry on till they come. I already phoned Dr. Cummings. He's medical examiner, an' till he gets over all we can do is wait. Don't you think you better rest?"

"No, no, no!" Mrs. Latimer's voice rose shrilly.

"No! Asey, this whole yarn of that girl's is crazy! She swears this isn't her car, or her trailer, or her uncle. And still, she swears that she started *out* in her own car, with her own trailer, and her uncle, too! And she claims that she didn't get out of the car until she came to the field here. And that she stopped up in town only just long enough to ask the way to a beach. She says that her trailer really was a Tootsy-Wheetsy contest trailer. But this one isn't. Asey, it's absurd! And all of it happening here in my field!"

Asey looked at her curiously. Her pettishness, in view of the circumstances, puzzled him. "You know," he said, "this is sort of a serious affair, Mrs. Latimer."

"I know! Headlines, and more headlines. It's my irritation about those headlines to come that's eclipsing all the sympathy I feel for that poor man yonder, whoever he is. I can see those headlines. 'Widow of Latimer Millions'—sometimes I wish they'd refer to Gregory by name, and not as 'The Latimer Millions.' . . . And, besides, Asey, it's all so crazy!"

"Some parts is normal enough," Asey said. "Here's the girl's licenses an' registrations. She's Cordelia Alcott, five feet five, hazel eyes, brown hair. Her car's a Tracy roadster, her trailer's a de luxe Wander Bird. That's sane enough. Only, the roadster here now, an' the Wander Bird tacked on to it, they're different

makers' numbers entirely from hers, an' they got New
York instead of Massachusetts plates. In a way, that's
clear, too. She thought she had her own outfit—"

"But she did, Asey! She says so. She talked with
her uncle before she set off. And if," Mrs. Latimer
said, as if she were trying to reassure herself, "if they
were hers when she started out, and if she didn't stir
from behind that wheel till she got here in this field,
then they've got to be hers now! She says that her
trailer was a Tootsy-Wheetsy trailer—you know, I
told you this looked like one. But this isn't. It hasn't
any insignia."

"I wonder," Asey said, "if you'd explain to me
about these contest trailers of yours? What insignia
do they have?"

"It's an enlargement of our trademark on the side.
A pixie holding up a blue bowl of Tootsy-Wheetsy—
what did you say?"

"I just choked," Asey told her. "Go on."

"Well, there are exactly twenty-five trailers marked
with that insignia, scattered by districts over the
United States. There aren't so many of them that this
girl should expect every trailer to be a contest trailer
like hers. . . . Asey, where's this uncle, if that man
inside isn't her uncle? You don't just misplace uncles
like—like—"

"Collar buttons," Asey suggested. "True enough."

"Still," Mrs. Latimer went on, "the Alcott girl swears that this Uncle Wilbur of hers was in his bunk in the trailer, having arthritis and bad temper, when she started. If the dead man isn't Uncle Wilbur, who is he? And are you—? Asey, why don't you start in and *do* something? You're supposed to be a murder expert."

"I'm waitin'," Asey said gently, "for Doc." He restrained himself from adding that her presence was curtailing him considerably.

"But why can't you hunt clues?" Mrs. Latimer persisted. "Why don't you *do* something? What are you grinning at?"

"I was thinkin'," Asey said, "of Lizzie Chatfield. Somehow, she's stuck in my mind. My, what a day for Lizzie! She'll have more fun—I'll be right back," he added parenthetically as he got up. "I'm goin' to help that maid of yours with that chair."

From the sun deck of the Inn. Lizzie, herself, watched through the binoculars as Asey strode across the field and took a camp chair from Gertrude's hand. It was all most unusual, and most exciting—that trailer there in the field, and Nora sitting there on that rock, and Asey Mayo and the maids running around. And that strange girl. Lizzie didn't know what to make of it all, but if Nora didn't give any indication of returning to the Inn Lizzie decided that perhaps she would take a little walk over to South Point. Perhaps—yes, that was Dr. Cummings's old sedan, bouncing down the lane to the field! Yes, perhaps, on the whole, it might be better if she changed her shoes and started over to the Point at once. Dear Nora should be cautioned against overdoing. And at the same time Lizzie could find out what was going on, and tell dear Nora about those swing record people.

Lizzie put her glasses into their case, rolled up her tatting, and went indoors. As she bustled along the corridor to her room, she collided with one of the maids, whose armful of papers and portfolios tumbled to the floor.

"Oh, Mrs. Chatfield!" the maid said. "Are you hurt? I'm sorry— Oh, *look* at Mr. Warren's sketches, all over the floor! He's moving— Oh, dear, here he comes now! He'll ruin me when he sees 'em on the floor—"

The maid scuttled away, but Lizzie waited for Jere. She was curious about those sketches.

" 'Morning, Mrs. C." Jere spoke as though he were very tired. "How are you?—Whee! What happened?"

"It was an accident," Lizzie explained. "I bumped

into Ethel. I'm so sorry. Are these really yours, all these nice sketches?"

"Chunks," Jere told her, with a touch of bitterness, "of my youth."

"Tch, tch"—Lizzie clucked her tongue reprovingly—"you shouldn't talk like that! You're not a day over twenty-six! Has dear Nora seen these lovely sketches here?"

Jere drew a long breath. "Nora," he said, "prefers the later Warrens. That's why she gets 'em. These items distress her, Mrs. C., so you'd better not refer to them. Say—wait! Have you got a lunch date? . . . No? Listen. Will you come over to Nora's with me? Now, right away?"

"But, my dear boy, I haven't been asked!"

"Mrs. C.," Jere said earnestly, almost desperately, "I went to school with your husband's nephew; my father did business with your brothers. Mrs. C., as a special favor to me, will you please come to lunch at the Point? Please?"

"Well—" Lizzie wavered.

"That's fine!" Jere patted her shoulder. "Be ready in five minutes. Hurry!"

It never occurred to Lizzie, as she did a little primping in her room, to wonder why Jere was so anxious for Nora Latimer to have another luncheon guest.

that particular day. To her, it was sufficient that her plans were working out in a perfectly beautiful manner. All the way over to South Point in the beach wagon Lizzie chatted blithely, entirely unaware of Jere's set jaw and tightened lips, and the whiteness of his knuckles as he gripped the wheel.

"My, my!" Lizzie said as they came over the crest of the hill. "Why, there's Nora, still down in the field! Why don't we drive down there and see what's going on?"

"You'll get terribly bounced," Jere said.

"But I do want to see that trailer," Lizzie told him honestly. "I've never seen one, and I've always wanted— What did you say?" she added, as they left the graveled drive. "What about a condemned man?"

"I said," Jere laughed shortly, "that the condemned man ate a hearty breakfast. Old song. I'm just joking —you'd better hold on!"

Nora Latimer smiled as she watched the beach wagon bump its way into the field, but the smile faded at the sight of Lizzie. Asey, emerging from the trailer, looked at Nora's face and whistled softly under his breath. Dr. Cummings, just behind him, moaned as Lizzie got out.

"Who told you?" he demanded. "Lizzie, who told you about our murder?"

"What!" Lizzie's scream was so piercing that a sea gull overhead flapped its wings and swooped off to sea. "What? What!"

"Oh, you didn't know? Just your instinct for news, I suppose. Well, we do have a murder— Lizzie, don't you dare faint! . . . Oh, well, faint away, then!"

"*Do* something!" Nora commanded.

"I know Lizzie's faints," Cummings said wearily. "Where's her handbag? Get it, Jere. . . . There, take the smelling salts out of it. . . . Yes, that little bottle. I know that bottle—there. . . . Now, Lizzie, snap out of it!"

"Who?" Lizzie said. "Who's been killed?"

"We don't know," Cummings answered. "That is, everything indicates that he's a Mister John Smith, but of course that's foolish. He can't be. It's impossible. No one is ever named John Smith. . . . J. Pierpont Smith, or John Vanderbilt Smith, or Jon Smythe, yes. But plain John Smith, never."

"What does he look like?"

"Well, Lizzie," Cummings said judicially, "he looks the way any man looks who's been hit with great force and a heavy piece of wood. Oak, Asey says. I'm sure you don't want to see him—"

"What does he look like?" Lizzie insisted.

"He's medium height," Asey said, "an' darkish.

Around forty-five or fifty. Black hair, sort of thick features, an' he's wearin' orange bathin' trunks. . . . Mrs. Latimer, let her have that chair, will you? Thanks. . . . An' he's got a mustache. Do you know him?"

"Of course not!" Lizzie said. "He doesn't even sound like anyone I know!"

"Good," Cummings said. "If Lizzie doesn't recognize him, Asey, he's never been to Weesit before. Now, I'll leave it to you to find out who he really is. I've got to— Oh, Jere, will you—? Where *is* that boy? Where's he going? I want him to—"

But Jere was dashing up the path toward the house. Lizzie, watching his headlong rush, caught on to the reason for it before any of the others did. "Why, he's racing to meet that girl!" she said. "The one that wore the bathing suit. Why, he knows her! He's kissing her! Now, isn't that nice? I've never seen him so happy and so animated since he's been here. I said to the chambermaid only the other day, if he'd just find some nice girl and— *Isn't* she a charming-looking girl! Who is she, Nora dear?"

"A tourist." Nora's voice was like a thin piece of ice as she stood up suddenly—too suddenly, Dr. Cummings thought, watching her with a professional eye. She wasn't well enough to jerk around like that. He'd tell her so later when she calmed down. For an intelligent woman Nora was displaying an amazing lack of emotional control in this mess.

"A tourist? Who?" Lizzie asked interestedly. "What's her name? Is she—?"

"This is the most fantastic muddle," Nora said angrily, "that I ever encountered. Lizzie, someone will take you back to the Inn. I don't feel equal to entertaining. Tell Jere I know he won't mind if I cancel lunch. I'm going to retire until this whole muddle is cleared up. Doctor, please keep the reporters away. And, Asey, I'm sure things will be cleaned up by tomorrow, won't they? I'd hate to be forced into applying pressure."

Dr. Cummings's eyes narrowed as he watched her return to the house. "Why that crack?" he asked. "Jangled nerves, I suppose. It's incredible, how nasty she can be sometimes."

"She meant," Asey said, "that she has lots of political friends, an' lots of money. She don't want her field littered up with us, or anyone, or anything. I'd imagine that if we don't get results by tomorrow, she will— Well, let's get to work. Hanson'll be here soon, Doc. You stay till then. You know the story. . . . Oh, here you are, Jere. You stay too, please. I'll take Mrs. Chatfield back, an' you too, Miss Alcott. We

got to find your own trailer an' car an' uncle, an'
such. Doc, tell Hanson I'll phone him. . . . Just
two shakes, Mrs. Chatfield, an' I'll have my car down
here."

Lizzie glowed at the sight of Asey's long, su-
perstreamlined Porter Sixteen. Involuntarily, she
thought of the bellboys. There wouldn't be any dallying about their bringing her hot milk at night, now,
after they saw her return to the Inn in that car, with
Asey Mayo!

It seemed to her that she had hardly got settled
on the pigskin seat before they drew up at the Inn.
Lizzie made a rather slow and deliberate exit.

"Now, Mrs. Chatfield," Asey said warningly, "you
mustn't tell anyone anythin' until after the police
come. It'd disturb Mrs. Latimer, to have folks yowlin'
around. I'll come back later, an' tell you every single
thing. I promise. You'll wait till I come before you
say a word, won't you?"

Lizzie hesitated, and then she nodded. "If it would
be better for poor, dear Nora, I'll do as you say."

The Porter Sixteen sped off.

About a mile from the town Asey stopped by the
side of the road and looked quizzically at Cordelia
Alcott. "Had some mornin', ain't you?" he observed.

"My friends call me Cordy." She drew a long

breath. "Oh, what shatters me, aside from losing Uncle Wilbur, is the story I have to tell! But it's true! Asey, whatever game the police decide to play, I'm going to be *it*, aren't I?"

"Unless we solve a few problems"—Asey pulled out his pipe—"I think so. I got great respect for the state cops, but there's some angles to your story that's awful transcendental. An' with Sister Latimer shootin' sparks an' breathin' fire—that was a bad time for Jere Warren to clasp you to his bosom, you know."

"I gathered that," Cordy said, "but I didn't know at the time. I haven't seen Jere for two years."

"So?"

"Yes," Cordy said sharply, "so! Look; let's iron out Jere, in passing. We were engaged. Then Jere lost his job, doing commercial art for an advertising firm, and then what little income he had just up and blew, and— Well, the poorer he got, the prouder he got. We fought, and that was that. It didn't seem to penetrate that I was even poorer than he was. Am poorer, for that matter."

Asey raised his eyebrows.

"The trailer outfit belongs to Uncle, and really," she said with a grin, "he *did* win it in that Tootsy-Wheetsy business. Uncle doesn't drive, and he asked me to. I lost my job two months ago, and stew in a trailer was paradise compared to Mrs. Moriarty's boarding-house, nine weeks owing. I hocked things and paid her, and here I am. And if Uncle Wilbur's lost— Well, even stew on his pension is at least stew."

"Speakin' of food," Asey said, "my lunch is in that compartment in front of you. Dig in, an' pour me some coffee from the vacuum bottle. An' while you eat tell me your story twice, please. I want to see where you got mixed. Begin back when you got up this mornin'."

"That was at seven. Uncle snores, and we're separated by a denim curtain. I made my bunk, and set out with the family purse for that farmhouse I told you about, those people named Snow. Uncle called out as I left, and said his arthritis was bad and his head worse, and his stomach simply terrible, and he wanted a cup of hot water with lemon in it, quick. I got it, and then went to the Snows' for things."

"Thinks like what?" Asey asked.

"Eggs, milk, butter, fresh bread, water in a jug, and then Mrs. Snow presented me with clams and a hunk of ice, and a basket of vegetables and a bunch of flowers. I had rather a load."

"It sounds," Asey said, "like an inventory."

She grinned. "Halfway back, I had to stop and put

down the vegetables and flowers, but I dragged the rest along to the trailer. Uncle yelled as I started to open the door, and told me to wait, because he was dressing. I told him to take the things in before the ice melted any more, and he said he couldn't move his arm because it was stiff, and I was a lazy, unfeeling thing to expect him to carry ice. I resented that, and we went on at some length, all pretty heatedly. Finally he said he was so ill and so agitated, he was going straight back to bed. On the whole, he annoyed me considerably."

"I'm beginnin' not to like Uncle," Asey remarked.

"Oh, but he's great fun! We were just out of sorts, both of us. I said he could go back to bed, but that we were moving the very minute I returned. I wanted a swim, and I was going to have one. He was still spluttering when I left. That sounds as if we were nasty people, doesn't it? But the squabble really began three days ago, when I wanted to visit the Randalls."

"The ones at Horseshoe Beach?"

"Yes, they knew I was going to stop by, and then they asked me to spend a few days, and I wanted to take the car and go. But Uncle refused point-blank to be left alone. After all, the car and the trailer are his and it wasn't really reasonable of me to get mad, but I did. Principally, it was the rain. I tell you, Asey, last week was hell. Anyway, to get back to my story, I got the vegetables and flowers, and marched back to the trailer—"

"An' slung 'em in the front seat," Asey said.

"Yes. I was so hot and mad, and Uncle had taken the other stuff in. I started off. In the village, I asked the way to a beach, and then drove to Latimers'. You know all that. But, Asey, where's my car? Where's the trailer? Where's Uncle?"

"Probably," Asey said, "Uncle's sleepin' hearty in the trailer, with the ice melted an' the clams gone bad in the sun. Soon, we'll go see—"

"I've grasped the fact," Cordy interrupted, "that I got the wrong outfit. But how? Where?"

"You was hot and tired," Asey said, "an' wrought up from the rain an' Uncle, an' from being thwarted on your visit to the Randalls'. There's pinewoods around the Snows' house. On the second trip for the vegetables you took the wrong path back. You thought you got into your own car, but you got into another just like it. Natural mistake. Same sort of roadster, same sort of Wander Bird trailer. No insignia on the side, but you wouldn't bother to look."

"Yes, that must have been how I switched. But

who's this man in the trailer in the field? Who killed him? When was he killed?"

"Last night, the doc says—"

"Who *is* the man?"

Asey shrugged. "One John Smith, if you want to believe the evidence. Well, it's time we set out to find Uncle. Ready?"

She nodded. "Except, before we go, will you explain to me about Jere and Mrs. Latimer?" She colored under her tan. "The last time Jere and I met we mutually decided never to meet again. But I've thought about him, and wondered about him, and I'll admit I was delighted to see him today. He seemed glad to see me. But Mrs. Latimer appeared to own him. In a nutshell, Asey, I'd like to know all before I see Jere again."

Asey hesitated. "I don't know much, Cordy. He's painted near my house. That's how I met him. He lives at the Inn."

"Go on."

"Mrs. Latimer owns the Inn," Asey said. "Her husband was a Cape Codder, one of those successful dabblers. She owns most of Weesit, an' half a dozen outfis, like Tootsy-Wheetsy—did she tell you that? Well, she also owns the station wagon Jere drives."

"I think," Cordy said slowly, "that I get it. And people say—?"

"People," Asey said, "say all the things that people usually say when a middle-aged woman has a youngish man apparently at her beck an' call. Me, I don't think Jere likes bein' a lap dog an' a surrealist. He done good work when he was paintin' over my way, an'—"

"I see. Definitely."

"Yup, but it's a lopsided situation, with Latimer doin' the loppin'. I wouldn't be harsh—"

"She's mad about him," Cordy said. "You can tell it with your eyes closed. Just the tone of her voice. . . . Asey, haven't you any ideas, or clues about all this mess?"

"John Smith," Asey said, as he started the roadster, "or whoever he is, was bashed from behind, last night between twelve an' two, the doc thinks. We think he was sittin' on the side of the bunk, an' someone bashed him sudden an' hard. There's a spot on the back an' base of the skull where a quick, hard blow is more definite than the electric chair. I can't think of a nicer way to kill anyone. You can track down knives an' bullets, an' poisons. But when someone's banged over the head you don't even know what sort of blunt instrument was used as a weapon. My guess here is a small block of hardwood—the cops'll check on that.

Somethin' that someone could pick up anywhere, an' throw away anywhere. It's a clever way to kill. The only problem is to get your victim where you want him. Either you got to sneak up an' bash, or else he's got to suspect you so little, you can maneuver him where you want. So, it might be the murdered man's best girl-friend, if you see my point, or a total stranger."

"Why are you and Cummings so sure he's not John Smith?"

"Everything was so awful John Smithy," Asey said. "So many monograms. Fishy, like. Now, tell me again what sort of place your trailer was parked in, an' we'll get Uncle an' take him back, an' see if he's a one to cast any light."

"If this man was killed last night," Cordy said, "isn't Uncle my alibi? Because he told me this morning that he never closed his eyes until after four, and I can't twist in my bunk without his knowing it. He has uncanny ears, anyway. He hears field mice, he claims."

"He's goin' to be a fine alibi," Asey said. "Now, this is the road, ain't it?"

"Yes. Around this next bend," she said; "past this knoll, right in this clearing. Right—"

She stopped short and stared at the clearing as Asey

stopped the roadster. "He's gone!" she said. "The trailer isn't there!"

Asey looked at her searchingly. "Are you sure this is the right place?" he inquired. "There's a lot of clearin's, an' you might have picked the wrong one."

"Listen," Cordy said; "I looked at the same spindly pines and bayberries and brambles for one solid week! Get out, and I'll show you where I buried our tins. Here—come along."

She took Asey by the hand and led him to a spot just inside the pines. "There; see? This is our dump. . . . Asey, where is Uncle? Don't tell me he's driven away, because he can't drive!"

"You're certain positive sure he can't?"

"Well," she said, "he can drive in the sense of holding the wheel while I light a cigarette, yes. I asked him to put on the parking brake once, and he yanked out the choke. . . . Asey, what's happened to him? If I can't find him— Oh, you don't think anything's happened to the poor lamb, do you?"

Asey was busy looking at tire tracks. "Here's where it was, an' here's where it pulled out. Not an expert job. Huh. Let's go into the woods an' see if we can straighten out what happened to you."

"Here," Cordy said after they had walked for some five minutes, "is—"

"Where you dropped your load. There's an apple, an' a zinnia. Now, here's traces of an old path. You went back on this one—"

"I don't remember, but it must be. Yes, there's another apple!"

"An' here," said Asey a little later, "is another clearin', on the same road but farther up. Looks like the same. . . . Yup, here's tire marks. That's what happened."

"But what about Uncle?" Cordy persisted.

"Prob'ly he figured you'd lit out on him," Asey said, "an' got someone else to drive him to other places, after you."

"Maybe he's gone to the Randalls'."

"If he did," Asey said, "he won't get far. I gave Hanson the numbers of your car and trailer plates, when I phoned from Mrs. Latimer's, just in case something like this happened. By now, the numbers'll have gone out over the teletype from Provincetown to the bridges."

"In case? You think of things, don't you? Asey, d'you really mean that you didn't expect to find Uncle?"

"Well, there was you an' him," Asey said, as they walked slowly back to where the Porter roadster was parked, "in the trailer. A little ways off, there was

John Smith. Uncle's your alibi, but are you his?"

Cordy shook her head. "I sleep like a log," she admitted. "But, look here, Asey, you can't suspect Uncle! You don't know Uncle!"

"Maybe not in the flesh," Asey returned, "but I'm gettin' to feel I've known him forever. Let's wander back to Latimer's. An' if Hanson should send down a feller named Harrigan to take charge, don't let him rile you. Don't let anyone rile you. You know your story. Stick to it."

"You're being pretty swell," Cordy coughed and blew her nose. "I don't know why you—"

"Your grandfather was Courtney Alcott, wasn't he?" Asey asked. "Yup. You're named for your grandmother. I took 'em to Frisco once, on Porter's yacht. Your chin sticks out like your grandmother's. I thought so this mornin', when you stuck it out at Mrs. Latimer. Well, let's get back—"

At the entrance to the Latimer grounds, a state policeman jumped on the running board. "Asey, Hanson's tearing his hair out to find you."

"Didn't he send Harrigan?"

"And how. But he's gone. Asey, you missed plenty, you have!"

"What's happened? Where's Hanson—down by where the trailer is?"

"Where," the trooper said, "the trailer *was.*"

"What's happened?" Asey demanded again.

"Go take a look," the trooper said. "I got to stay here an' keep the crowd out. Just you go give a look!"

Cordy gripped the door as the Porter shot off up the drive. The field below the Latimer house was dotted with cars and groups of people. But the trailer was gone!

"Asey, what's happened?" Cordy asked.

Asey was too busy hailing Dr. Cummings to answer. "Hey, Doc! Hey, come here!"

The rotund doctor hurried to the car. "Peachy time for you to show up," he said. "Asey, someone set that damned trailer on fire, and burned it up!"

"An' what," Asey asked, "happened to J. Smith?"

"By the grace of God"—Cummings mopped at his forehead with a handkerchief—"he'd been taken uptown in the ambulance. Oh, Asey, you should have been here, if only to have seen Harrigan!"

"He was here, then?"

"Up at the house, chatting with Nora, and one of his troopers was here in the field with Jere Warren. The other'd gone up the drive to the entrance. And, Asey, you ought to hear Nora now. She's wound up like a top. Just after she'd got herself calmed down, too. . . . Come see what's left."

Asey looked thoughtfully at the wreckage, and then he smiled. "You took pictures," he said, "before you moved Smith?"

"Harrigan did," Cummings told him. "And I know it'll charm you to hear that he left his camera, films, and kit inside the trailer. Nothing but ashes now."

"I don't understand this," Cordy said. "D'you mean that someone deliberately burned the trailer up? Why? Who did it?"

"Here's Warren," the doctor said, before Asey had a chance to answer. "Jere, come here. Give Asey an eyewitness account."

"Whoosh!" Jere said. "That's all. The trooper and I were sitting over in the beach wagon, and suddenly we smelled smoke. We rushed over, and the place was an inferno. The gas tanks blew—see my pants? That's where something hot landed. We couldn't save the trailer or the car. It was all we could do to put out the grass fires here."

"See anyone lurking around?"

"Not a soul."

"Who was here after I left?" Asey asked.

"Nora," Jere said, "and one of the maids came down with some sandwiches. The doctor and I were here, and then the troopers came. And Lizzie. She plodded over on foot to retrieve her pocketbook and smelling salts. She didn't stay long enough to speak a hundred words. She said she had orders from you about everything, and back she plodded to the Inn. I suppose she's sitting there in her first row orchestra seat on the sun deck, with those binoculars riveted to her eyes."

Hanson, the police lieutenant, came over to them. "Asey, I could wring Harrigan's neck for letting this happen! Why'd you leave? Whyn't you come back? Is this the girl? Well, come over to my car and get me straightened out on things. I'll all twisted."

Obediently, Asey and Cordelia told him all they knew.

When they finished, Hanson stared at them.

"All clear now?" Asey asked.

"Sure." Hanson spoke with elaborate sarcasm. "Oh, sure. Yes. Miss Alcott starts out in her outfit, but it isn't hers. It's another outfit when she lands here, and it's got a dead man named John Smith in it. And Miss Alcott has an uncle, and a trailer like Smith's, but right now they've disappeared."

"You sound confused," Asey said, "but you think it over, an' it's like lookin' through plate glass. Now, I got to go—"

"Come back here!" Hanson yelled. "You can't run out on me! What'll I tell the papers? What'll I tell Latimer? Mayhem's the least she's threatened me with if I don't clear this up. Asey, come back and help!"

"I'm goin' off an' help," Asey said. "Meantime, chase this mob out of the field. That'll do more to soothe Mrs. Latimer than anything else. Then get this wreckage towed away. Leave one of your men at her house. That'll help the Latimer feelin's an' give her a sense of security an' bein' waited on. 'N' en, find out about the trailer. Oh, you already got people goin' on that? Well, find out who John Smith is. An' find Uncle Wilbur an' the other trailer—"

"What'll I tell the papers?"

"Tell 'em anythin', as long as you make it sound good. Promise startlin' revelations tomorrow. Who knows? You may have 'em. Now, I'm goin' to see Lizzie Chatfield. If she happened to be huggin' her binoculars around the time the trailer was burned, we may get somewhere. I'll stay at the Inn, tonight, Hanson. Drop over later."

"What about the girl?"

"She can stay there, too," Asey said. "I'll be responsible for her, an' Lizzie can chaperon her all proper. Now, you let me go see Lizzie."

At the Inn, Lizzie greeted Asey and Cordelia effusively. "Such an exciting day! And now this fire! I'm so glad you came, Asey, because I wanted to ask you about that. Was it spontaneous combustion?"

"Most any fire," Asey said, "can be spontaneous combustion. If you mean, was it set—"

"That's just what I mean," Lizzie interrupted. "Because it was set, wasn't it? Just like a book I read from the Inn Library last week. Jere Warren recommended it to me. It was a murder, and, in it, the murderer set a fire and burned up the scene of his crime. Only, in the book, it was a stable. Not a trailer, of course. It was awfully clever, the way he did it in the book. There weren't any fingerprints left, or any footprints, or anything for the police to work on at all. And this amounts to the same thing, doesn't it?"

Cordy looked at Asey. "I begin to get it," she said. "I begin to percolate. It did just that, didn't it? It demolished all the things that might have led to discovering who John Smith really was. Instead of having a trailer full of things that would tell you all about the man, you've nothing but ashes."

"An' some numbers," Asey said. "Mrs. Chatfield, were you lookin' through your binoculars around the time of the fire?"

"Oh, yes, I always look around every so often,"
Lizzie said. "And do you know what I think? I think
someone came in a car and set the fire. The beach
lane comes very near Nora's grounds. Anyone could
jump her wall, easily. And, with those woods, he
could easily get to the field and not be noticed. Jere
and that officer were over on the other side, in the
beach wagon. They wouldn't have been able to see
anyone, from that direction. I couldn't, either, with
the trees in the way. So that's what I think, that someone came in a car, and sneaked— Oh, by the way"—
she turned to Cordy—"your uncle. Have you found
that uncle of yours?"

"Not yet."

"Isn't that strange!" Lizzie said. "Well, Asey, some
one must have come in a car—"

"Did you have your glasses on the field all the
afternoon?" Asey wanted to know.

Lizzie shook her head regretfully. "I was over there
earlier, and when I came back I talked with some
friends. I'm sorry now that I didn't really keep a
watch, but, of course, I never expected that the murderer would come back and do anything like that! I
wouldn't have gone back for my pocketbook if I'd
thought he might come back! I didn't even think of
the murderer—where are you going, Asey?"

"Phone," Asey told her succinctly. He called Hanson at Mrs. Latimer's. "An'," he wound up his conversation, "find Uncle if you have to turn out the National Guard!"

On his way back from telephoning he arranged for a room for Cordy. Later, after a fruitless period of searching back roads for Uncle Wilbur, Asey and Cordelia and Lizzie dined together at the Inn.

"There's Jere Warren!" Lizzie said, during the meal. "Let's have him join us."

"Please," Cordy said quickly, "no. I'm tired. I don't feel like talking. I—I'm worried about Uncle. D'you mind not asking Jere?"

"Why, no." Clearly, Lizzie minded a lot. "Only, well, he does seem to be so very interested in you. He has that look."

"What look?" Cordy asked.

"Oh, I can't explain it, but I know it," Lizzie said happily. "I've got five sons, you see. All married. They all had that look just before—there's Hanson, Asey!"

Asey followed the lieutenant out on the porch.

"Listen," the latter said; "I've got twenty men hunting Uncle and his damned trailer, and no soap. Now what?"

"Go through hotels, camps—"

"We have. I had those number plates flashed on

the Boston commercial stations in the early evening news. No soap. We've checked all wharves and boat landings. He hasn't left the Cape."

"Then he's here," Asey said. "Find him. If I thought I could help you, I would—"

"I know all about that," Hanson said, "an' I don't want you to go dashing around any more than you have to. Well, we'll carry on."

"Got anything on the burned trailer?" Asey asked. "Haven't you got anywhere with that?"

Hanson shook his head. "They've only checked through as far as the distributor. I'll see you later."

Shortly before midnight he returned. "No news," he told Asey. "You might as well go to bed. We'll keep it up. There's one man in Hyannis who's got a Tracy roadster and a Wander Bird trailer about a million years old, and he just phoned me that if he was picked up once more, he'd sue the state. What the trailer tourists think of us isn't printable. We're stopping all of 'em. . . . Asey, where is this damn' uncle?"

Asey wondered, himself, as he got ready for bed. This missing uncle, with his missing trailer, interested him. He wondered how Uncle Wilbur looked. There'd probably be pictures of him in the paper next day. Asey laughed. It was a crazy situation.

He got into bed and went to sleep at once. He even slept through half of a typical August thunderstorm. But the sound of someone fumbling at his door wakened him in a split second.

Automatically, Asey's hand slid underneath his pillow. But his pistol was back home in Wellfleet. He hadn't thought to ask Hanson for a gun. Not for a moment had it occurred to him that he needed one. A convenient flash of lightning confirmed his feeling that no one, yet, had entered his room.

Grinning, Asey slipped out of bed and crept over to the windows. To keep one of them from rattling he had whittled out a wedge earlier in the evening, and that small triangle of wood was going to come in handy now. The Inn rooms had two doors. The outer one was a swinging, latticed thing for ventilation, and the inner one a regular door that opened in.

Pulling out the wedge, Asey crept back to the door and carefully inserted it between the bottom of the door and the threshold. It fitted beautifully.

Let 'em try to get in now, Asey thought. Even though they worked his key out of the door, or managed to turn it from the outside, they'd have a fine time trying to shove through over that wedge. In the meantime, he'd get the trooper Hanson had left down by the switchboard. Just removing the receiver on the phone by his bed should bring the fellow hopping. To make sure, he'd tap out some code on the hook. Whether or not the man knew code, that should be enough to send him into action.

He tapped, and waited. Nothing happened. He tapped again. Still nothing happened.

Mentally, Asey summed up his opinions of the trooper in a few stark nautical phrases.

As he started back to the door, his elbow caught the cord of a table lamp and sent it crashing to the floor. He heard a sound in the corridor. The person outside was departing.

"Damn!" he said. He unlocked the inside door and pushed at the outside latticed door.

But the latter didn't give. He tried again, but the door would not open.

He chuckled. "Dose," he said, "of my own medicine. The lad didn't want to come into my room, but to make sure I stayed put inside it. So, he sticks a wedge in, on the swing. Very smart, mister!"

He went back to the phone and jiggled the hook, but the line was dead. Two sharp flashes of lightning inspired him to snap on the bed light. As he suspected, that didn't work. The storm had cut off all the electricity, and the phone circuits as well.

Asey sat down on the bed and listened to the thunder. If he could outshout that he might raise that trooper, but he'd also rouse the whole hotel. And probably, by now, whoever put the wedge on the outside of the door was miles away, tending to his own business, secure in the knowledge that Asey Mayo was effectively hemmed in. Except, of course, for the windows.

Asey got up and looked out of them. He could tie sheets together and climb down, like the eloping bride in an early movie.

He twitched off one sheet, before he laughed and put it back on the bed again. He must be getting old!

"If I was this feller," he said, "tryin' to hem Mayo in, an' I knew I'd waked Mayo up, first thing I'd expect would be for Mayo to take to the windows. So, I think I'd give up my hemmin' plan, for the time bein', an' wait to take a crack at Mayo, leavin' via the windows. With all this crackin' an' bangin', I could pump Mayo full of holes, an' nobody'd be the wiser."

He stood and peered down into the Inn's famous rose garden. If anyone was waiting—yes, there was someone, under the second pergola!

Asey's fingers itched for his automatic. If only he had something in the line of a weapon!

He sat down in a chair, over the arm of which was

his canvas duck coat with its innumerable pockets. If he were a proper detective, he thought, there'd be something—by golly, there was! Not much. But those two lead sinkers left over from last week's flounder fishing might, with luck, do just what he wanted.

There was an inside screen, he remembered, on the bathroom window. After ten minutes of careful work, he had the screen out and the window up without the person under the pergola apparently being aware of it. Then he waited, a lead in either hand. The person down there wouldn't wait very much longer, Asey decided. Just long enough to make sure that Mayo hadn't been sufficiently disturbed or aroused to do any window climbing.

A few minutes later a flash of lightning showed the person moving away. Asey pitched both sinkers simultaneously. In the crash of thunder that followed, he couldn't tell whether the fellow made any outcry, but Asey was willing to bet money that his wild left pitch had hit home. He'd seen a hand half raised to the fellow's head.

"An'," he said with satisfaction, "if it did touch you, you'll be marked, mister, as good as if I'd carved my initials on you!" . . .

Around five o'clock the electricity came back, and, shortly after, Asey got the trooper on the phone.

Together they examined the large rubber wedge that had been thrust under the door from the corridor.

"The bellboys," the trooper said, "took dozens of these to different rooms tonight. They keep 'em in a basket in the office. Shall I take it, and see what they can do for prints?"

Asey nodded. "You can try. See anyone in particular wanderin' around last night?"

"Three or four bunches dribbled in late, all pretty high, from the Yacht Club. That Warren fellow was around a lot. He said he never got to sleep till after three, so he'd given up trying. Want me to bring up the night clerk? He'll know people's names."

"Get him," Asey said. "An' so Jere was around, was he? Huh."

The night clerk yawned at Asey's question. "Sorry," he said; "usually I get some sleep, but, with the storm—what a night! Sure; a lot of people paddled down. The Ferguson brat had a stomach-ache and I had to call the nurse. Then there was a new guest who blew in just a little while ago, and he had to have his bed shifted around so his head pointed north and he could vibrate. I guess he vibrated plenty with that last thunder! Lizzie Chatfield came down twice for wedges."

"Go on," Asey said. "You interest me greatly."

"Oh, I got a lot of complaints about windows rattling, and the phone, and the lights."

"But about Lizzie. When did she come down?"

"After Colonel Belcher, and before Miss Champion. . . . Say, you two want breakfast now? It's time for mine. Come along to the lobby."

"One more thing," Asey said as they started downstairs, "does everyone comin' in late have to pass through the lobby, or are there other doors open besides the main one?"

"Everything's locked except the one opposite the desk," the clerk told him. "Everyone has to come through here after twelve, maids and all. Manager locks up, himself, and he has the keys. Anyone fooling with your door would have to be a guest, or someone who came in before twelve, if he wasn't a guest. And if he was a stranger I don't see how he could get out except through the main door. All those other doors are locked, and the keys taken out."

It was during their picnic meal that Jere Warren came in the front door. His flannels were soaked, and his shoes made slushy sounds as he walked over to them. "Hi!" he said. "Got more coffee? Asey, can I have—? Say, what's the matter? Why do I get stared at so?"

"How'd you get that bruise on your cheek?" Asey asked in a soft purr.

"That? Oh, that's nothing. Look." He drew a sketchbook from his pocket. "See what Jere did. Rose Garden in Storm. That little item, in time, is going to buy Jere a car. Isn't that good?"

Asey looked at it. "Very. Got any others?"

"The top three pages," Jere said. "They're damp, but good. They'd be better if my flash hadn't given out and my umbrella turned turtle on me. Some nice, windy storm. You try balancing a flash and an umbrella and a sketch pad and a pencil—"

"Warren," Asey said, "what sort of game is this you play? First, fancy art for Nora, an' then this stuff in your off moments?"

"I'm not playing games," Jere answered stiffly. "I don't turn out any fancy art for Mrs. Latimer. And, furthermore, I'm pretty damned sick and tired of all this chatter. Look, Brooks, did I pay my hotel bill yesterday?"

The night clerk nodded.

"And I moved to a cheaper room in the other wing, and I— What the hell am I telling you this for?" he wound up angrily. "It's none of your damn' business!"

Asey watched him stalk through the lobby and

up the stairs. "Mike," he said, "watch that lad, will you? Begin now, an' stick. I'll tell Hanson. Brooks, what's the story on this Warren, anyway?"

The night clerk produced a sleepy leer. "Every year," he said, "Latimer has a— Hell! let's be polite and call him a protégé. Once it was a violinist. He didn't have long hair, but he used the same kind of perfume as my girl. Then there was an artist. Then a writer—what a twirp he was! All the same sort, all of 'em. Warren's different. He *did* pay, yesterday. None of the others even gave the maid a dime. And Warren's left his beach wagon up at South Point, too."

"Rebelled, huh?"

"Looks like it. My idea is, he was broke, so he took up her offer to come see her sometime, and he didn't realize what he was getting into. He gave her her money's worth. Painted that fish daytimes, carted her around the rest of the time. About three weeks ago she went West on business, and got sick and had an operation—"

"I had," Asey said, "a snip-by-snip description of that."

"Well, she came back last week. While she was away he sold some of his regular paintings. After that he asked how much he owed, Henry said. Henry told him he was Latimer's guest. He didn't think Warren meant it, of course. But Warren got mad and demanded his bill, and Henry said he'd have to talk with Mrs. Latimer, and Warren said the hell with her. They almost had a fight—"

"An' Henry broke the news to Nora?" Asey asked.

Brooks grinned. "He passed the buck to old Greening. He's the manager. He's away, and the notice about it's still on his desk. But, boy! Nora's sure crazy about this one, I'm telling you! This time she's got it bad. The others were just light cases. Watch her look at him sometime—say, what's the trouble with *her?*"

Cordelia Alcott, in one of Lizzie Chatfield's ample nightgowns, lurched down the stairs. "Asey!"

He hurried over and took her arm. "What's wrong?"

"Asey, go look, quick!" She sat down abruptly on the bottom step.

"Look at what?"

"Here." Brooks presented her with a paper cup of water. "Drink this. What's the matter?"

"Go look out of that window, Asey Mayo!" Cordy said, pointing. "No, the other side. Go look, and see if you see in that field what I see in that field! Go quick! I want to be sure I'm sane."

Asey walked to the window. His face, when he returned, was a study.

"Do you see it, too?" Cordy demanded.

"Yes." Asey sat down beside her. "I see it, too."

"A black Tracy roadster," Cordy said, "with a de luxe Wander Bird, special finish, in Mrs. Latimer's lower field. And it looks like that damn' pixie with the bowl of oatmeal on the side. And in the same place where I parked yesterday. What does it mean?"

"Wa-al," Asey said, "I don't think it just sprouted here, from a whale's tooth, or something. Cordy, go get dressed. I want you to come over with me. Brooks, get her somethin' to eat."

"What are you going to do?" Cordy asked.

"Right now? I'm goin'," Asey said, "to address some forceful words to Hanson. Cops beatin' the underbrush, radio flashes jammin' the air, an' then that car an' the trailer turn up so near that if they was bears we'd be chewed up. Hanson's goin' to get the well-known earful!"

Hanson escaped the earful only because he had already left for Weesit.

As Asey turned from the phone, Jere rushed over to him. "Say, have you seen—?"

" 'By the dawn's early light,' " Asey said. "Yup.

How'd you get that bruise on your cheek, Mr. Warren?"

"None of your damn' business!" Jere retorted. "And listen—call off that cop! I won't be trailed—"

"It's disgraceful," Asey said. "A downright disregardin' of your rights. Uh-huh. . . . Oh, you all ready, Cordy?"

"All set." She ignored Jere. "Let's go."

"Cordy," Jere said, "you can't— See here, Cordy Alcott, you've got to listen to me! Stop this nonsense and listen to me!"

"The first rule in handlin' what is known as the gentler sex," Asey said, "is never to give 'em orders. Mike, you keep on watchin' him."

Cordelia was very silent as Asey made an inspection of his roadster in the Inn garage. "Routine," he said, in answer to her question. "Sometimes folks that don't like me, they take advantage of my drivin' so much. Huh. I don't like the looks of the front tires."

"You don't mean they've been tampered with?" she asked incredulously.

"Look close, an' you'll see how some smarty's driven in a needle, it looks like. Too thin for a nail. . . . Hey, feller, got a spare car I can borrow?"

"Take mine," the garage boy said. "But it ain't—"

"Thanks. An' will you change them front tires of mine, an' put on the spares, an' get some new tubes?"

"You want me to touch your car?" The boy remembered Asey's definite instructions to the contrary, the previous night.

"Yup, you do the tire changin'. How's the doors here at night, all closed an' locked?"

"Closed after the last guest gets in. But we don't bother to lock 'em, because I'm here, or someone is. Did the tires get—?"

"This yours?" Asey pointed to an antique touring car.

"It's old," the boy said, "but I'll get the manager's if you wait till I call—"

"This'll do fine," Asey said. "Get in, Cordy, an' listen to the best engine Cap'n Porter ever built. It was a corker fifteen years ago, an' it'll be a corker fifty years from now. Drive mine to Mrs. Latimer's, feller, when you're done. They'll tell you where I am."

The boy scratched his head as he watched them roar off. Never before, to his knowledge, had Asey Mayo ever allowed anyone but himself to touch any of his cars. It wasn't like Asey. It was queer.

At the entrance to Mrs. Latimer's, Asey slowed

down to wait for Hanson, just arriving. In another car, behind, was Dr. Cummings.

"That's some relic you got there," Hanson said, as he got out and walked over to them. "Asey, man and boy we've combed the Cape since yesterday afternoon, and we can't find a trace of Miss Alcott's car, or her trailer, or her uncle. Not a trace."

"So?" Asey said. "Huh. Ain't you up early, Doc?"

"No," the doctor said wearily, "I'm just getting to bed late. I spent the storm delivering triplets. For almost half an hour there," he added wistfully, "I hoped for quints. Somehow, I never get a break. . . . Hanson, haven't you found out anything yet? Haven't you got anywhere with this John Smith? . . . You haven't?"

"I can't help it," Hanson said. "We sent the numbers in, and we've got to wait till they trace 'em. The trailer came from California. At least, it was sold there. And you can't say that we haven't hunted for that damn' uncle! Asey, he must have beat it out of the state before we began hunting." Hanson put one foot on the running board and leaned his elbows on the door. "Have you any idea where that man can be?"

"Uh-huh."

"Oh, you have?" Hanson said irritably. "You have,

have you? I suppose if you'd been running this search, you'd have had him by now, wouldn't you?"

"Get in," Asey said. "Get in back, Hanson. You too, Doc. You're about to go on a long, long journey with Houdini Mayo. Now you see it, now you don't. Observe, gentlemen, I got absolutely nothin' up my sleeve— That reminds me, Hanson; don't forget to provide me with a gun this mornin'. . . . Nope, I got nothin' up my sleeve. An' yet, as we climb over this here rise, look what we find! Hanson, ain't it startlin', the way the hand is quicker than the eye?"

He stopped the car, and allowed Hanson and the doctor to take a good look at the car and the trailer parked in the field.

Dr. Cummings found his voice first. "That," he said, "is the sort of thing that comes of delivering triplets all night long. That's the sort of thing you find yourself seeing. And I watched that car and trailer burn to ashes yesterday! My God, I'm speechless! Is that real, Asey, or is it something you thought up with mirrors?"

"It's real, all right," Hanson said bitterly. "Uncle Wilbur, huh? Asey, drive down. I want to see Uncle Wilbur. I want to see the man who can outsmart half my force! Asey, drive down before he disappears!"

Leisurely, Asey steered the old Porter down the

hill. Hanson jumped out and opened the gate. "That's ours, all right!" Cordy said. "But I don't see how Uncle managed to drive here all by himself! Oh, look! He had a flat! See? The spare's off."

Asey drew the car up alongside the trailer, and Cordy jumped out.

"Uncle Wilbur! Uncle!" She knocked on the door. "Will you unlock—? Why, it *is* unlocked! He's the most careless man! Uncle— Oh, Asey look! Look what's lying inside on the floor!"

"Now what, for God's sakes?" Hanson asked.

"Look," Asey said, after peering inside the trailer. "Doc, you better look, too. This is your department. She's alive."

Hanson and the doctor stared with bulging eyes at the trussed-up figure of Lizzie Chatfield, lumped on the trailer floor. Then, simultaneously, they crowded through the narrow doorway into the trailer. Deftly, Hanson cut the silk stockings that served to bind Lizzie's wrists, while the doctor removed the scarf with which she was gagged.

He expected Lizzie to have hysterics all over the place, but, amazingly, Lizzie rose to the situation. When the gag was removed, she spoke with the utmost calmness: "Thank you, Doctor. That thing was awfully tight."

"Lizzie!" Cummings said. "What happened? Who did this? Are you all right?"

"Well"—Lizzie rubbed her wrists—"I should like some smelling salts, if you have any. That bump on my head—"

"What bump?" Asey demanded, from the doorway. "Mrs. Chatfield, how in the name of all that's holy—what happened?"

"Why," Lizzie said, "I saw the trailer here, when I first looked out of my window this morning, and I simply couldn't believe my eyes! It's a mirage, I said. And then I tossed some clothes on, and I hurried over here just as fast as my legs would carry me."

"Whyn't you tell me?" Asey demanded. "Whyn't you tell Cordy? . . . Oh, it don't matter now, I suppose. You rushed over here. Then what? Who hit you?"

Lizzie shrugged.

"Don't you know?" the doctor demanded.

"I just opened that door"—Lizzie pointed to it—"after knocking, of course, and stepped in. I've always wanted to see the inside of these things. I told Jere so yesterday. And after I stepped in—well, that's all I remember, till a little while ago; and I waked up, and here I was, tied up like a roast chicken. Mercy me, I might have been seriously hurt, mightn't I?"

"I think," Asey said, "that you might, Mrs. Chatfield. How did you leave the hotel?"

"Oh, I didn't want to disturb anyone," Lizzie said, "so I just crept out by the gangway. The sun deck gangway. I didn't want to wake anyone. . . . What time is it now? . . . Oh. Well, it was only an hour or so ago. Why, I have quite a lump on my head!"

"Don't faint now!" Cummings said. "Here, take this pill. . . . Asey, what do you make of this?"

He shook his head. "All I know is, Mrs. Chatfield got bumped. An' instead of bumpin' her again an' finishin' her off, someone tied her up an' gagged her—"

"With my old stockings," Cordy said. "And my scarf. And those are Uncle's sneakers there beside her on the floor. Mrs. Chatfield, did you see anything of Uncle? . . . You didn't? Asey, where can that man be? There's someone out there at the door—maybe it's—"

"It's just one of Nora's maids," Cummings said, with a sigh. "Probably Nora's got colic again. Last night she kept pestering me—nothing would convince her that she wasn't having acute appendicitis all over again. All right, Gertrude!" He raised his voice. "Tell her I'll be up presently."

Lizzie got to her feet. "I must say," she said, "I

never knew such things to happen on Cape Cod
before. Asey, when you find the person who hit
me, I want to give him a good piece of my mind."
She paused. "Asey," she said, in a weak voice,
"that couldn't really have been the murderer, could
it?"

"Wa-al," Asey drawled. "I think—"

"How perfectly awful! Doctor, give me those smelling salts! Why, I never—but, of course, murderers
always come back to the scene of their crime—"

Dr. Cummings broke in on her monologue. "Asey,"
he said, "take her back to the Inn before I go nuts.
. . . Lizzie, I'll be around and look you over, if you
want, as soon as I've seen Nora."

Hanson followed them over to the old Porter.
"What—?"

"If you're goin' to ask me what you think you
ought to do next," Asey said, "don't bother. I still
think what I thought last night—that you might find
Uncle Wilbur, an' you might track down something
about John Smith—you got the chassis numbers!"

"Listen, I told you they phoned me from Boston
that they had that trailer number traced to a distributor in Hollywood!"

"You never said Hollywood, you said California!"
Asey told him. "Hollywood, huh? Now, I wonder—

Well, Hanson, keep tryin'. I'll take Mrs. Chatfield
back, an' then I'll come back here—"

But, after leaving Lizzie at the Inn, Asey swung
the old car off in the opposite direction. "Tell me,"
he said to Cordy, "just how did Uncle get that
trailer?"

"Oh, he wrote an ode, or an essay, or something,
and sent it off with box tops."

"Have you seen any other of the contest trailers,
around on your travels?"

"No. Of course, we might have seen one where
that damn' pixie insignia had been taken off. I
yearned to take ours off, but Uncle wouldn't let me.
He signed some agreement or other that he wouldn't
remove the thing, and Uncle's the soul of honor. He
loathed that pixie as much as I did, too. More. He
has a phobia about publicity."

"But didn't he get a dose of publicity when he
won?"

"He should have, but he shoved it off on me. I
took delivery of the thing for him, and posed for
pictures. I felt safe enough, because no picture ever
looks like me. Asey, if you're brooding about the
Tootsey-Wheetsy angle, how about Nora?"

"Hanson had that same brain wave yesterday,"
Asey said, "but I couldn't see it, myself. To begin

with, she's just gettin' over her operation. That rules
her out at the start. And just because her company
strews trailers around ain't no reason for her to kill
a man named John Smith because he was in a trailer."

"Haven't you got some ideas about it all?" Cordy
asked. "Some clues you're cherishing in the back of
your mind—? By the way, where are we going?"

"Up the Cape. I got one idea from somethin' Hanson said. Also, I got another idea that this whole
thing's an accident."

"What? You mean, you don't think John Smith
was killed?"

"I certainly don't think he's alive," Asey returned,
as he stopped the car before a large, rambling white
house. "He was very much killed, an' I don't think
Lizzie understands yet how near she come to bein'
killed the same way. But I don't think John Smith
was meant to be killed, an' I don't think Lizzie was
meant to be hit over the head. I think someone was
baffled, just like I am now. Cordy, wait here while
I see Carl Bartlett. I think it's possible that he might
maybe cast some light—if only Hanson had said
that about Hollywood sooner!"

Half an hour passed before Asey returned followed
by a tall, bald man who, like the night clerk, couldn't
seem to stop yawning.

"Miss Alcott, Carl Bartlett," Asey said. "He's sleepy because he got in from a deep-sea fishin' trip just about three hours ago, an' he's been seasick for two days. He—"

"I never heard a word about this murder," Bartlett said. "We hadn't a radio on the boat. It's the most appalling thing I ever heard of! Poor Sampson!"

"Sampson?" Cordy said. "Asey, does he—d'you mean, you knew John Smith?"

"He's Johann Sampson—"

"The movie producer, that one?"

"That's right," Asey said. "Bartlett used to be a director, an' when Hanson said Hollywood, it sort of seemed to me that maybe we had an actor incognito, an' I thought Bartlett would know. John Smith is Johann Sampson."

"Sampson himself," Bartlett said. "He stayed with me last week. He was touring around the Cape, studying it as a movie locale. He has to travel as John Smith. Otherwise, he just gets mobbed."

"How'd he happen to have one like the Tootsy-Wheetsys?" Cordy asked.

"It seems he was a judge in that contest."

"Of course he was!" Cordy said. "How stupid of me! I remember his name."

"And he was so delighted with those trailers that

he ordered one like them. Shall I sit with you in front?"

"Squeeze over, Cordy," Asey said, as he got in the car. "Carl's goin' back to Weesit to make sure about this. Tell me, why are you so sure that Sampson had no enemies?"

"I know it sounds absurd," Bartlett said as they set off, "but he didn't. He's a bachelor, he lives alone, he hasn't any near relatives. They died when he was a boy. Two years ago he almost went broke, and his office was packed with stars and ex-stars all fighting to pawn their pearls and town cars for Sampson. He was the sort who sent his scrubwomen home in cabs on rainy days. I simply can't understand anything like this happening to him."

"You say he was just tourin' around?"

Bartlett nodded. "Once or twice a year, he knocks off and goes driving around, always in this country, so he can keep a finger on the pulse of the public."

Back in Weesit, Bartlett looked at the body in the back room of the local undertaker's. "I was right," he said. "That's Sampson. I never had any doubt, after your description. Asey, are you sure someone wasn't trying to rob him?"

"There was a big roll of bills in the trailer yesterday," Asey said. "Silver-backed brushes, a platinum watch. Nothin' had been touched. I think robbery's out."

"Well, what was the motive, then?" Bartlett asked. "When I saw him, he'd just come from Newport. Before that, he stayed a while in Connecticut. And so on, in various stages, back to Hollywood. If someone were tracking him down, with murder in mind, it does seem as though they might have got to it before this. After all, if you're going to kill someone, why dawdle across a continent first? I'd like to know the motive. Why do people kill other people?"

"In general," Asey said, "love, an' money, an' their ramifications."

"Well, Sampson's money is tied up in his business. You wouldn't kill him for that. As for love, he was too busy for women. Lived like a deacon."

Asey sighed. "Look; Hanson'll want you for some odds an' ends. Will you help him all you can, an' then I'll have someone take you back to bed. The boy's outside with my car. I'll take that over, now, an' he'll drive you home in the antique. Thanks a lot."

The boy from the Inn garage glowed at Asey's praise of his old touring car, and announced that he'd be glad to drive Mr. Bartlett home. "That roadster of yours!" he said. "What a car! I was careful with her, too. Say, you didn't tell me to, but I brought over those needles from the front tires I changed. They look like the kind my mother uses to sew up chickens with after the stuffin's in."

"They're the kind," Cordy said in a strained voice, "that I have in the trailer, in my workbasket, to embroider in wool with."

Asey nodded.

"You don't seem at all surprised!" she said.

"I ain't," Asey returned. "I seen one in your pocketbook yesterday, threaded with white wool. I decided it was what you used to embroider the initials on that bathin' suit." He put the needles in his tobacco pouch. "Thanks, feller. I'll see you later."

Before they left, Asey went back to the undertaker's. When he returned, he was grinning, and Cordy asked why.

"I wondered about Bartlett, in passin'," Asey said. "But the feller that runs his boat is my cousin, an' he says Bartlett was out in the boat, all right. He's just been describin' Bartlett's reactions to a ground swell."

On the beach road, he stopped the roadster and pulled out his pipe. "I feel," he said, "like meditatin'.

Tell me all about Uncle Wilbur, his early life, an'
if he folds up bath towels. Keep on till I tell you
to stop."

Obediently, Cordy lighted a cigarette and attacked
the life history of Uncle Wilbur. Asey didn't hear one
word in a hundred. He was too busy meditating.

Johann Sampson, alias John Smith, had been killed
in his trailer the night before last. Making a perfectly
natural error, Cordy had driven his trailer off for
her own, the next morning. Falling for a Main Street
humorist, she'd brought the trailer to Nora's field.
That was all clear and distinct. For all anyone knew
she might have killed Sampson. But, with Lizzie
chaperoning her in the Inn last night, Cordy had
no chance to stick needles into his tires, even if she
happened to have similar needles. She couldn't have
been the person who knocked Lizzie out. So much
for that.

Somebody had burned the trailer. Probably the
murderer found it simpler to fire the whole works
than to try to destroy fingerprints and footprints.
And burning the trailer had thrown them off from a
more prompt identification of Sampson. It was a
nice stall.

All that business outside his room at the Inn was
enlightening, Asey thought. Someone had wanted

to make sure there would be no chance of Asey intervening in any plans he had. Arousing Asey, the fellow had waited by the windows. Later, he made sure of discouraging pursuit by sticking those needles in the tires.

Who had brought Cordy's trailer to Nora's field? Asey didn't know. Wilbur seemed the logical person, but where was the man, anyway, and how had he driven the car and the trailer over that bumpy field, if he didn't know how to drive?

Asey sighed, and clamped his teeth down on his pipestem. That was about all there was to work with —the trailer firing, the wedge inserting, the needle business, and the tire changing. And the fact that possibly one of those lead sinkers had socked the guy.

And, no matter from what angle you viewed it, Jere Warren fitted into the picture beautifully.

"But where," Cordy asked for the third time, *"is* Uncle?"

Asey came back to earth. "Can he change tires?"

"You do ask," Cordy said, "the silliest questions! Of course not. Don't you get what I've been telling you? Uncle used to have lots of money. He never drove, because he was always driven. That's my whole point! Uncle is as helpless about most things as a

Pekingese lost in a blizzard. Uncle only got to be a bookkeeper after the crash. He's been a retired book-keeper only a few months. Nothing was ever farther from his thoughts. When his business went—"

"What business?" Asey asked.

Cordy drew a long breath and let it out sharply. "You haven't listened to— Oh, and I made such a swell story out of it, too! He was W. W. Alcott, of the grocery firm, and they went bust, don't you remember? The warehouse burned, and the treasurer beat it, and everything happened all at once. That's how Uncle won the trailer, don't you see?"

"No," Asey said honestly, "I don't."

"Why, it's not only that Uncle has always eaten that foul Tootsy-Wheetsy! In his day, he sold it in carload lots! Alcotts' were the distributors! . . . Look; let me tell you everything, or you won't—"

Before she could continue, Cummings drove up. "Hanson says," he informed Asey, "no fingerprints within a mile of that trailer. None on the jack, or tire, or that wedge. And you'd ought to see Nora!"

"Temper again?"

"Plus colic. I told her, if that's what tomatoes do to her, she'd better eschew them for life. That place is a madhouse. Phones ringing, reporters yelling,

Nora's businesses howling about their advertising, and some lawyer screeching about a trust. And a dog chasing a Persian kitten. I'm exhausted."

"Nora seems to have a lot to do about her businesses," Asey remarked.

"A lot of to-do," Cummings corrected. "Actually, I don't think she can do much. The Latimers were trust fiends; all of their businesses are tied up. But Nora can't keep her fingers out of things. I suppose they let her play with the advertising to keep her quiet. I can't understand that woman, she always seems on a hunt for something to fasten onto, like—like—"

"Like Jere," Cordy suggested.

Cummings shrugged. "Maybe. I don't know. Asey, haven't you found any trace of Uncle, yet? No? . . . Well, if you solve this one, you'll be good."

"Cheery soul," Asey said as Cummings departed.

Cordy looked at him. There was an odd note in his voice.

He grinned at her. "Let's go back to the Inn an' find some food. An' I want to know more about Uncle, an' I want to see Jere. He's got a bruise on his face that— What's turnin' you so pink?"

"I'm afraid," she said, "I'm the bruise. I socked him, last night."

Asey leaned back against the seat. "Go on."

"It's nothing, really. He knocked on my door just after Lizzie and I went up to bed, and asked me to come down and talk with him, and I did, and we— Well, we still seem to be able to hurl each other into a temper. That's all. I socked him, I got so mad at him, and came back to bed."

"So, the two of you was roamin' around, huh? What time did you go back to bed?"

"I don't know. My watch is in the trailer. What did you say about Lizzie?"

"Somethin' I want to take up with her," Asey said.

But what, he thought on the way back to the Inn, was the sense of talking with Lizzie? He'd told her to lock Cordy's door, and she hadn't. So both Jere and the girl were running around loose the night before. And when you came right down to it, Lizzie had been running around loose that morning.

He drove the roadster back to the garage. If people were sabotaging his tires, it might be well to have someone watch over the car. He called to one of the mechanics: "Will someone watch this, like a hawk?"

"Sure; I will. I'm sorry you had trouble."

"Is that a mirage," Asey interrupted, "or is that Lizzie Chatfield out there, shovin' that oil drum to one side?"

The mechanic snickered. "That's her. I'll hand it
to the old girl. When she's got her car here, she sees
to it that it's kept in order. Her chauffeur isn't half
the mechanic Lizzie is. Right now, she's trying to find
something a friend of hers that came last night thinks
he may have lost on the way in. She's been pawing
all over the drive, helping to find 'dear Wilbur's'
wallet—"

In two strides Asey was out of the car, with Cordy
at his heels.

"Hello," Lizzie said brightly. "Dr. Cummings is
really marvelous, isn't he? I can't even feel that bump
on my head."

While Lizzie ran on about Dr. Cummings, Asey
found his eyes riveted to her open knitting bag. And
the paper of large needles that were in plain sight.
He was hardly aware of the man who came down
the drive and around the corner of the garage until
Cordy clutched his arm.

"Asey, it *is* Uncle Wilbur!"

Asey sat down on a wooden sawhorse, leaned back
against the wall, and laughed until the tears ran
down his cheeks.

Uncle Wilbur was not the fussy little dyspeptic
he had imagined. Uncle Wilbur was tall and well

built. His white flannels were immaculate, his blue coat would warm the cockles of a tailor's heart. A beautifully clipped white mustache and pince-nez on a black cord provided the final touches. Uncle Wilbur was elegant.

"Uncle," Cordy said, "where have you been?"

"My dear Cordelia," Wilbur said with perfect equanimity, "I might well ask you the same thing! How absurd of you, dashing off into all this mess! Really, my dear, I feel you owe me an explanation!"

"Mr. Alcott," Asey said, "yours is the honor of explainin', first an' rapid."

"He's Asey," Lizzie explained. "*The* Asey Mayo."

"Splendid!" Wilbur extended his hand. "I can't tell you how pleased I am, I've read so much about you. And, of course, you were Porter's sole topic of conversation, in the old days. Now—"

"Let's begin with yesterday mornin'," Asey said, "when you found the provisions outside the trailer. The clams an'—"

"Spoiled," Wilbur said sadly. "I threw them out."

"Then," Asey said, "what?"

"Oh, I called Cordy, of course," he said. "I called and called. She'd been gone four hours, then. Much longer than she usually stays away, even if it's good swimming weather. It was really unusual. So I went over to the Snows'—those nice people who sold us things. Mrs. Snow insisted on giving me lunch. Most hospitable person. And she gave me something for my stomach. I don't know if Cordy mentioned my digestive system, but it's been behaving very badly lately."

He spoke of his digestive system as though it were some neighbor's child who had ravaged his delphiniums.

"She did," Asey said. "So?"

"Mrs. Snow's remedy," Wilbur said, "made me feel much better, but sleepy, so I had a nap. When I waked up, Mrs. Snow suggested that I wait until her husband came back from quohauggin'—what *is* that?"

"A quohaug," Asey said, "is what New Yorkers like to think of as clams. Snow quohaugs for a livin'."

"Well, she suggested that I wait till Mr. Snow came back, and he would drive me around in his car and hunt for Cordy. He had their car, you see, and neither Mrs. Snow nor I could drive enough to cope with the trailer."

"Ever think of phonin'?" Asey asked.

"Who?" Wilbur retorted simply. "Besides, the

Snows hadn't a phone. If they had, Mrs. Snow and
I doubtless would have found out that Snow was
marooned at his wharf with his car broken down,
after he'd got back from—er—quohauggin'."

"Didn't it occur to you"—Asey grinned at Wilbur's
pronunciation of "quohauggin' "—"to go somewhere
else, and call the police an' ask em' to investigate?"

"What could I have asked them to investigate
about?" Wilbur asked. "I couldn't just say, 'Oh, by
the way, I've lost a niece somewhere,' could I? I decided, finally, that Cordy really had been angry with
me when we had words in the morning, and that
she'd gone scooting off to the Randall place, in a
pique. She's left me alone before—"

"Uncle, only that time when I ran out of gas."

"Say no more about it, my dear. . . . Oh, yes,
Mayo, actually I did think of the police, but it seemed
such an extreme step to take. And if she'd gone to
the Randalls' wouldn't that have been silly? I felt
sure I'd have known at once had there been any sort
of accident. Bad news always travels so rapidly. And
there was the publicity angle. I hate people poking
around, asking questions, taking pictures. Usually,
if you let them alone, things solve themselves."

"Uncle," Cordy said, "did you know that the man

who was killed—Lizzie's told you everything, hasn't she? Well, he was Johann Sampson, one of the judges who won your contest for you!"

"He didn't win it for me," Wilbur said. "I wanted the first prize of ten thousand dollars. I've told you repeatedly, this trailer was worse than nothing. Anyway, Mayo, I hate publicity, and I was in no mood to create a sensation all because of an errant niece—"

"Uncle, you're being nasty!"

"Well, really," Wilbur said, "for a time I began to wonder if you were taking after your Aunt Belle, the one—"

"D'you mind," Asey said, "gettin' back to your story? What happened next?"

"Oh, I stayed at the Snows', waiting for Mr. Snow to come back. After dinner we listened to the radio—"

"You did, huh? An' you didn't hear that the cops wanted you?" Asey interrupted. "Or any flashes about the murder?"

"We were listening on the short wave," Wilbur explained. "The Snows had just got a new short-wave set from a mail-order house, and we didn't listen to anything nearer than Brazil. Then that storm came up, and the electric current went off, and finally Snow came back very late. That was when we learned that his car had broken down. He'd walked all the way home. By then, Cordy, I was beginning to be genuinely annoyed with you, and, somehow, Mr. Snow felt very intensely about your absence. You seem to have charmed him. He said you were a nice girl and we must find you right away. So we went out to the trailer—"

"Now, just a sec," Asey said in his purring voice. "Cordy an' I hunted you yesterday afternoon from Dan to Beersheba, an' that trailer wasn't where she left it in the clearin'. S'pose you explain that part."

"Oh, didn't I tell you? Just after lunch Mrs. Snow thought it would be a good idea to drive around and see if we could locate Cordy. So, she and I took the trailer from our camping site—"

"You told me," Asey pointed out, "that neither of you could drive."

Wilbur smiled. "Let me assure you that that statement," he said, "was no idle boast. It was the result of experience. We got the trailer from our camping site along the road and conveyed it to a spot behind the Snows' barn, on a lane, at which point we mutually decided that we could not drive. Besides, we'd done something drastic to the hitch, and we'd also picked up a flat. Snow fixed the flat last night when he returned, and we drove to the village. We couldn't uncouple the trailer, because of that jammed hitch.

It was pouring, then, and thundering and lightning, and Snow began to get anxious about his boat. We could see the whole bay, when the lightning flashed, but his boat wasn't where it should be. He was worried, so I suggested that he drop me off at the Inn, and go investigate."

Asey sat up straight. "Were you—did you have the bed moved, so you headed north? Were you the feller that Brooks told me about, the one who came in late?"

"Asey!" Cordy said. "If only you'd listened to me this afternoon! I told you all the parking troubles we'd gone through because of that little idiosyncrasy! He has to sleep heading north, like a compass. Uncle, d'you mean you left Snow wandering around with the car and trailer, and came here?"

"Where else could I go?" Wilbur asked plaintively. "I didn't know any more than the general outlines of the town. It seemed to me it was a silly expedition and we'd have done better to have stayed at the Snows' place. I thought over the possible lines of action, and the Inn and a nice, warm bed seemed the most sensible objective. I shouldn't have started out if Snow hadn't been so persistent, and when he shifted his enthusiasm to his boat—well, I came here.

Then, this morning, I saw that Snow had left the trailer over in the field."

"Why?" Asey asked. "Did you tell him to?"

"Certainly not," Wilbur said. "I told him to leave it in some convenient place when he got through with it, and I suppose that was it. I thought so when I saw it. He couldn't very well leave the trailer in the rose garden. I thought he was very logical. I suppose someone gave him a lift home. Then, Cordy, I found Lizzie. Her husband's one of my very good friends, and I've known Lizzie—"

"You never told me, dear," Lizzie said reproachfully to Cordy, "that you are one of the *W. W.* Alcott family! To think that I lent you a cotton nightdress to sleep in!"

Asey swallowed hard. "Mrs. Chatfield," he said, "have you got any more needles like them in your bag?"

"Oh, yes," Lizzie said. "I lose them so. Just like those window wedges—it seems as if they lose themselves, just to annoy me."

Cordy broke the silence: "Uncle, have we, by any chance, enough cash to pay your hotel bill? Or mine?"

Wilbur looked acutely distressed for a moment. "Oh, well," he said, "I'm sure the Inn will be glad to take the trailer for the bill. I'm fed up with the trailer. It doesn't seem to me that it works out a bit well."

Cordy looked at Asey, and bit her lip.

"And, as for you, my dear," Wilbur continued, "have you eaten your Tootsy-Wheetsy this morning? Or yesterday, either? You know, Mayo, the girl's anemic, and you'd think she'd want to do something about it, but no! I have to force her to eat her breakfast food. I practically have to shove it down her throat. . . . Oh, Lizzie tells me that Jere Warren is here. I do hope, Cordy, that you'll be more sensible this time!"

"Where," Cordy asked Asey, "are you going?"

Asey grinned. "Me," he said, "I know Waterloo when I meet it. The Department of Utter Defeat is retirin'."

Asey went into the garage and sat down behind the wheel of his roadster. Cordy followed him, but he waved her away. The gesture didn't disconcert her at all.

"That's often the way Uncle affects me," she said. "I want to be alone. D'you blame me now, Asey, for mixing trailers? It's simply the will of God that I haven't done anything worse. Are you really sunk?"

"I thought," Asey said, "with Wilbur, an' with Lizzie an' her needles an' wedges, I might be on the

track of somethin', at last. But there's some yarns you
have to believe, crazy as they seem. Some people just
tell the truth. Lizzie does, except maybe in a social
way. So does your uncle, except maybe for the same
thing. A hundred thousand men could tell me the
yarn he spun, an' I wouldn't believe 'em. But I believe Wilbur. I know perfectly well that when I
check up his story with the Snows it'll be just as he
said. I believe Lizzie, too."

"So do I," Cordy said. "What now?" she added
as Asey started the car.

He shrugged. "I don't know, just. Maybe a kindly
bird'll hop on my ear an' whisper into it. I hope it
does. Meantime, will you keep Wilbur an' Lizzie out
of mischief, an' away from trailers?"

Going down the hotel drive, Asey noticed Jere
Warren and the trooper, Mike, playing croquet on
the lawn. Apparently they were on the best of terms.
Grinning, Asey drove along the beach road to the
Latimer estate. A number of people milled about the
field, and he spotted two press cars and a group of
photographers.

He swung the roadster off the beach road into a
meadow, pushed through a brook and up the sandy
slope of a hill to the rear of the house. He even managed to park his car in the Latimer garage without

being seen by anyone other than Dr. Cummings, who had watched the entire proceeding with a quizzical smile.

"I gather you're evading the press?" Cummings said. "Asey, tell me why someone killed Sampson, alias Smith. Hanson's stunned. He's talking with half of Hollywood by phone, and he says no one can supply a motive."

"So Hanson's been investigatin' Sampson?"

"Everything he found out checked with what Carl Bartlett said. And Hanson found out the reason for the New York plates, and for some of the delay, too. Seems that the outfit was re-registered in New York. Bartlett said because New York plates aroused less comment than California ones. . . . Asey, why was he killed?"

"I think," Asey said, "it was an accident."

Cummings snorted. "Accident my eye! No man was ever less accidentally done in. Whoever killed him meant to kill."

"Uh-huh," Asey said, "but I wonder if that some-one meant to— Say, is that the beach wagon that Jere Warren returned to Nora? What do you think of Jere, Doc?"

"Not much. No more or less than I think or have

thought about any of Nora's young men. She wants to see you, by the way. Go get it over with, and then come back and tell me things—oh, something else has been bothering me. How was that trailer set on fire yesterday?"

"For all I know," Asey told him, "someone rubbed two sticks together an'—"

"Be sensible! If something highly explosive was poured around inside the trailer, and someone tossed in a match, we'd be able to pick our man from his complete lack of eyebrows. How was it done?"

"I wondered about that considerable," Asey said. "It must have been a delayed job. I think, Doc, someone plugged in the little electric iron, after first settin' the iron on something like Harrigan's film—"

"That it!" Cummings said. "He had a couple of packs of film, and he left 'em on the table. And that iron was sitting there. And that gasoline stove was right there."

"Yes," said Asey. "Iron to film to stove is as good a guess as we'll probably have. I'll run in an' see Lady Latimer."

He found Nora on a chaise longue in the living-room. "Better?" he inquired.

"Cummings says it's tomatoes," she said. "I suppose he knows. They virtually ruined me, anyway. And now all this new hurly-burly. Why don't you arrest that girl?"

"You mean Cordy? You think she's—? I see. You don't like her much, do you?"

"You certainly can't deny that she's apparently the motivating factor, can you? Out for publicity. I looked into the matter, and I find she posed for the contest-award pictures, though her uncle actually won that trailer. That ought to prove my point. Just one of those motivating girls—why, she hadn't been here ten minutes before she started making lunges at Jere."

"I see," Asey said, "but I don't think you do. At the risk of makin' you sore I might as well tell you that Cordy an' Jere is old friends. That bruise he's got on his face come from Cordy tellin' him where to get off. Does that make you feel more kindly disposed toward her?"

Nora shrugged. "She really doesn't interest me." She paused to disentangle a small Persian kitten from a ball of yarn in her sewing bag. "Have you found her uncle?"

"Of all places, at the Inn."

"The Weesit Inn?" Nora asked blankly.

"Believe it or not, that's where he was, while people peered under toadstools for him. You'll like Wilbur. He's refreshin'."

"Where's he been all this time?"

"Hither an' yon," Asey said. "He's a hither-an'-yonny sort. Tall an' elegant an' Beacon Street. A New England colonel, if you know what I mean."

· Nora laughed. "I somehow thought of him as a fat little man with a red face."

"So did I. Have they told you about Lizzie gettin' biffed when she come over to investigate the trailer?"

"Cummings told me. Personally, I'd say that Lizzie'd stuck her nose into things once too often, and— Is it that lawyer again, Gertrude? . . . Sorry, Asey, I've got to stagger out and be forceful again. If I had him here I'd annihilate him. He knows that, so he phones from a safe distance."

While she was gone, Asey obligingly dragged strings across the floor for the benefit of the kitten.

"That man and his wills and his trusts!" Nora said, when she returned. "What farsighted folk the Latimers were. And the operator says a Chicago call is coming in ten minutes. That'll be that advertising manager, with more stupid notions— Puff, get down from that mantel!" She deposited the kitten on the floor.

"Somehow," she continued, "cats have a feeling for the better things, don't they? Puff won't be entirely happy until she's knocked that jade—oh, my God, Martha's let Skippy in! Grab him, Asey, before he gets Puff again!"

A young Airedale bounded joyfully into the room. But before Asey could get him Mrs. Latimer picked him up and with difficulty shut him out on the porch. With a flick of her tail that was almost the equivalent of a thumb to her nose, the kitten scrambled up a chair back and stared longingly at the mantel.

"Cats," Asey said, "have a feelin' for a lot of things —Whee! What's goin' on down there in the field? Look! Say, look here, Mrs. Latimer. That's Uncle Wilbur, the one in the blue coat an' flannels, next to Lizzie."

"Run, see what's going on!" Nora said. "Oh, here comes a trooper rushing up!"

The trooper thundered breathlessly into the room. "I want to phone— Oh, Asey! Hanson said I was to call you. This Uncle Wilbur—what's his name—"

"What about him?"

"He's just tried to set *this* trailer on fire!"

"How?" Asey asked.

"Cigarette lighter fluid. He spilled it all over the floor. He claims he just wanted to fill his lighter, but he was already smoking. Hanson says he was just ready to drop the lighted butt, or a match—"

"Well, well," Asey said. "My, my! Tch, tch! So Uncle Wilbur— Feller, go back to Hanson. Tell him to march Wilbur to—to the Inn. To his room. Tell Hanson that I'm leavin' now, an' when I come back I hope to have some interestin' items for him about Wilbur. Tell him, came the dawn. Got it?"

"What is this dawn?" Nora asked as Asey picked up his yachting cap.

"Kind of a belated, daylight-savin' dawn," Asey said. "Wilbur bein' the sun. So long."

Dr. Cummings yelled at him as he backed the roadster out of the garage and started for the road by the same circuitous route he had taken earlier. "You! Hey, Asey! You nut! Why you don't break your blessed neck, God knows," he added as the Porter splashed through the brook and circled a cow.

Better than anyone else, he knew that things were happening when Asey began to race around at that pace. Philosophically lighting a cigar, he strolled down to the field. He arrived in time to witness Wilbur's departure in a police car.

Lizzie and Cordy rushed over to him. "It's all a horrible mistake!" Lizzie said. "They mustn't arrest him! Can't you explain that he's *W. W.* Alcott?"

Patiently, Cummings extracted the story of the lighter fluid. "And Asey knows?" he asked. "He—"

"Where is Asey?" Lizzie demanded. "We've got to do something! Asey'll know what to do! Where is he?"

Hanson overheard her question. "Asey ordered it himself," he said; "if you mean about Wilbur's exit."

"He did, did he?" Cummings grinned.

"It's outrageous!" Lizzie said. "I can't get over it, their arresting him! I feel faint!"

"Smelling salts in your handbag," Cummings said. "Here, sniff! Now, don't worry about Wilbur. Asey knows what he's doing. He's just left here driving as if he was after the Vanderbilt Cup."

Cordy's eyes narrowed. So Asey had just left. If she had a car and could only follow! If— She saw Jere standing in the crowd, and after a moment's hesitation she walked over to him. She still definitely meant what she'd told him about never wanting to speak to him again, but this was no time to carp.

"I'm sorry, Cordy; it's all a mistake," he said before she could speak. "Can I help? The reporters are going to pester the life out of you."

"They already have. Can you get a car? I want to find Asey."

"Sure." Jere turned to the trooper: "Mike, get your

car. We're finding Asey. Hustle, before Hanson—
Here. Scoot through the crowd."

"You hadn't ought to," Mike said. "Besides, no
one living can catch Asey in that car."

"We'll try."

In their ensuing two-hour search they missed Asey
at the Snows', at the telephone office twice, at a garage,
at the post office, and at the public library.

Cordy sighed wearily. "Go back to the phone
place," she told Jere. "He'll phone plenty if he's
delving into Uncle!"

Mike's sharp eyes picked out the Porter, parked
behind a lattice in the rear of the telephone exchange.
"Now," he said, "sit and wait, and don't bother him
and get me in Dutch! Hear me?"

It was nearly half an hour before Asey came out.
His set jaw and look of grim determination sent chills
colliding on Cordy's spine. "Sorry I had to act so
with Uncle," Asey told her. "I can't help myself.
Want to follow me back to the Inn an' let me explain
there? I'm in a hurry."

Forcing Mike's car to its utmost, Jere just managed
to reach the Inn as Asey strode in and spoke to Hanson.

"Got Alcott?" he asked.

"Yeah," Hanson said. "He's sore, too. Mrs. Latimer

just came over and blew me to hell for keeping him here and giving her Inn a bad name and a black eye."

"Mrs. Latimer? Where is she?" Asey demanded.

"I don't know. That was ten minutes ago."

"Hustle," Asey said briefly. "Come on!"

With Hanson and two of his troopers following, and Cordy and Jere after them, he took the stairs to Wilbur's room four at a time. Swinging aside the lattice door, he grabbed the inner door handle, and then called for a key.

"It's just stuck," Hanson said.

"It's wedged," Asey told him, leaning over and removing Hanson's gun from its holster. "Bust it in, quick! Hurry, you guys! Hustle!"

He shot twice, almost as the door crashed down, and before the others could grasp the scene in front of them.

Wilbur, with blood trickling down his forehead and cheeks, was trying to get up from the bed. Above him stood Nora Latimer, staring with glazed eyes at her bleeding wrist. At her feet was a short, stubby piece of wood. Oak, from the wood basket by the fireplace beyond.

"Grab her, Hanson," Asey said evenly.

Hanson blinked.

"Oh, hurry!" Asey said. "Before she comes to her

senses. . . . That's it. . . . Now, help Wilbur. . . .
Now, take your handcuffs an' lock her to someone.
Fine."

"You shot that billet of wood out of *her* hand!"
Hanson said. "But you had told us before to take
him!"

"To keep him safe an' whole, of course. I couldn't
tell you about her then," Asey said. "All I really knew
was that she was fakin' about her operation. . . .
Call Cummings, someone. Both of 'em need attention.
But don't call any reporters! . . . Oh, there you are,
Mrs. Chatfield. I wondered why you weren't in on
the excitement."

Lizzie, for once, was speechless. Uncle Wilbur was
the only one of the onlookers who could match Asey's
calm.

"Asey, I'm tremendously grateful, you know," he
said. "In another second I fear I should have been
liquidated. Really, that was amazing! I was lying
here resting, about nine tenths asleep—I really had
an exhausting night, last night! And I felt someone
near me, and I looked up just as she belted me with
that piece of wood. She was just going to polish me
off, when you burst in. She would have done it, too.
I was too dazed to move. . . . Oh, my head!"

"Lie back," Asey said. "Hanson, sit Mrs. Latimer

down in that chair. . . . Mrs. Latimer, will you tell
the story? All right," he went on, as Nora gave no
sign of having heard; "I'll save time an' tell it. You
killed Johann Sampson, alias John Smith, because
you thought you was killin' Wilbur Alcott—"

"What!" Wilbur sat up. "How quaint of her! No
two people were ever less alike, I'm sure, to judge
from Lizzie's description, and the picture of him in
the papers."

"There," Asey said, "you have the point. Pictures.
Did you ever have your picture taken, Mr. Alcott?"

"Once. Just once. For my class album. I turned
out to be a black-haired ape, a creature to be viewed
with loathing. That was the only picture ever taken
of me."

"An'," Asey said, "from what I just been rakin'
up of your past an' your business, you was one of
them remote men, wasn't you? You kept out of pictures an' headlines, you didn't dash around in society,
an' the person that got by your third secretary was a
genius."

"I told you I hated publicity," Wilbur said simply.

"Exactly. Now, you had a trailer. A specific trailer,
with a specific label. Old Tootsy-Wheetsy. Mrs. Latimer knew that. She knew where you parked in it.
She knew you was there personally."

"How?" Wilbur asked. "What with rain and arthritis, I hardly stirred from my bunk from the night we landed here in town until the sun came out yesterday. How, Asey?"

"She checked by way of your mail an' the post office," Asey said. "To begin with, she knew you two was tourin' about in your trailer, an' from the Randalls she found out that you were plannin' to stop by an' see them. She planned for Cordy to be out of the way, by suggestin' that the Randalls ask her to stay a few days with 'em. Casual, but she suggested it. She arranged that visit for you, Cordy. She phoned 'em night before last, an' they said they expected you. They didn't get your note about not comin', till yesterday. Got the background?"

"No," Wilbur said.

"Look; she's sure of your trailer. She knows what it looks like. She's sure of you. She knows what you look like. She spent last week kitin' around in her car, lookin' into likely campin' sites where you might go."

"So that's where she went!" Lizzie said. "I wondered about those trips she made! I tried to find out."

"She spotted you on Snows' clearin'," Asey said. "She gets Cordy asked elsewhere. Now do you get it? She goes to this trailer parked on Snows' clearin', findin' there a darkish-lookin' man. A man lookin' like you, Wilbur, in the only picture existin', from that class album. . . . Oh, sure, she'd asked about you, too. She'd asked two of the men I phoned today. But your hair's been white only in the last five years, an' durin' that time your old friends ain't seen hair nor hide of you. Their descriptions of you tallied with the dark-haired picture, an' with this dark-haired man. So she kills the dark-haired man in the trailer on Snows' clearin', an' departs."

Lizzie's eyes nearly bulged from their sockets. "She —she hit me, too?"

"I'll get to that," Asey said. "What Nora Latimer didn't know was that she'd got into another trailer that'd pulled up late that evenin' on the same lane. Why, not even the Alcotts knew about that other trailer! Her gettin' into Sampson's outfit was as natural a mistake as Cordy's takin' it the next mornin'. More so. An', by the way, consider Nora's feelin's out in the bay the next mornin' when she sees the scene of her crime bowlin' along toward her; No wonder she got worked up, presumably over trespassers! Me, I'd of fainted. So, there's the story of her killin' Sampson. Then, when she seen the trailer in the field this mornin', she hustled over. She was waitin' for Wilbur, but she got Mrs. Chatfield—"

"Asey," Wilbur interrupted, "why was she so anxious to kill me? I never knew her. I knew Greg. What was her motive, if she had one?"

"She had two sterlin' motives—love an' money. Nora's pretty fond of Jere, an' she wanted money."

"Well, I'm the last person," Wilbur said, "to be killed for his money! I have one dollar. I borrowed that from Colonel Belcher. I did have a wallet, which I lost last night, but it was empty!"

"Yup," Asey said. "But among the Latimer trusts, one's mighty interestin'. I just been findin' out about it over the phone. It gives her a whoppin' yearly income, but if she marries again she forfeits it, an' all connection with the Latimer estate. Greg thought out everything. There's not a single hunk of cash money Nora can lay her hand on at any time, an' she'd lose her income if she married again. Mind that, 'cause it's important. Now, if Nora died, a large sum was to go to Wilbur W. Alcott, if he was still alive. But, if he was dead, then Nora could have that chunk any time, to do just what she wanted with. It was the only loophole in the whole business where she could get her hands on a large amount of cash."

"Why, I'd forgotten that will of Greg's," Wilbur remarked. "There was some clause about me, wasn't there?"

"You forgot," Asey said, "half a million dollars?"

Wilbur's casual wave of a hand would have struck Asey as being phony theatrics an hour ago, before he'd learned the approximate size of the private fortune that Wilbur had turned over to his company's creditors.

"Just a gesture of Greg's," Wilbur said. "He was a master of gestures that cost nothing. Of course, the chances of my surviving Mrs. Latimer were and are remote. Well, well. So she wanted money. Why? Did she want to marry again?"

"Jere," Asey said.

Nora nodded slowly.

"You thought you could buy me!" Jere was incredulous, and he paid no attention to Cordy's restraining hand on his arm. "No, Cordy, I'm not going to stop. I'm going to get to the bottom of this! . . . Nora, what made you think I would—? Why, it's—it's fantastic!"

"When I met you last winter," Nora said, "you told me that you thought artists should be subsidized. And supported, so—"

"So," Jere interrupted, "that their creative ability wouldn't be hampered by material things, like finding the rent money. Yes, I used to say that, before I was subsidized and supported by you this summer, and then I learned that self-respect plays a part in creative work, too! But I never said I wanted to marry you! I never— No, Cordy, I'm not going to stop! I want the truth of this. I'm not going to let everyone think this is all my fault, that I said I'd marry her, that I wanted to marry her, or even suggested it in passing! I never did!"

"You told me," Nora said, "time and time again, over at South Point, that you wanted to live there, and you wished you had the money to!"

"I said I'd like to live on the Cape! I didn't mean in your house! I *did* wish for money, but not yours!"

"The trips you said we'd take," Nora said. "The places you wanted to see. With me. All those things you said we'd do together! You kept saying we'd do them together, if only we had the money!"

Jere looked helplessly at Asey. "I did tell her it would be fun to go here and there or do this or that! And I probably said 'we.' But I never meant with her, even if she's convinced I did. I—Asey, she just twisted things the way she wanted them to be! She— she thought I wanted to be bought!"

"When a woman in love wants to believe somethin'," Asey said, "she usually does. Every rose is a bouquet, if you know what I mean. An' then, folks with lots of money sometimes overestimate what it'll buy. Those other lads Nora helped, they all wanted money. They did almost anythin' for money. Nora knew that. So, why shouldn't you, Jere? Particularly if you kept talkin' about 'we' all the time! But, you see, to marry you she needed money. An' to marry you meant losin' everythin', unless Wilbur was to die. It's as simple as that. . . . Now, Mrs. Latimer, you fired that trailer with the electric iron an' the film, didn't you?"

"I told them I was going to look inside the trailer," Nora said. "They saw me go. It took about thirty seconds to plug in the iron and pull out the films."

"Now, why?" Lizzie asked. "Had you read that book? Was that why you set the trailer on fire?"

"What book?" Nora returned. "I set it on fire because Asey stared so at my feet, yesterday morning over in the field. I'd thought of fingerprints, so I'd worn gloves. And I'd wiped the linoleum floor before I left. But Asey stared so at my feet, I began to worry about footprints and if maybe I'd missed one and left muddy prints in spite of the care I took. It was raining that night, you know. The more Asey stared at my sandals, the more I worried. Then I remembered that iron—"

Asey avoided meeting her glance. He had not consciously stared at Nora's feet, or at her sandals, either.

But he did remember Nora's purple-lacquered toe-nails. They had disconcerted him every time he tried to think.

"Besides," Nora continued, "I hope that if the trailer was destroyed you'd never find out who that man really was."

"I thought out *that* part," Asey said truthfully. "Now, you played with the wedge in my door last night. It was easy for you with your passkeys to get in an' out of the Inn the back way. The needles in the tires come from that sewing basket the kitten played with at your house today. An'—"

"And to think she hit me!" Lizzie said.

"It was lucky for you," Asey said, "that she recognized you. She didn't want to make any more mistakes, so she pulled her punch an' just tied you up, an' left. . . . Mrs. Latimer, where'd you hunt for Wilbur last night? . . . Well, it don't matter if you won't answer. You probably hunted all over. An' before you set out, an' just after you returned, you phoned the doc that you felt terrible. Yup. But you'd ought to of washed the mud off the beach wagon. That caught my eye, an' I knew Jere hadn't used the machine. An' just one more item—where did that sinker hit you?"

"My shoulder," Nora said in a toneless voice. "It

made my arm stiff. That's why I missed just now when I tried to kill Alcott. That's why he got that crack on the scalp instead of on the base of his skull. But if you hadn't come I'd have got him the next time."

"Then," Asey said, "you'd have come pantin' down an' said you found him like that. Or else sneaked away. You was pretty safe, either way."

"Asey," Lizzie said, "*how* did you know that she didn't have appendicitis?"

Asey grinned and sat down beside Wilbur on the bed. "Well, what sort of tied things up in red ribbons, she lifted a squirmin' kitten off a mantel an' dumped it down on a rug, an' then lifted up a wrigglin' dog an' lugged it bodily an' against his will some twenty-five feet to a door. I couldn't do that without wincin', you know. I couldn't change a tire. I didn't try, this mornin'. I all but ruined myself drivin' around yesterday, an' runnin' up the stairs here now—"

"What do you mean?" Lizzie demanded.

"I got out of the hospital, myself, a week ago," Asey said. "Matter of a nasty little appendix, only I didn't make it public. You had the surgical details down pat, Mrs. Latimer, an' you mostly winced at the right places, but your act slipped up on the dog an' the cat."

"But why should she pretend to have appendicitis?" Lizzie asked. "Why appendicitis?"

"A physical disability," Asey said, "is about the nicest alibi a body can have. It's the simplest. Most any hale and hearty person is capable of committin' a murder. But you don't suspect invalids or convalescents. So, Nora pretends she's had an operation an' is convalescin' from appendicitis. I don't know why she picked appendicitis, particularly, except it's common enough so she could find out all about it, an' people wouldn't ask her questions she couldn't answer. An' it ain't so complicated that she couldn't move around. She took me in. I ruled her out at the start because she was still too delicate an' seedy an' out of health to go dashin' around doin' the things this murderer done. An'—"

"Why didn't someone *see* her?" Lizzie asked.

"People did see her fire the trailer," Asey pointed out. "They knew she went in, but they didn't connect her with the firin'. Why should they? I tell you, she was convalescin'. She was ruled out at the start. She slipped around the Inn without bein' seen. Why not? She owns the place. She knows it. She knows the roads around. An', after all, you don't take a cheerin' section with you when you set out to kill someone!"

"But the maids at the house!" Lizzie persisted.

"They live in the far wing," Asey said. "If they heard a car at night, they wouldn't have thought of Nora as drivin' it, because she was supposed to be sick. Last night they'd have thought any cars belonged to cops, an' the cops would have thought it was other cops. If anyone seen her, they wouldn't have thought it could be her. An' even if someone recognized her for sure, they wouldn't have connected her with this affair."

"How did she track me down?" Wilbur demanded. "After the—er—crash, I've kept out of people's way."

"She found that out. She'd been huntin' you for some time, when your name bobbed up in the Tootsy-Wheetsy winners. Then she found out from the Randalls that you planned to come to the Cape. So, she went away, presumably West on business, an' when she came back, she had her appendix an' hospital story. No one ever checks up on folks's operations. She had a perfect alibi for anythin'. She just had to let you come within driving distance, that's all. The Randalls are relations of hers—"

"They know nothing of this," Nora said. "I just encouraged them to ask the girl to stay with them. I had to get her away. It was hard to— Oh. Oh!" She gave an odd little cry, and Hanson grabbed her as she swayed forward.

Suddenly she pushed his arm away and sat bolt upright. "What on earth"—she spoke in her usual brisk voice—"is the matter? What's the matter with my wrist? It's all bloody! It's bleeding!"

Asey looked at her curiously.

"I can't remember— Lizzie, what are you staring at me like that for? My wrist—fix it quickly, Asey! It hurts! Do something! How did I—what's happened?"

Asey bit his lip as he took the handkerchief Lizzie offered, and started to bind up Nora's wound.

"How did I get here?" Nora demanded. "What's happened? Who is—"

"Say!" Hanson said. "Say, what's the matter with you?"

Asey grinned. "Temporary insanity," he said, "an', with the Latimer millions, I'm glad my job ends here."

"She—say, she was all right! She knew—"

"My God!" Cummings bustled in. "My God! What now?"

"You fix Mrs. Latimer up," Asey said. "Maybe you an' her can work it out together. Wilbur, come along to my room an' let me start in on your forehead, an' the doc'll carry on later."

Lizzie followed Asey and Wilbur up the hall. "It's extraordinary!" she said. "Nora, of all people! But I always said she had a hard streak. That temper of hers, and always so emotional about her—er—young men. Was she really temporarily insane?"

"I'd hate," Asey said, "to be the judge of that. She may not have been, but it'll certainly seem so, in time."

"Oh. Oh, I see. Well—" Lizzie sat down heavily in the easy chair in Asey's room. "Well, there's always the silver lining, isn't there? Those two."

"What two?" Asey asked.

"Why, Cordy and Jere. Out in the corridor; see? They've made up. But I knew they would. He had that look. I knew, all along. . . . Asey, let me have that washcloth. That's *no* way to wash his face!"

While she expertly cleaned up Uncle Wilbur, Asey pulled out his pipe and lighted it.

"Asey," Wilbur said suddenly, "I've thought what you can call this episode in your career. It's—"

"Trailer," Asey said. "I thought of it too."

"Trailer?" Lizzie asked. "Why?"

Asey and Wilbur smiled at each other.

"Trailer," Wilbur said. "Trail her. Or, as the French say, Lizzie, '*Cherchez la femme.*' "

THE SWAN BOAT PLOT

THE
SWAN BOAT PLOT

T HE FIERY glow of the rising sun practically
guaranteed Boston its third sizzler in a row,
Asey Mayo thought, as he parked his long,
black Porter Sixteen roadster by the Boylston Street
curb and looked expectantly toward the Public Garden for the plump form of his housekeeper cousin
Jennie.

It was exactly 5:30 A. M., and Jennie should be
poised by the subway entrance back of the Channing
monument with her suitcase in hand, ready to leap
into the car and be driven posthaste back home to
Cape Cod. For today, June first, was the official open-
ing of Jennie's annual house-cleaning season, and
she wouldn't permit anything to interfere, not even
the difficulties involved in her return from a family
funeral in Chicago.

Asey grinned as he contemplated the relays of
relatives pressed into service to rush Jennie home

in time to get her curtains down and into the washtub at the proper moment. But his grin faded when
no figure bustled toward the car.

"Golly!" he murmured. "Ain't she *here* yet?"

He was in no mood to hang around Boston. He
had his own plans for the day—a sail out Cape Cod
Bay for tautog, and then a session with the bass on
North Beach. He was already dressed for it, in dungarees and a blue shirt and his oldest yachting cap.
His rubber boots were on the car floor, next to a
pail of lines and tackle.

"I wonder, now, if I got this wrong." Taking
Jennie's letter from his pocket, he scanned the final
page.

" '*Lisha will pick me up Sunday night at 7 at
Cora's,*' " he read. " 'He says the Salty Codfish Sherlock (he means you) could probably make Boston
in 5 hours, the way you drive, but it'll take him 8 or
so. Allowing for everything, I'll be there sure by 5:30.
You meet me then. Everyone asks me if you done
any murder detecting lately. I declare, out here they
don't realize you're so busy at the Porter factory making those tanks you don't hardly ever get home! Why,
Cora didn't even know you was a director of Porter
Motors; she thought you was still Captain Porter's
hired man and yacht captain, like you was years ago.

She said, why would anyone call you a Lithe Hayseed Sleuth, you don't look like a hayseed! Can you
beat it? Now, 5:30 Monday morning, back of the
Channing monument. Don't be late. I got to start
cleaning.' "

Asey replaced the letter and mentally gave Jennie
just half an hour. If she didn't appear by six, she
could take the train home.

Sliding out from behind the roadster's wheel, he
walked over into the Garden. Perhaps Jennie might
already have come and be wandering around. The
Public Garden was her favorite spot in Boston. She
loved its statues and prim flower beds, and particularly its swan boats. If it were later in the day and the
boats were out paddling their leisurely course about
the tiny artificial lake, Asey knew he would have
found Jennie perched on the front bench of one,
gurgling with pleasure while she fed peanuts to the
ducks. Maybe even at this early hour she might have
strolled over to the boat landing by the bridge.

Asey shook his head as he started off down the
dirt walk. Perhaps, as Jennie claimed, the swan boats
took her back to her childhood and made her feel
young again. But it still didn't seem right for her
to get such a thrill from a flat-bottomed water barge,
foot-propelled by a stern paddle hidden in a metal

swan, and capable of a top speed of two miles an hour!

"For the love of Pete!"

He stopped short at a turn of the path and stared blankly ahead at Jennie's new tan suitcase with the brown stripes and red initials, sitting forlornly on its side in the middle of the walk. Beyond it lay the brown pocketbook he'd given her for Christmas!

But there was no sign of Jennie herself.

"Jennie!" He opened his mouth and bellowed in his best quarter-deck roar. "Jen-nie May-o!"

His voice echoed across the pond, and two moth-eaten gray squirrels stopped their scampering and looked at him.

But Jennie didn't appear.

Asey picked up the pocketbook, peered inside, and then hastily shut it before the miscellaneous hodgepodge of its contents started to spill over. There was only some small change in the money compartment, but that didn't signify anything. When Jennie traveled, not even the Gestapo could find where she hid her funds.

"Ahoy, Jennie! Ahoy, Jennie Mayo!"

Frowning, he tucked the bag and pocketbook under his arm and walked slowly toward the boat landing. He couldn't imagine any situation that would have prompted her to dash off of her own accord and leave her precious belongings behind. She never would have been duped into rushing off with a stranger. Once away from home, Jennie was inclined to view her fellow men with deep suspicion. And, if anyone had tried to rob her, the chances were that the prospective thief and not her two bags would have been stretched out prone on the path.

Asey's bewilderment increased, halfway around the lake, when he came upon her best brown straw hat on the grass by a clump of trees. "She's *been* here!" he muttered. "Where *is* she?"

Slinging the bags on a bench, Asey shinnied up a near-by maple, braced himself, and made a slow survey of the Garden. But the place was deserted except for the ducks bobbing around the lake and the squirrels romping under the trees, and a flock of pigeons waddling along the footbridge railing.

His gaze automatically followed the line of the rail, and then went down the angle of the steps leading to the swan-boat landing. What he saw there sent him sliding down the tree and propelled him at a gallop along the path.

"By gum!" He paused at the edge of the landing's worn planking, looked ahead, and winced.

For the body of the gaunt young man in gray slacks

lying there behind a settee was not a pretty sight. Decidedly not.

Someone, Asey decided thoughtfully, had done some very expert shooting. The bullet hole in the fellow's forehead was almost mathematically centered, and the condition of the back of his head, turned slightly sideways, indicated that a considerably powerful weapon had been used. The fellow had gone down like a log without even knowing what hit him.

Scattered around near the body were several small cardboard cartons and leather cases, and almost at the water's edge stood a camera, set up on a tripod and aimed at the little fleet of swan boats moored a few feet away from the landing.

Asey opened his eyes wide as he looked at them.

He'd ignored the boats entirely in his haste to convince himself that the crumpled body he'd spotted from the tree was not that of his cousin Jennie. He discovered now that the metal swan on the nearest boat had a framed background of blue velvet propped up behind it. And posed with her arms around the swan's neck was an amazingly likelife dummy of a girl, scantily and bizarrely clad in red and white striped shorts and a blue, star-spangled bra! Her straight blond hair dangled to her shoulders, and she stared at Asey with the bland, disconcerting disdain of a store-window model.

Obviously, the murdered man had been taking pictures of the dummy and the swan, although why he should choose to take them at all, and particularly at this hour, was a puzzle to Asey.

"Let's see!" he thought out loud. "This fellow turned around from his camera—yup, that's it. He's still got a plateholder gripped in his hand. Maybe he heard or saw somethin' behind him. Anyway, he turned, an' that's what someone was waitin' for, an', bang, that was that! Wonder who he was—"

Asey bent over and read the printing on the metal-edged tag attached to the handle of one of the leather cases:

"RUDI BRANDT, STUDIO 5, ARTS BLDG.,
ARLINGTON STREET, BOSTON, MASS."

Since the initials on the breast pocket of the fellow's shirt were "R. B.," Asey decided he could reasonably assume that the fellow was Rudi Brandt.

He rubbed his chin reflectively as he glanced around. There was no trace of any weapon hurriedly discarded by Brandt's murderer. There were no lipstick-stained cigarette butts or shreds of Harris tweed, or anything a movie detective would have pounced on as a vital clue. The only small, extraneous objects on the landing were peanut shells, left over from the swan boats' customers of the day before. And still, in all the Garden, there was no one but himself, and the ducks and pigeons and squirrels.

There must, Asey thought, have been a good, hefty report from the gun firing that shot, and he wondered why the sound hadn't brought some of Boston's cops running to the scene. Someone must have heard the shot. Probably a lot of people had, and promptly dismissed it from their minds. That was the trouble with city folks. They took it for granted that every loud bang was a car backfiring.

Asey tilted his yachting cap back on his head. He could guess, now, what had probably become of Jennie. Arriving earlier than she'd figured, she'd started over for the landing and then—perhaps the shot had launched her off—she'd seen fit to rush in and mix herself up with this nasty business. Heaven only knew where she might be now. He only hoped she hadn't really dashed off on her own in a wild attempt to catch or track down a murderer who blazed away at people as accurately as this one did. But it wouldn't be the first time his firm-minded cousin had barged into a situation where the average angel would fear to tread!

Asey replaced his cap. He was forgetting himself. He shouldn't be dallying around, brooding like this. This was neither his bailiwick nor his business, and he ought to report the affair to the cops, and trust that Jennie would sooner or later come back to the Garden and her belongings. No one as efficient as the person who shot Brandt would ever let himself be hampered for long with Jennie's meddling.

He tried to figure, as he returned to collect her hat and bag and pocketbook, the location of the nearest phone. He couldn't remember any stores open on Boylston Street. Probably the drugstore on the corner of Beacon and Charles was his best bet.

With the bags under his arm he emerged a few minutes later on Beacon Street, just in time to see a girl in a knee-length red coat streak around the corner opposite him and dart up the side street. It occurred to Asey that she looked strangely familiar. He frowned, and then slapped his thigh.

"The dummy!" he said. "That's it! She had the same color blond hair, wore it the same way, an' had on the same red-heeled pumps— Oh—oh! Oh—oh!"

A cop had loomed in sight on the corner where the girl had first appeared. And he had a typical cop's grip on the arm of Jennie!

Asey rushed across Beacon Street in nothing flat.

"Thank goodness, you've finally come!" Jennie's tone insinuated that if anything out of the ordinary were happening, it was all Asey's fault for not being there sooner. "Asey, tell this cop who I am, and who *you* are—see?" She joggled the cop's arm. "Recognize him, don't you? He's Asey Mayo, and I'm his cousin, and you let me go, you!"

"Listen, lady; I seen you snatch that girl's purse!"

"I did not!" Jennie said hotly. "I—"

"Look," Asey said; "both of you stop breathin' fire an' listen to me. Over in the Garden—"

"He's a director of Porter Motors, too!" Jennie joggled the cop's arm again.

"Yeah?" The cop leaned back against the basement railing of the house before which they stood, and gave Asey's fishing costume a critical once-over. "Yeah? I took him for a millionaire. Now, I seen you grab that purse—"

"I never! I was only trying to grab *her,* and all I got hold of was her bag! . . . Asey, did you see a blond girl in a red coat run past? . . . When? Where'd she go to?"

"Around that corner, about two shakes ago." As Asey pointed to the side street, the cop casually turned his head in that direction.

Instantly, in a single swift gesture, Jennie grabbed the red purse from under the cop's arm and shoved him squarely in the stomach. Then she grabbed Asey's belt and started to run. "Hurry up!"

Asey, as he was yanked along, looked back over his shoulder, to see the cop lose a desperate battle with his balance and disappear in a spectacular tumble down the basement steps.

"Hustle!" Jennie almost dragged him around the corner of the side street, glanced along it briefly, and shook her head. "Oh, dear, I've lost that girl *again!* Well, it won't matter so much, now you're here to help get her. Come along quick, before that fool cop sees us!"

Nonchalantly, as if she'd lived there always, Jennie reached out, shoved open the wooden alley door of one of the low brick houses, pushed Asey into the narrow alley, and closed the door behind them. "There! We'll wait till that fool's gone. . . . Asey, the time I been havin'! I never seen anything like it!"

"Neither did I!" Asey told her severely. "D'you realize what you just done? You assaulted a cop, an' city cops don't like bein' assaulted!"

"I never assaulted anyone!" Jennie protested. "I just accidentally pushed that fellow, and he happened to slip. Listen; we've got to find that blond girl, because she's just shot and killed a man on the swan-boat landin'! I heard the shot, and saw her and everything, with my own eyes!"

"You seen her? Then why, instead of chasin' around like a hen with her head cut off, didn't you *tell* that cop so?"

"You saw why!" Jennie retorted. "He wouldn't listen. Asey, she shot him and then ran away, so I dropped my bags and ran after her. Now go on and ask me why I didn't call a cop!"

"None around?"

"Not a soul, an' *somebody* had to catch her! I almost did, too. That's why I know about this alley," Jennie added parenthetically. "She hid here, once, but I found her and followed her across these back yards. Finally I was so near that I reached out to grab her, and just then that cop turned a corner on Charles Street and seen us. When I turned to call to him to come, the girl jumped ahead, and so I only got her purse. And then that fool cop grabbed *me* for stealin' it! Asey, we can't stand here like bumps on a log! We got to get her!"

"Seems as if we had," Asey agreed. "Golly, if only you hadn't got yourself in Dutch with that cop!"

"I don't care a fig for him! It—it's—" From the quaver in Jennie's voice, Asey suddenly realized she was on the verge of tears. "It's the *other* one I'm scared of!"

"What other one?"

"The other cop that was standing near the Beacon Street Garden entrance," Jennie said, "when I was chasin' the girl. He'd heard that shot, Asey, and he *seen* me tryin' to catch her, but he never paid a speck of attention to her at all! He thinks *I* killed that fellow! He even shot at me to make me stop!" Jennie said.

"A *cop*," Asey said slowly, "shot at *you*, while you was chasin' the girl out of the Garden? A cop did?"

"Yes, and the bang scared me half to death! I'd have run away from him after that even if I hadn't been chasin' her!"

"Look here; you tell me the whole yarn from the beginnin'," Asey said.

"We haven't time! We got to catch the girl! . . . Asey, what're you lookin' so upset for? After all, it isn't as if he hit me!"

"What'd the cop look like?"

"Like a cop, naturally!" Jennie said with asperity. "Dark blue visored cap, white shirt, dark pants. He was standin' near a car. You think I don't know a cop when I see one? Now, let's go after the girl; if we don't catch her now, we'll lose her forever!"

"I don't think it's that fateful," Asey said. "She's too different-lookin' to lose easy, an', besides, we can give a pretty good description of her. . . . Peek in her bag an' see if there ain't somethin' with her name on it."

"I forgot I had it." Jennie snapped the bag open. "Oh, what a lot of powder an' rouge! That's more than I ever owned in my life—but there's no name card."

"No matter. From all that stuff," Asey said, "I'd guess she's a professional model, an' I think we can get onto her track. Right now I want to clear up this other cop trouble."

"The real trouble," Jennie said, "is time."

Asey sighed. "Honest, ten minutes one way or another ain't goin' to affect the tracin' of that girl!"

"I don't mean that. I mean just time. Time out West is all mixed up, Asey. I couldn't get it straight. I figured it'd be five-thirty when 'Lisha dropped me off, but it was *three*-thirty!"

"An' you been wanderin' about the Garden since then?"

"'Course not!" Jennie said. "I went and sat in a

bus station in Park Square. Then I had breakfast and
sat some more, but, come daybreak, I was so fidgety
from waitin', I went over to the Garden and—"

Although he seemed to be listening raptly, Asey
was too busy with his own speculations to hear much
of Jennie's scenic description of the Public Garden at
daybreak. He was sure that the person who potted at
Jennie was no cop. If a real cop had heard the shot
that killed Brandt, and suspected that the shooting
involved a killing, he wouldn't have stood still and
contented himself with firing a warning shot across
Jennie's bow. A real cop would have rushed after her
and the girl, nabbed them, and found Brandt's body
long before Asey, himself, arrived.

"You listenin'?" Jennie inquired acidly. "Or detectin', or what?"

"I think," Asey said, "I'm detectin' a strong odor
of fish. How near was you to that cop? How good
a look did you get at him?"

"I don't know; I didn't stop to examine him! I was
busy chasin' the girl!" Jennie said. "I naturally
thought he'd chase her, too! If only you'd listen,
you'd never ask such silly things! You see, I was
lookin' at the flower beds and half watchin' for you—
it was ten after five, but you're usually early—and I
seen this couple come into the Garden from the cor-

ner of Boylston and Arlington. It was the blond girl and the fellow who got shot."

"His name was Rudi Brandt." Asey told her about finding him and reading the tag.

"Well, Brandt and the girl was almost runnin', they was in such a rush. He had his hands full of boxes and cameras, and she was carryin' that dummy. Then this other young fellow in white pants and a blue shirt come runnin' after 'em, and stopped 'em."

"Where was you?" Asey asked. "Didn't they see you?"

"No, I was down by the water's edge, feedin' the ducks with some roll I'd saved from breakfast. I heard 'em and saw 'em, but the bushes hid me from them. Anyway, this fellow—his hair was light brown and awful rumpled, like he hadn't combed it, and he wore a pair of those funny triangular spectacles that make you look slant-eyed—well, wasn't he worked up! Wanted the girl to turn around and come with him. But she wouldn't. Told him to leave her alone, and smacked him in the face. Then the boy shook his fist under Brandt's nose."

"So? What'd Brandt do?" Asey asked.

"Just shrugged, and said somethin' I didn't hear, and the boy slammed off, mad as a hatter. Then Brandt and the girl rushed to the landin'. You know,

I guessed when I first saw his camera that he was goin' to take a picture," Jennie added, "but d'you know what it was going to be for?"

"What? I wondered, myself."

"A magazine cover for *Fashion-Allure*. The girl told the boy with spectacles so. You know I always buy that every month. There's a copy home on my sewin' table this minute."

"Uh-huh. I glanced at it," Asey said. "Wa-el, I s'pose a picture of swan boats an' that dummy couldn't be crazier than the cover on that copy. Two purple lions an' a head of lettuce—what was it s'posed to mean?"

"It's modern art, I guess," Jennie said. "They always have covers like that. Anyway, they rushed to the landin', and Brandt set up his camera and draped the dummy over the swan. Then he helped the girl hop to the boat, posed her on the boatman's seat, and started takin' pictures lickety-split."

"The girl? *She* was in the pictures, too?"

"Sure thing. She was dressed just like the dummy. Didn't you know that?"

"All I noticed was her hair," Asey said, "when she rushed past. Her coat covered the rest. Huh! Brandt's pictures'll settle her bein' there an' who she is, an' all. I don't know why it never dawned on me she might've been in the picture along with the dummy. Jennie, now I see why Brandt was out so early, an' in such a rush. He couldn't do a job like that later in the day, with crowds millin' an' gapin' around. This begins to make more sense. Go on. Then what?"

"Well, Brandt helped her jump back off the boat to the landin' and started to fix her hair different, and she didn't like the results one bit! Slapped his face, and grabbed her coat and put it on, and turned to leave. Brandt called out and started after her, and then, *bang!* Down he went. And I begun to run after her, and as we run out of the Garden that cop shot at me—"

"Uh-huh," Asey said as she paused for breath, "only he wasn't a real cop. Firin' a shot at that point wouldn't't've stopped either you or the girl. Not unless one of you was hit. A shot'd only do what it did—scare the two of you into runnin' harder. No, I don't think he was a cop. I think he was the feller that shot Brandt!"

Jennie planted her hands on her ample hips and looked at him defiantly. "Oh, you do, do you? Well, let me tell you, the girl got mad with the way Brandt fixed her hair, started to leave, and shot him when he started after her! I seen it!"

"Not likin' the way someone's done your hair ain't much of a motive for murder."

"I can't help that! She shot him!"

"But where'd she get the gun? Where'd she been keepin' it?" Asey persisted. "There's no room to cram a gun into that red purse of hers. An' if she was dressed like the dummy—or undressed, as you might say—she hardly had any place to hide a gun on herself. Did you honestly *see* her shoot him?"

"Land's sakes, you can't see what's goin' on when someone's back is *to* you, the way hers was to me! But I seen the next best thing. I seen her throw the gun away afterwards!" Jennie concluded with triumph.

"Why," Asey asked gently, "didn't you mention that before?"

"With you askin' so many fool questions, I never got to it!" Jennie returned. "Listen; after she shot him, she stood there a second, lookin'. Then she reached down and picked the gun up from the grass. She'd dropped it after she fired; see? Same thing I always did when I tried shootin' with the Women's Defense Corps at home. Anyway, I seen her pick up the gun and heave it out to the pond. Only, she missed the water. I was runnin' along the path toward her, then, and I heard the gun hit the wood of a swan boat. She don't know that, either, because she was already rushin' off. And I followed her, and then that cop shot at me. How *could* that cop have anything

to do with this, Asey? He *had* a gun—and remember
I already *seen* the murder gun thrown away!"

"There's no law against a body packin' two guns,"
Asey said.

"Land's sakes, Asey Mayo, this isn't a cowboy
movie, it's the Boston Public Garden!" Jennie said
indignantly. "I tell you, he was a plain cop, and no
murderer about it!"

Asey grinned. "In the light of your amended story,"
he said, "I'll grant you he ain't the murderer. But I
still don't think he was a cop. No cop'd blaze away
at you like that, without knowin' any more of what
was goin' on than he did!"

"You can't ever tell what cops'll do," Jennie said.
"Give me my hat, Asey. That other fool cop must be
gone now. Let's get started after the girl. Haven't
you got enough evidence to do somethin' about
her?"

"I'd think so. Besides all you seen," Asey said,
"there's Brandt's pictures to prove she was there, an'
the gun to clinch things. Only, first I want to see if
the coast is clear."

He walked down the alley to the back yard, disappeared for a moment, and returned wearing a denim
coat and bearing an ash can.

"Where'd you get them things?" Jennie demanded.

"From an ash house. Take my cap while I look around."

He lugged the can out to the street, set it down by the curb, and straightened up, to find two policemen striding down the brick sidewalk toward him.

"Hey!" the taller hailed him. "You seen a fat woman with gray hair and a brown print dress around here anywheres? Or a tall guy with a yachting cap?"

"I just come here," Asey said with perfect truth. "Anything the matter?"

"That bag-snatcher again. Sometimes it seems to me there can't be a bag left in this district! They must've cut back up the hill, Mike. You say Riley's ankle was sprained when he took that tumble down the stairs?"

"Yeah. It's his bad ankle, too. This dame always worked alone before, but Riley says the guy with her had a bag and a pocketbook they'd already got so far this morning. The nerve of her! When dames get so fresh they start shoving us over railings, they ought to get learned a lesson, if you ask me!"

"Me, too. Let's get 'em. Let's try the hill."

Asey's eyes narrowed as he watched the pair stride up the street. No matter how you figured it, Jennie was in hot water. These cops wanted her—as much to avenge their friend's sprained ankle as for being a supposed bag-snatcher. The cop who shot at her, if he was real, would begin wanting her as soon as Brandt's murder became known. If he was a fake cop— "I wonder!" Asey said. "Could he have been in cahoots with the blond girl?"

After all, a waitng car with a man standing near suggested a planned quick getaway. Making up an accomplice to look like a cop was an old trick, but it still worked. Suppose the girl had taken a quick look at the pursuing Jennie and decided that out-running her was wiser than fleeing under her nose? If something like that were the case, and if Jennie were seen hanging around now, it was possible that the next potshot in her direction wouldn't miss her by any mile!

Clearly, his most pressing problem was to remove Jennie from the scene and keep her away till he sorted out some of this mess. It would be a waste of breath to order her to visit someone and stay put till he called for her. The pursuit and capture of that girl loomed so in Jennie's life now that she'd even for-gotten about her annual house cleaning. What he really needed was some seemingly important mission to send her on.

He grinned suddenly, and returned to her. "Jennie," he said gravely, "we're in a jam. They're not huntin' only you. They want me— Don't interrupt. Without my yachtin' cap on an' in this coat, I'm safe for a while. But I got to have other clothes. You got to help. First, I'm goin' to put you in a cab. You go to the South Station ladies' room, change your dress, sit there till nine, an' then go to Blanding's."

"Porter's tailor, the one makes your suits?"

"Just so. You're to stand over 'em an' make 'em finish up my new suit in a rush."

"I didn't know you'd got a new suit! What kind?"

Improvising rapidly, Asey described an entirely imaginary new Palm Beach suit. "So you fetch the suit back to the roadster," he concluded. "It's over by the Channin' monument. I'll watch for you. Remember to get shoes an' socks an' all, too. Got a pencil an' paper? I'll write Blandin' a note."

In a masterly six lines, Asey summed up the situation for his old friend Blanding, and begged him to invent things, anything at all, to keep Jennie busy till noon.

"Now"—he gave her the note—"I'll find a cab— Say, was anyone else around the Garden you forgot to tell me about?"

"Only an old man walkin' some dogs, but he left

long before Brandt an' the girl come. Before him, there was a woman in evenin' clothes that hustled across the Garden— You sure you'll be all right?"

For his part, Asey thought ten minutes later, as he watched her sail off in a cab, he was going to worry a lot more about her staying put. But, now she was gone, he could start to work. Stuffing his yachting cap into the pocket of his appropriated jacket, he turned back toward the Public Garden.

People were beginning to appear, now that it was nearly seven, he noted as he came to Beacon Street. A maid was halfheartedly sweeping the basement steps down which Riley had tumbled, a boy listlessly trundled a grocery cart along the sidewalk, and half a dozen dogs were being walked by sleepy-looking owners. The only wide-awake person in the group was a bearded man in a white linen suit who was trying to unsnarl the leashes of his two Chows.

Asey slowed down at the sight of that white hair and flowing white beard, which he recognized, although he hadn't seen them in the ten years since their owner, Judge Thatcher Sudbury, sold his shooting box on North Beach and left the Cape. Under less urgent circumstances, Asey would have enjoyed stopping and chatting with him, and he was rather relieved to see that the Judge also appeared to be in a hurry, for he whistled to his dogs and ran with them up the front steps of a brownstone house.

At least, Asey decided, it was comforting to know there was someone of importance and integrity living in the neighborhood who would probably go to bat for him if the need arose.

Once back in the Garden, he made a beeline over the grass toward the swan boats. The absence of police and the general lack of hubbub confirmed his suspicion that no one had as yet discovered Brandt.

He made rapid plans as he strode forward. After another look about the landing he'd visit Brandt's studio. Somehow he could get in. Somewhere he should be able to find a clue to the girl's name and her address.

There was no sense in worrying about any possible problems that might surround his contemplated projects, or any use in trying to locate any of his friends out at the State Police barracks. They couldn't help him in Boston. On this job, Asey thought, he'd have to trust to luck and ingenuity.

An involuntary whistle escaped from his lips as he came to a stop by the swan-boat landing. Even if no one had officially found the body, someone had been there, all right! For Brandt's leather case of plate-holders had been opened and tipped over, and the plates themselves, used and unused, spilled out on the planking under the glare of the sun, were now exposed and worthless.

Nothing else had been moved or touched as far as he could determine. But those ruined plates were sufficient to convince him that the blond girl was no dummy, no matter how much she was made up to look like one. After escaping from Jennie, she must have circled back here and, with a couple of simple gestures, blotted out the ultimate, damning evidence of her presence on the landing. Now the proof of her being here depended solely on Jennie's word, which at the moment wasn't worth two cents, in the estimation of the police.

Stepping past the settee to the water's edge, Asey gazed out steadily at the moored swan boats for some trace of the gun.

At last he caught sight of it, lying on a rear bench in the shadow of a rolled-up awning top. Again he whistled.

He'd guessed right about its being a powerful weapon! That was a model you couldn't mistake, a Smith & Wesson .357 Magnum, famous for shooting the most powerful revolver cartridge in the world. He understood now the condition of Brandt's head, he thought, as he walked slowly off the landing back to the path.

"For a girl like her to pack a gun like that!" he murmured. "I can see how droppin' it would be easier than carryin' it—"

The sudden sound of pounding heels sent him scurrying off the path to the refuge of a clump of low bushes, and a moment later he thanked the impulse that had prompted him. The two men rushing toward the landing were the same two cops who had seen him taking the barrel out of the alley.

Behind him, apparently winded, walked a young man wearing white flannels and a blue shirt. His rumpled mop of light brown hair caused Asey to wonder if this mightn't be the fellow Jennie described as butting in on Brandt and the girl when they first entered the Garden. When the boy put on a pair of spectacles with triangular-shaped lenses, Asey decided his surmise was correct. He was somewhere in his early twenties, Asey judged, and neither the griminess of his mussed flannels nor the grubbiness of his saddle shoes could disguise the fact that both were expensive.

The boy sat down on the grassy slope above the path and watched in a detached manner while the two cops scurried about the landing. The tall cop called out some question Asey couldn't catch. But he saw the boy shrug, and heard his answer:

"I tell you, I just happened to walk past, and I found him, that's all!" His accent was so thoroughly Bostonian, Asey thought, you could cut it with a knife.

"How'd you know who he was? See anyone around here?"

"Everyone knows Rudi. I didn't see a soul. I merely found him," the boy returned. "Er—d'you think you could bring yourselves to do something about it all? Like calling detectives?"

Asey grinned at the expression on the cops' respective faces, and looked with renewed interest at the boy. It was one thing to own a genuine broad "a," and something else to quell cops with it. For all his sloppy appearance and his air of detached weariness, this boy knew what he was doing. That he didn't mention having seen the blond girl with Brandt probably meant that he didn't intend to mention her at all. And, if people questioned him, they were going to smack themselves up against the barrier of that super-nonchalant broad "a."

It wasn't the first time Asey had seen an untidy-looking Boston youth stump people with similarly bland passive resistance. Cap'n Porter's son Bill had the same backfield physique and boyish look—and he ran the Porter factory like a Prussian field marshal. Later on, Asey decided, he'd seek out this young man and have a chat with him. Within an hour, a phone call to any Boston newspaper office would elicit the name and address of the discoverer of Brandt's body. That part wouldn't be hard, and the boy would be something to fall back on in case he drew a blank at Brandt's studio.

But right now, he thought, as he quietly retreated from the clump of bushes, he ought to tackle the studio before the place became littered with cops. He'd nothing to gain from hanging around the Garden. The cops could see nothing he hadn't already seen, and he rather doubted that they'd notice that gun right away, either.

Ten minutes later he tried the knob of Studio 5 on the third floor of the Arts Building, found the door unlocked, and entered a small waiting-room whose walls were almost obliterated by framed photographs, most of which looked like *Fashion-Allure* covers.

Asey glanced at them, then crossed the waiting-room's plum-colored broadloom and pushed open the door at the opposite end. That was the studio proper, a barnlike room stuffed with a miscellaneous clutter. There were screenlike backdrops, disjointed arms and legs and plaster heads, a duplicate of the dummy out on the swan boat, and a fat, masculine dummy wearing a green top hat. There were odd chairs and tables, stray bits of bric-a-brac, piles of draperies, and at least a dozen bizarrely decorated screens.

Peering behind one of the latter, Asey came on a stack of prints. Not only was the top picture a study of the blond dummy and the blond girl, but so, he found, were all the rest! They were posed with practically everything under the sun, including a washtub and some dead trees. The longer he looked, the less Asey liked the girl and the harder it was for him to tell her from the dummy.

"If she come here first to change to that costume," he said aloud, "her own clothes ought to be around somewheres. They might lead to— By gum!"

He almost crowed as he spotted an opened magazine on the floor beyond the screen. There, staring up at him, was a full page photograph of the blond girl in evening dress! Grabbing up the magazine, he eagerly read the caption beneath the picture.

"Lissome, impulsive Liss," it was headed. "Virtually unnoticed at the time of her debut, Liss Lathrop

has been glamorized into national prominence by the genius of photographic wonder-work, Rudi Brandt, and now graces magazine covers, tobacco ads, mink coats, beer. A member of one of Boston's oldest families, Liss is newly engaged to the young tycoon Jackson Poor. Wiseacres wonder if Romance will abruptly cut off a career bound to end on Broadway or in Hollywood. Liss says it won't. Next pages show Liss in her younger days, Liss in her delightfully charming Old-World home." (*Pictures by Brandt.*)

Asey flipped over the page, to discover, in a picture headed *Sub-deb at Hunt Club,* that the boy with the rumpled hair and glasses was Liss's older half-brother, Craig Lathrop.

"So!" Asey said.

He glanced at snapshots of *Liss at Seven in Tartan,* and *Liss at Leggy Eleven with Mother,* and memorized the address of her home, where Brandt's pictures showed her. Throughout the series, he noted, she somehow managed to maintain the same slightly petulant expression of a sulky child.

Asey looked back meditatively at the picture of her tousle-headed brother, and then looked up and listened as the outer door of the waiting-room squeaked open. It couldn't be the cops slipping in so quietly, he thought, nor could it be clients, at seven-thirty in the morning. He ducked behind a screen as light footsteps padded toward the studio.

A good-looking black-haired girl entered, made for a tablelike desk he had missed entirely in the studio's confusion, and, with the casual confidence of one familiar with the place, yanked out the top drawer.

Peeking around the screen, Asey watched while she extracted a checkbook and wrote a check. Asey could see the nervous flush in her cheeks and hear her rapid breathing. She knew the place and she knew where things were, he thought, but she was sufficiently ex-cited to make a mistake on her first check, and have to rewrite it. Then she reached down into a lower drawer, drew out a small, red, leather-bound volume, thrust both it and the check into her pocketbook, and audibly sighed her relief.

Asey waited until she turned away from the desk before he opened his mouth to speak to her. But his request for fuller explanations of her actions died on his lips as the waiting-room's outer door squeaked open again, and the girl, uttering a startled little cry, darted for the very screen behind which he was hid-ing!

Never had Asey seen any eyes open as wide as the

girl's when she found him there. Her expression reminded him of nothing so much as a close-up of an
old-time movie heroine registering intense emotional
upheaval.

Asey looked at her speculatively. The instant she
started to scream, he was going to be forced to imitate
an old movie, himself. It was going to be a Douglas
Fairbanks Senior act for him, out the studio's side
window and down the antique fire escape into the
great unknown below.

But the girl, to his amazement, accepted him as
casually as if she'd met him at a dinner party. Entirely
at ease, she put her finger to her full red lips, and then
pointed toward the door in a gesture which indicated
that she thought he ought to take a look and see who
was out there.

Cautiously Asey ducked down and peered around
the edge of the screen.

A tall, broad-shouldered young man stood uncertainly on the threshold of the studio. He was well
tailored and well dressed, and his disapproval as he
stared around at the studio's litter was obvious.

"Who is it?" The girl prodded Asey.

He shrugged and motioned for her to look.

"It's Jackson Poor!" She breathed the words in his
ear as she straightened up.

"What a pigsty!" Poor's muttered comment sounded as if he were viewing the place for the first time.

"Pompous ass!" the girl whispered indignantly in Asey's ear. "What's the mighty tycoon want?"

"S-sh!" Asey shook his head warningly, and squinted through a crack of the screen's frame in time to see Poor start to inspect the floor beneath a broken armchair.

In the course of the next quarter-hour the girl and Asey took turns watching Poor while he carried on a survey of the floor space under every stick of furniture in that section of the studio. Once he stopped to mop his perspiring face with a handkerchief which he jerked irritably from his coat pocket, and when the contents of the pocket jerked out, too, Poor's annoyance bordered on high dudgeon. Muttering to himself, he crawled around the floor retrieving cigarettes, a length of string, and several stubby pencils.

"How utterly absurd of him! What's he hunting?" The girl penciled her comment on an envelope taken from her pocketbook. "Jack Poor never set foot in here before! He hates Rudi. What do you think the egotistical stuffed shirt *wants* here? Why—"

The rest of her question was cut off in mid-air by

Asey's hand descending on the pencil. "Watch out!" he hurriedly scrawled.

Poor was looking directly toward their sheltering screen. Suddenly he strode over to a chest in the corner beyond them, grabbed off its top a crumpled white silk dress, rolled it into a ball, and stuffed it into his coat pocket. It was inevitable that he should see them when he turned around.

"What the—" he paused. "Oh. Peg Whiting. What's the big idea, anyway?" he demanded peremptorily.

"We might," the girl said crisply, "ask the same thing of you! Because, if that's Liss's dress you just picked up, the police aren't going to like it!"

"What're you talking about?" Poor asked. "What've the police got to do with Liss's dress? She phoned and asked me to get it for her, and I did." His critical gaze traveled over Asey's denim jacket and dungarees. "Who's he?"

"As far as I'm concerned," Peg informed him, "he's a bundle straight from heaven. He's probably the only person who can save Liss from the police. You will, won't you, Mr. Mayo?" she added.

Asey looked at her quizzically. "So that's why you didn't scream!" he said. "Recognized me, huh?"

"I spent two summers at the Meweesit Girls' Camp on your road," Peg said, "practically panting every time you roared past in your chrome-plated Porter Bullet. D'you still drive that gorgeous, gleaming thing?"

"In the interests of National Defense," Asey said, "the current model's black, an' looks like a hearse. Miss Whitin', what d'you know about—?"

"Look here," Poor broke in, "I want to know what's going on, and why the two of you hide behind screens. If you were here when I came, why in hell didn't you *say* so?"

"You know," Asey said gently, "anybody listenin' to you might almost think you had more business bein' here than we have. Now, s'pose you put that dress back!"

"I will not! Peg, who is this fellow?"

"He's Asey Mayo, Cape Cod's gift to the detective world," Peg said. "And I don't know how he stumbled into this mess. It's enough for me that he's here. Mr. Mayo—oh, I can't 'mister' you! No one at camp ever did. Asey, you know about Rudi Brandt, don't you?"

Asey nodded. "Uh-huh. But I don't know about you, Miss Whitin'. Or about Mr. Poor. Just when did Liss Lathrop ask you to get her dress? Where was she when she phoned you?"

"What's the matter with you? I don't understand this damn' nonsense!" Poor, Asey thought, was working himself up to a good, lathery mad. "Liss begged me to get her white dress she'd left here, and I rushed off without my breakfast. She claimed it was a matter of life and death!"

"It happens to be a matter of death," Peg said. "Rudi's been killed." She spoke in a forced voice, rather flatly, as if she had drilled herself not to break down.

"Oh. Car accident?"

"He's been shot," Peg said. "Murdered."

"Oh! Too bad," Poor said perfunctorily. "That's a nasty business. But I must say I'm not surprised. That fellow seemed to enjoy making enemies. Who shot him?"

Asey watched Peg's face as she answered. He felt that she was furious with Poor, but she spoke calmly enough: "I don't know. Liss was with him."

"Liss? She *was*? Well, she's got nothing to do with it!" Poor said belligerently. "Liss liked the fellow— frankly, I could never see why! Always stood up for him. Always. *She's* got nothing to do with it!"

"I hope not," Peg said. "But Chub—that's her half-brother, Craig," she added parenthetically to Asey; "Chub said Liss was with Rudi when he was setting out to take pictures this morning in the Garden. I don't know where Liss is, now. But Chub found Rudi's body, and called in the police."

"So *Chub* found the body, eh?" Poor said. "How'd that happen?"

"If you want to know"—Peg was making a valiant effort to keep her temper—"Chub was trying to keep Liss from having her picture taken in red and white striped shorts and a blue, star-spangled bra, posed on a swan-boat swan in the Public Garden. For a cover. And with Brenda, too!"

"With that damned dummy? On a *swan boat?*" The veins in Poor's neck were bulging so that Asey expected the fellow's collar button to pop any second. "Nonsense! I don't believe you! Liss promised me she'd never do any more of that sort of stuff! I explained things to her very carefully, and proved that Brandt'd gone far enough with that duplicate-dummy angle— Why, damn it, he's been making Liss look more and more like—what's Rudi call the dummy?—Brenda. I tell you, Liss promised me all that dummy and cover tripe was out!"

"I know she did," Peg returned. "Chub knew it,

too. And he knew how furious you got the last time
she posed with Brenda. That's why he rushed into
this mess! You see, he got up early because he was
going sailing at Marblehead, and on the hall table he
saw Rudi's message. Apparently Maggie'd taken the
call last night and left the note there for Liss to see
when she came in. After Chub read what Rudi wanted
her for, he tore over here to the studio, and finally
he caught up with her and Rudi as they were going
over to the swan boats, and stopped 'em, and begged
Liss to drop the idea and come along home. But she
wouldn't."

"I don't understand this!" Poor said. "Liss promised me! She gave me her word! What reason did she
give Chub for going through with it?"

"If she gave any, Chub didn't tell me what it was,"
Peg said. "I only know she told him to mind his own
business, and smacked him, and went on with Rudi."

"It's all Brandt's doing!" Poor said. "Because he
took a few pictures of her that attracted attention he
thought he could make any demands on her he
wanted to! Why, only last week Rudi hounded her
about that damn' underwear ad till she finally gave
in and posed for him. I *told* Liss she wasn't to let him
bully her again. She's got to consider *me*, now! I
can't have my future wife running around in under-

wear ads! Chub should have argued her out of it. He shouldn't have quit so easily!"

"Chub knows Liss well enough to know when argument's useless!" Peg said. "Besides, he didn't quit. He went to a phone and called me, and asked if I'd come and see what I could do with Rudi. So—"

"Wait up a sec," Asey interrupted. "Why'd he call you? How d'you happen to come into this, Miss Whitin'?"

"I work for Rudi," she explained. "I'm a combination secretary-receptionist, printer and photofinisher, and general soother. I used to be his model. Anyway, Chub wanted me to talk to Rudi, so he phoned me. I still don't see," she added, with a frown, "why he couldn't get me then! I was there in bed, and the phone was beside me on the table, and it never rang! I'm sure he must've called the wrong number, though he swears he didn't. He says the bell rang and rang!"

"How'd he get hold of you?" Asey asked.

"He came after me—I live a few blocks over on Beacon Street, you see. And of course the apartment's outer door was locked, so he couldn't get in the vestibule to ring my bell, and had to ring for the janitor, and the janitor didn't choose to be roused. So Chub finally left and phoned me from a drugstore. That time, he got me. And I dressed and met him down-stairs, and we came here."

"Why here?" Poor demanded. "If Rudi was taking pictures in the Garden, why didn't you go there and stop him?"

"Because Chub had wasted an hour trying to get hold of me, and I was sure Rudi'd be through and back here long before six-thirty!" Peg said. "I knew Rudi planned to do his work in a rush at the first crack of dawn, so—"

"You mean that you knew all along he intended taking these pictures?" Poor broke in angrily. "Then why in hell didn't you stop him from using Liss?"

"Rudi never told me he was going to use her!" Peg retorted. "When I helped him run up the costumes last night he gave me to understand they were for Brenda and the other dummy, the new one, Bella! Anyway, by the time Chub reached me, I knew the only sensible thing was to come here to the studio and inveigle Rudi into hustling back to the Garden while he could, take the two dummies, and discard the pictures he'd made of Liss and Brenda. You see, there was so little time!"

"Did you persuade him?" Poor asked.

Peg made a helpless little gesture. "I never had a chance to say anything! When Chub and I finally got here, Liss and Rudi hadn't come back. We waited a while, and then decided to hunt them up. Time was so short! So Chub went over to the Garden to see if they might still be there, and I went around the corner to see if they might be having a cup of coffee at the diner. Chub came back and said Rudi'd been shot over on the landing and Liss was gone! He hadn't called the police, so I told him to. But—"

"But what?" Asey asked as she hesitated.

"Well, Chub said he didn't want to be the fall guy and get involved with the police."

"Thinking of the family name, I suppose!" Poor commented.

"He was thinking of Liss!" Peg said. "He said if he called the cops, they'd want his name and ask if he knew who Rudi was, and he'd have to say yes, and so on and so forth, and ultimately Liss's name would get dragged in by way of his. But I finally persuaded him to get a cop, and I stayed at the diner till I remembered my check— Oh!" She stopped short.

"What's the matter now?" Poor asked.

"I just thought— Asey, what must *you* have thought when you saw me writing that check? But it's really all right. I write all Rudi's checks and handle all his bills and accounts, and I forgot to pay myself yesterday. Over there in the diner it dawned on me I'd have to wait until his lawyer or someone got around to paying me—maybe months from now —and I really needed the money. And—well, I suppose it was wrong; but was it *very* wrong, Asey?"

"Where's Liss now?" Poor spoke up before Asey had a chance to answer.

"Where was she when she phoned you?" Asey returned.

"Home, I suppose. I wonder if she—" Poor was silent for a moment. "Who do the police think shot him?"

"I haven't even seen any police," Peg said. "I *hope* they won't try to drag Liss into it because she was with Rudi, but I'm awfully afraid they will."

"Have you seen 'em?" Poor asked Asey. "D'you know anything about it?"

"I'm not in any position to guess what the cops might be thinkin'," Asey said, "but, accordin' to the person who seen all this business happen, Liss got sore at Brandt while he was rearrangin' her hair-do, an' got mad enough about it to shoot him. I—"

He broke off as his ears caught the sound of heavy footsteps clumping somewhere in the hall beyond the waiting-room. With a grin, he darted across the studio, softly closing the door into the waiting-room, locked it, and pocketed the key. He knew police turmoil when he heard it, even though he had never before happened to be on the receiving end.

"What—?" Poor began.

"Those are cops, Mr. Poor," Asey said, "an' at this point I don't feel like meetin' 'em, so I'm—"

"My God, neither do I! Not *here!* Not *now!* How can we get out? Where's that corner door lead to?"

"That's the darkroom," Peg said, "but it's just a blind closet. Asey, I've nothing to hide, but, if you two are going to leave, I'm not going to stay here and face 'em alone! Only, how can we get out?"

Asey took her arm and steered her over to the side window. "Fire escape," he said, raising the window. "Give her a hand down, Poor. Okay?"

"Aren't you coming?"

"Just a sec. Forgot somethin'." Asey, running nimbly across to the desk, caught up Peg's pocketbook, and smiled at the hubbub out in the waiting-room.

The studio door was being rattled now, and several voices were clamoring for someone named Kenny to get the key. Someone else was all for breaking the door in, and quickly.

As far as he, personally, was concerned, Asey thought, they could blow the door down with trumpets as long as he had half a second more in which to get out of the place. His leg was on a level with the sill when the window suddenly, and of its own accord, slid down with a quiet little thump.

Asey reached out a hand to open it again, and, when it refused to budge, he hitched Peg's pocketbook under his arm and used both hands. Then he knelt precariously on the sill and slammed the palms of his hands under the top frame. Then he tried tugging and shoving, simultaneously, while beads of perspiration broke out on his forehead. He was aware suddenly of the growing heat and of an odd odor which he couldn't quite place.

"Smash it in!" The voice of the impatient door-breaker reached him clearly.

It was advice he'd take himself, Asey thought, if only the window glass weren't wired!

Shoulders thudded against the door, and Asey put every ounce of strength he possessed into one final shove. But the window remained stubbornly and irrevocably shut.

The studio door was all but bending under the force of shoulders battering against it when the crown of Poor's hat appeared at the window, and a second later his anxious face peered in. In response to Asey's urgent gesture, he reached out and shoved the window open without any apparent effort.

Asey heard the inside door go down with a crash as he and Poor jumped from the lowest landing of the fire escape onto the brick areaway below.

"Hurry," Poor said. "They may look out that window. Duck through this alley here. . . . Well, that was a close one! I couldn't imagine what'd happened to you till I noticed the window was closed. What was the matter? Did it jam?"

"There was one period"—Asey wiped his forehead with the sleeve of his denim coat—"when I'd have said it was welded, if I'd had the breath to say anythin'! I don't know *what* happened. It just plumb stuck! It might've been an old side-catch fixture, or maybe an old wedge got stuck in it. Your guess's as good as mine. What become of Peg?"

"She ripped her dress jumping down, and she's gone home to change. Frankly"—Poor fanned himself with his hat—"I just think it's an excuse to get away. I think she's come to the end of her emotional tether. She really feels wretched about Rudi's death. She liked him—although what she and Liss ever saw in the fellow—well, I suppose it doesn't matter now. . . . By George, that was exciting for a moment there, wasn't it?"

"Uh-huh." If the little episode had accomplished

nothing else, Asey thought, it had succeeded in altering Poor's point of view.

"Funny thing," Poor continued, "going down the fire escape, I suddenly remembered that you're in Porter Motors, aren't you? I know young Bill Porter slightly."

"Uh-huh," Asey said again, and wondered if that slight acquaintance might account for Poor's changed attitude.

"Brilliant fellow. Mayo, I owe you an apology. I felt pretty silly there in the studio, knowing you'd seen me pawing around for Liss's dress. Besides, I was already upset about Liss. The instant I heard her voice over the phone this morning, I knew she was in some sort of trouble. But she wouldn't tell me what was wrong. Only made me promise to get that damned dress. Believe me, I'm not unmoved about this business of Rudi! I know how serious it is—What's the matter?" he added, as Asey stopped short.

"I just got a horrid feelin'," Asey said slowly, "that the woman in the blue dress who just went into that corner drugstore is someone I know! Golly, I better look! Take this pocketbook of Peg's, will you?"

It couldn't be Jennie, he told himself, as he hurried back to the corner. He'd watched her pack, unpack, and rearrange the contents of her suitcase a dozen times, the night before she left the Cape. He was sure that she owned no dress that color of blue. Still and all, it had looked awfully like her!

"See her?" Poor sauntered after him.

"No. Wait a sec. I'm goin' inside."

"Hurry," Poor said. "Peg's going to join us at the diner on the next corner. Then I'll get my attorney, and Chub, and we'll all go see Liss and straighten things out, and get her out of any possible trouble—d'you hear me?"

"Uh-huh." Asey swung open the drugstore's screen door and stepped inside.

The place was empty, without even a clerk in sight.

Asey peered into the two phone booths, then walked around them and surveyed the side door which they partly blocked.

Even if, by some mischance, the woman had been Jennie, and even if she'd popped out this side exit, he still had no business letting himself be sidetracked into following her. He had no time now to worry about Jennie. He had frittered away enough precious minutes listening to Poor and Peg Whiting, in the vain hope that they might drop some hint of the one thing he would have liked to know more about before seeing Miss Lathrop. They'd filled in many little chinks, but they hadn't suggested any possible motive the girl might have had for killing Rudi Brandt.

The thing for him to do now was to get to Liss before the cops or Poor and his cohorts did. If Poor, pacing restlessly up and down in front of the store, thought he had any priority on his services, Asey thought, Poor was sadly mistaken in that highhanded assumption.

"I think," he murmured, "that I'll be leavin' you right now, mister, before I get into any more distractions!"

Without further ado, he slipped out the side door.

Back in the studio he had memorized the Lathrop's address, so now he headed again toward Beacon Hill.

It came to him as a distinct surprise, however, to find that Liss Lathrop's home was the brick house in whose adjoining alley he and Jennie had spent so much time earlier in the morning.

It was just possible that Liss herself might have overheard their conversation in the alley, and that Jennie's insistent pleas to "get the girl" might well have been the inspiration for Liss's phoning Poor to retrieve her dress. Anyway, under the circumstances, it might be wise to call on the girl in a backhand way instead of barging along in any direct, frontal attack.

The plate-glass window of a fruit store caught his

eye. He grinned, went in, and when he emerged he was carrying a beribboned, fruit-laden wicker basket.

Five minutes later he was ringing the service bell at the rear of the Lathrop house. "Present for Miss Lathrop," he told the worried-looking maid who came to the door. "She's got to sign for it first."

He started to walk past her, but the maid thrust her foot quickly across the threshold.

"You wait here," she said. "Give me the slip. I'll have her sign it."

She grabbed the slip and closed the door. But she didn't trouble to lock it, and a moment later Asey was in the basement hall.

He glanced around. It was a typical city layout of two large rooms to a floor. Making for the back stairs, he ran quietly up to the living-room-dining-room floor, and ducked behind a portiere as the maid panted back downstairs.

From his hiding place he listened to the sound of her footsteps clumping along the basement hall to the rear door, heard her drag in the heavy basket, and waited while she lugged it to the floor above. "Miss Liss, will you please open the door?"

Asey slid out from behind the portieres, crept to the bottom step, and looked up expectantly. He couldn't hear the girl's words, but only the sound of her voice, high, rather shrill, and imperious.

"Miss Liss, I'm afraid of dropping it— There; see? It's only one of the baskets Mr. Poor's always sending us, like I said. The man left it. I told you he was all right. He'll be coming back for his slip later, after he's delivered over to the Garrisons'. He often does that to save waiting!"

Asey sneaked hurriedly back to the shelter of the portieres while the maid clumped down to the kitchen. He waited until it seemed that she was again busy with her own work, and then he mounted the stairs to the floor above. There was little doubt in his mind now that Liss Lathrop had overheard Jennie and himself. She was on guard, suspicious even of a basket of fruit.

Pausing, Asey considered the four doors leading from the hall, and picked the nearest as being the likeliest. All he could do now was to take the bull by the horns, march in, and bluff her. He swung open the door, and entered a bedroom whose walls and ceiling and furniture appeared to be all the same color of silver-gray. His basket of fruit stood in the center of the deep-piled rug. The girl wasn't to be seen, but his ears caught a rustling sound in the connecting room, whose door was ajar.

Asey tiptoed over to it, thrust it open, stepped in, and then made a valiant effort to duck back and away. His last conscious thought was that he had certainly walked right in and asked for it! . . .

Later—how much later he had no way of telling —he rubbed the throbbing lump on the side of his head and told himself ruefully that he couldn't even have the satisfaction of claiming that he didn't know who or what had hit him. Miss Liss Lathrop had done a bang-up job on him with the heel of a well-swung riding boot, and he hated to consider what the results would have been had she got him before he started to duck away.

He groped tentatively in the darkness. He was in a good-sized closet—without doubt Liss Lathrop's own. Somewhat unsteadily, he got to his feet and reached a hand up over his head in an attempt to find a ceiling light. In a lucky fumble, his fingers closed over a cord. He yanked it, blinked at the sudden glare, and surveyed his quarters.

There were enough dresses to stock a small shop, dozens of hatracks and elaborate stands that seemed to sprout shoes. But it was the closet door which interested him far more than the girl's wardrobe. It was thick, sturdy pine, and he knew even before he tried the knob that he would find it locked.

Asey tapped the wood reflectively. That was not a door you butted out with your shoulder or carved up with your pocketknife.

He thought once again that, for a girl who looked so much like a dummy, Liss Lathrop was far from being one. She'd taken him in as neatly as anyone ever had, and left him in what he could only sum up as a spot. Even if he yelled and someone—say, the maid—heard him, his presence in that closet was nothing he could lightly explain away. If Liss, herself, heard him and chose to let him out—Asey shook his head. You couldn't tell what she might be tempted to do!

Certainly this biffing business had dispelled any lingering doubt he might have had, despite Jennie's eye-witness testimony, that anger over a rearranged hair-do was no fit and reasonable motive for Liss's shooting Brandt. To judge from the force with which she'd wielded that riding boot, Liss was apparently a girl who didn't require such a whale of a lot of motive before resorting to violence.

The ceiling light above him suddenly flickered and went out, and a second later Asey started groping toward one of the shoe stands. Once the light went out, he was able to see the thin streak of daylight along the side crack of the door. There was a latch and, about eighteen inches above the latch, there was a bar about two inches wide. But there wasn't any latch bolt!

He found a shoe, jerked out the flexible metal shoe tree, and wrenched off the wooden toepiece. If luck was with him, that bar above would turn out to be a wooden, slatlike block attached to the doorjamb with an old hand-made screw, not unlike those that held fast his own closet doors at home. With the metal strip from the shoe tree he could turn up that block in no time!

Thirty seconds later he was out in the bedroom.

He was astonished to find that it was even hotter there than it had been inside the closet, and downright dumfounded to see the hands of the silver clock on the littered writing desk pointing to noon! No wonder he'd been feeling hungry, he thought, as he reached over to the basket of fruit and helped himself.

He was busily tackling a grapefruit, using a silver letter opener for a knife, when the hall door swung open suddenly, and a short, blond woman wearing a pink cotton housecoat stared blankly at him.

"Why, how perfectly amazing!" Her voice, high and twittery, reminded Asey of a sparrow. "I'd no idea anyone was here; Liss never told me! Now, let me think—I'm *sure* I've seen your face before. But I'm always so terrible with names, Mister—er—"

"Mayo," Asey said. "Asey Mayo, ma'am. Er—who—?"

"No!" The woman came in, perched on the arm of a chair, and clasped her hands delightedly. "My dear man, you'll never believe me, but I've just this minute finished talking with Judge Thatcher Sudbury—I simply *had* to ask his advice. And he said the only person he could think of to help me was a man named Asey Mayo from Cape Cod. But he didn't know how to get hold of you. However did Liss manage to locate you and drag you here? Of course, it *was* Liss who got you?"

"Wa-el"—Asey's Cape drawl was drawlier than usual—"I guess you could probably say she dragged me some. An' she sure got me! See my lump?"

"Oh, did she hit you, too? Liss is *so* impulsive—her artistic temperament, of course. She inherited it from me."

"Er—you're her mother?" Asey inquired.

"Why, certainly! Didn't she tell you? I suppose in her excitement she forgot I was home again. Really, Mr. Mayo, I've been *so* worried! What did Liss want you to do?"

"I ain't sure," Asey said, "just what her basic thought was, ma'am."

"Well, of course the poor dear girl *is* in frightful danger, no matter what she says! You *know* she's in danger!"

"So?" Asey said. "What from?"

"Why, those crackpots! The very minute her picture appeared in a national magazine last year all those people started writing her, wanting her autograph, and locks of her hair! I knew then that sooner or later, someone would try to kidnap her, or do something just as terrible. When she told me Rudi'd been shot, *I* knew at once that someone had really intended to kill her, and just accidentally hit him instead. But of course she told you all about that awful business, I suppose. I *do* think she was so clever to find you!"

"Uh-huh. What does Liss *really* think, herself?"

"Oh, she's sure someone meant to kill Rudi!" Mrs. Lathrop said. "But I think she's just saying that to keep me from worrying. Do you understand about the gun?"

"Frankly," Asey said, "she didn't—uh—take the time to explain. What about it?"

"It's so very confusing!" Mrs. Lathrop sighed. "She said she got annoyed with Rudi and was leaving him, and then she heard a shot, and, the next thing she knew, she was throwing away a revolver! —Did you say something?"

"No," Asey gulped.

Mrs. Lathrop babbled on: "But Liss thinks *she* knows who did it— Why, you look surprised! Didn't she tell you that, either? How careless of her!"

"Uh—who *does* she think shot him?" Asey inquired.

"Well, you understand that this is Liss's idea," Mrs. Lathrop said, "not mine. I always thought Peg Whiting was indifferent to Rudi. I'm sure she is vastly more interested in Chub than she *ever* was in Rudi. But then she made so much more when she worked as Rudi's model than she does now! And, as Liss said, jealousy is jealousy, and money is money. Oh, dear!" She sighed wearily. "Money *is* such a problem always, isn't it?"

"All this"—Asey indicated the room's silver-gray glitter—"wouldn't seem to show any lack of it."

"My dear man, we're as poor as church mice!" Mrs. Lathrop told him. "When Houghton—my husband—died, he left us this place, and the house in Beverly, and the shack in Maine, and all those awful brick buildings downtown here in Boston. It's just taxes and repairs all the time, and of course Chub won't sell a thing, because the Lathrops don't believe in selling, ever. What *you* have doesn't matter, so long as your great-grandchildren are sure of two per cent. Truly, until Liss took to modeling, I was at my wit's end about money most of the time. . . . Look; *is* there any chance of anyone thinking that Liss shot Rudi?"

"Wa-el," Asey said, "perhaps maybe—"

"Oh, dear!" Mrs. Lathrop was genuinely upset. "That's what Liss thought! Of course, she is a simply marvelous shot, but—"

"Is she," Asey said, "indeed!"

"Oh, yes! See her skeet trophies over on the corner shelf?" Mrs. Lathrop pointed with quiet maternal pride. "Houghton taught her to shoot."

"Say!" Asey suddenly became aware of the bruise on Mrs. Lathrop's wrist and the red, scratchlike streak on the side of her face. "Did Liss do that to you?"

"Well, of course, Liss always has been impulsive," Mrs. Lathrop said apologetically. "It's just her way. And of course she was so upset about this awful business of Rudi. Probably she knows best, but I *didn't* think she ought to go to Rudi's studio, really! I suggested that she just ask Peg over to lunch. So much simpler, I thought, and much better taste. But the idea irritated Liss terribly."

"She's gone to Brandt's studio?" Asey demanded. "To see Peg? Does she think that Peg shot him?"

"I didn't want her to go one bit," Mrs. Lathrop said, "but she was *so* determined— Listen; I hear the hall phone ringing. I'll have to run down and answer. Maggie's out. If it's that strange person calling again," she added, as Asey followed her down the stairs, "should I report him to the police?"

"What strange person?" Asey asked curiously.

"Well, of course he *said* he was a reporter, but he didn't sound like one! In fact, it's the oddest-sounding voice I ever heard. First I thought it was Peg, but then it sounded more like a man. He called twice before I talked with the Judge. He wanted Liss— Oh, stop ringing; I'm coming!"

She picked up the phone, said hello, and then covered the mouthpiece with her hand. "It's him again!" she said in a stage whisper. "Hello? . . . Miss Lathrop's not home. Who *is* this calling? . . . What? . . . I said, she's not home! And I'm going to tell the police about you. . . . I said, Miss Lathrop's not here, and the police are going to know all about you—" Mrs. Lathrop suddenly broke off,

smiled delightedly, and then continued with un-
wonted vigor: "All right; if you want to know, you
can find her at Rudi Brandt's studio!" Slamming
down the receiver, she turned to Asey. "That's the
oddest voice I ever heard! It might be either a man
or a woman with a mouthful of cereal. Wasn't that a
brilliant inspiration I had?"

Without giving Asey any chance to answer, she
rattled on: "It came to me in a flash! Now—don't
you see?—that person will go to the studio hunting
Liss, but *you* will go there too, and find out who it
is and what's going on. And, if it's some policeman
being tricky, just you explain to him that Liss's being a wonderful shot doesn't *mean anything*—"

The rest of her sentence trickled off into an ag-
grieved little twitter as she watched the front door
of No. 19½ close behind Asey.

Outside on the brick sidewalk, Asey paused for a
second. Faced with a one-way street and the snarl of
traffic beyond, he could probably reach Brandt's studio as quickly on foot as he could in a cab. Whatever
the impulsive Liss might be up to now, he wanted
to get hold of her before she met any odd-sounding
reporters, or anyone else. Particularly Peg Whiting.

"Mayo!"

Asey felt his arm gripped, heard a dog bark, and

turned to look into the beaming face of Judge
Thatcher Sudbury. Despite the glaring sun, he wore
no hat, and, despite the wilting heat, his linen suit
looked crisp and pressed. Asey wondered how the
man, in such an informal costume, still managed to
convey a distinct impression of judicial dignity.

"Hello, Asey! I thought I saw you earlier on Beacon Street!" He pumped Asey's hand heartily. "Well,
well, how are you? Didn't you just come out of the
Lathrops' house? I thought so! Been visiting my
cousins?"

"Uh-huh, an' I got sort of delayed," Asey said. "I
—er—I'm goin' to come back an' see you later,
Judge, but I'm in a rush now, so if you'll excuse
me—"

"What brings you to Boston?"

"Jennie's house cleanin'." Asey detoured around
the Judge. "I'll see you later!"

He dodged past the two Chows, which had been
watching him with thinly veiled dislike, and hurried
along toward the studio.

As he passed the Public Garden, he noticed that
the swan boats were paddling around as usual, and
that in spite of the heat there were more people in
the Garden than he ever remembered having seen
there before. The only policeman in sight was a

burly man in shirt sleeves who was giving a ticket to a woman driver.

Asey slowed down to buy a newspaper from a boy, glanced at the headlines, came to an abrupt stop, and wondered if the glaring sun had in some way impaired his eyesight. For under the screaming head of **"PUBLIC GARDEN SLAYING"** was an explanatory line in smaller type that said, **"Notorious Woman Bag-Snatcher and Pal Sought in Brandt Shooting, Robbery Motive, Police Assert."**

He shook his head slowly as he scanned the column beneath.

The gist of it, as the reporter pointed out with exquisite simplicity, was that, since Brandt had neither wallet nor money, and his pockets were empty, he had obviously been robbed. The police had at once connected the robbery with the bag-snatcher who had been at work in the vicinity that morning, and both she and her male companion were shortly expected to turn up in the police dragnet. Mr. Craig Lathrop, who found the body, had mentioned seeing a suspicious-looking milkman, and the police intended to track him down, too. There was no mention of the girl, or of the gun!

Asey thrust the paper into his pocket, wiped the

perspiration off his face, and continued thoughtfully on his way.

Something was more than screwball about all this business. Surely the cops must have found that Smith & Wesson by now, he thought. If they hadn't located it by themselves, certainly some one of the swan boats' passengers would have found it for them. And a weapon like that would undoubtedly be registered. Once they had the gun, they should—

"Hey, you!"

Asey realized suddenly that he was holding up traffic with his speculations, and, with a red face, he stepped onto the sidewalk and strode along to the Arts Building. He hesitated at the entrance and looked around. There were no cops about nor any police cars.

"Asey!" Jennie emerged from the doorway of the next building and marched up to him. "Where've you been? I've waited here so long!"

"So it *was* you I seen," Asey said reproachfully, "in the blue dress, back there in the drugstore! New one, huh?"

"If you saw me, I certainly wish you'd yelled at me!" Jennie said. "I've waited here so long, and I'm so hot!"

"I'm sore!" Asey said. "Didn't I tell you to go to Blandin's, an' stay there?"

Jennie sniffed. "You think you can shunt me off on a wild-goose chase like that? I knew you never bought any Palm Beach suit! You always said you hated 'em. So I just read that note, and changed my dress at the station—just to be on the safe side—and come right back here. My, my, what excitement! You never seen so many cops!"

"You mean, you went back there to the Garden? To the landin'? Under their very noses? Jennie, d'you know they want you, an' me?" Asey demanded. "Did you see the papers?"

"I read 'em," Jennie said, "but I knew it all, anyway. I heard the cops in the Garden talkin' it over. Honest, they haven't caught on to a single thing! And, Asey, that boy with the rumpled hair that tried to stop the girl from goin' with Brandt, his name's Craig Lathrop, and he never told the cops a thing about the girl bein' with Brandt!"

"He's the girl's half-brother," Asey explained. "Her name's Liss Lathrop— What's the matter?"

"Only her brother!" Jennie sounded disappointed. "I thought he might be her beau, and I made up a triangle— Well, anyway, I listened to the cops, and finally, I got so worried about you, I got Brandt's

address from the newspaper and come here, thinkin'
you'd go where he lived, sooner or later. D'you
know those fools never found the gun?"

Asey nodded. "I don't understand that."

"Neither do I. I watched 'em mill around the
landin', but I didn't see 'em find it, so of course I
thought they must've got it before I come back to
the Garden. But the papers say no gun was found!
I think it's awful queer, Asey! I'm sure I heard it
hit the wood of a swan boat!"

"You did. I seen it, myself."

"Well, then, where is it? The cops never found
it, and neither did anyone else that rode on the boats.
I couldn't find it," Jennie added, "and I certainly
tried to! I rode on every single boat, changin' my
seat and peerin' around under the benches till folks
thought I was daft. It's not on any of those boats
now, and I didn't see anyone take it. D'you suppose
that brother did? He went away, and then come back
with a pretty dark-haired girl and another big fellow."

Asey shook his head and shrugged. "Could be.
Jennie, you been here long? Did you see the Lathrop girl?"

"Now, you know," Jennie said, "I thought I *did*
see her just after I come—that was over an hour

ago. It looked like her, but her hair was done up. But I saw the brother and that dark girl go in. . . . Asey, where've you been? What you been doin'?"

"Come on," Asey said; "I'll tell you on the way. I want to look into things."

"Is it safe for us?" Jennie asked as they entered the building.

"If nobody's spotted us yet," Asey said, "I doubt if they will. Think of you, sittin' under their noses! Jennie, there's somethin' awful haywire about all this. It don't work out. An', by the way, if we should run into any trouble, try to break away an' call Judge Sudbury. It's three flights up, an', if you'll listen while you climb, I'll sum up my mornin' for you."

His brief summary was punctuated by Jennie's breathless and incredulous exclamations. "I never! . . . I absolutely never! . . . I never heard the like. . . . I never— Is this the place?"

Finding the door of Brandt's waiting-room unlocked, Asey squared his shoulders and strode in, fully expecting a cop to jump up and bar his way. But the room was empty.

"I s'pose," Asey said, while Jennie stared open-mouthed at the photographs on the wall, "these cops know best, but I'd have left someone here, or at

least locked up! Seems pretty casual of 'em to walk
out an' leave things wide open!"

"Probably they took pictures," Jennie said. "They
took millions of pictures over on the landin'. I heard
one plain-clothes feller say that was their system.
Soon's they got through, people prowled around all
over the place, and they let the swan boats start up.
Is that the studio in there?"

Jennie repeated her question and then crossed
over to where Asey stood silently in the doorway,
and peered in. "Never wasted time cleanin', did he?"
she commented. "Oh, look!" Her voice sank to a
whisper and she pointed to a figure on a couch.

Asey nodded slowly.

"Asey, that's the blond girl herself! She must be
asleep. So it *was* her I seen comin' in— Oh, Asey,
look at her head! She's been shot, too, the same way!
And look there on the floor! There's a gun! Asey,
d'you see it?"

"I see it," Asey said grimly. "That is the Smith
an' Wesson Magnum that nobody found!" He stared
around the room. "So that," he continued, "is why
the door was open. I s'pose she had a key. I wonder—"

"Asey, if—if she killed Brandt with that gun, then
who"—Jennie's voice quavered—"*who* killed *her?*"

"Same person who shot Brandt, I think," Asey said.

"But it couldn't be! *She* shot Brandt! I saw her!"

"I know, an' her mother says she's a wonderful shot. Jennie, listen. Back in the Garden you heard a shot, an' started to run when you seen Brandt fall. Right? The girl stood there a moment, then reached down, picked up the gun, an' threw it away. Right? You was runnin' along that curvin' path to the landin'. You seen her pick the gun up, but you honestly didn't see her drop it, did you?"

"If she didn't drop it," Jennie said, "I'd like to know who did! There wasn't a soul anywhere near the landin' but her! I couldn't have helped seein' anyone, if they'd been near enough to throw that gun into the clearin' there, after shootin' Brandt. That's what you're drivin' at, isn't it?"

"Somethin' like that," Asey said. "You see—"

"I seen it!" Jennie retorted. "You're the one that needs to do the seein'! You know it isn't easy to throw a gun! That girl could only heave it as far as the swan boats, not more'n twenty-five feet away! She'd have seen anyone, if there'd been anyone there! So would I, if they was within fifty yards of her; it's all clear, around there! We'd have seen anyone throw it! I told you, the only people I saw in the

Garden was a man with two Chows, and a woman in evenin' clothes, lots earlier— What are you mutterin' about?"

"Two Chows! Jennie, d'you remember Judge Sudbury? Was it him with the two Chows?"

"Land's sakes, I'm dumb!" Jennie said. "I'd ought to have recognized that beard! That's just who it was! Why, I haven't seen him for years!"

"Let me figure, now," Asey said. "After Liss Lathrop smacked Chub for buttin' in, an' went on with Brandt, then Chub phoned Peg. She said her phone didn't ring— Oh, Jennie, no wonder I been feelin' there's somethin' screwball about this! It was starin' me in the face, but I never looked beyond the tip of my nose! Golly, I should have caught on quicker!"

"I'm not catchin' on any!" Jennie told him bluntly. "I don't even know what you're talkin' about!"

"Chub said he phoned Peg. Peg said her phone didn't ring then. That may mean he never phoned when he claims he did. P'raps he followed Brandt an' Liss to the Garden, whether you seen him or not. On the other hand," Asey added thoughtfully, "maybe he was tellin' the truth, an' the phone rang in Peg's apartment, only she wasn't there; see? Peg knew Brandt planned to take his pictures early, in a rush. No reason why she couldn't have sneaked over to the Garden, herself. Jennie, it's a shot in the dark, but what did the woman in evenin' dress look like? Did you notice her at all?"

"I only glanced at her. She was blond, and short—"

"What?" Asey demanded.

"Blond and short, and she moved quick. Like a sparrow. She went past me so fast, I didn't think she saw me. She had on a pink dress with ruffles, and she carried an awful pretty beaded bag. Honest, I hardly noticed her!"

"Uh-huh. You just took a passin' glance," Asey with irony. "Just a peep. Huh! You know you just give a fine thumbnail description of Liss's mother? Golly, was they all roamin' around? I wonder if Poor was there, too!"

"But the papers said the Lathrop boy come from a fine old family, and his sister was engaged to a rich tycoon!" Jennie said. "And I'm sure the Judge's important. Would folks like that be mixed up in a thing like this?"

"They may be the best people," Asey said, "but they got some odd habits. The rich tycoon sneaked into the studio an' swiped Liss's dress so's the cops wouldn't find out about her, an' Chub Lathrop lied to the cops with the blandest broad 'a' I ever heard. An' Peg was so innocent—but still she remembered to write her pay check! An', golly, I forgot all about that book she stole out of Brandt's desk. An' that mother's most too good to be true. I swallowed her whole, an' put her down as a twitterer, but, now I look back, I'm wonderin' considerable about her!"

"She lie to you?"

"Wa-el, it's my impression she done a lot of skiddin' around the truth. Liss had smacked her. Liss smacked Chub. Poor was sore with the girl for posin'. Liss got Peg's modelin' job. Yup, Jennie, I'm beginnin' to understand a lot of things!"

"I wish I could understand how that girl could've picked up that gun and thrown it away unless she dropped it in the first place!" Jennie said. "You think it dropped from heaven by itself? Asey, it just come to me— Could someone have been hidin' up in the branches of a tree, maybe?"

Asey shook his head. "That's one thing I'm sure didn't happen. I saw Brandt's wound. That bullet he stopped was travelin' horizontal. Now—"

"What you goin' to do?" Jennie asked as he entered the studio. "Should you go in there?"

"I got to. But you stay put." Asey walked over,

picked up the Smith & Wesson by the checkered grips, slid the cylinder catch forward, and allowed the cylinder to swing out on its crane. "Huh! Two cartridges fired," he said. "Jennie, lock that outer waitin'-room door, an' stand by it. If you hear anyone comin', let me know."

"Then what do we do?" Jennie inquired.

"We pull another early Fairbanks down the fire escape," Asey told her. "Right now I'm goin' to find out who owned this gun. It'll take a bit of phonin' to Hanson an' the other state cops, but they can dig out the information for me."

It took twenty minutes, and, when the registered owner's name was finally divulged to him, Asey's long whistle of amazement brought Jennie running to the studio door.

"Did you find out?"

"Yup." Asey replaced the receiver. "It's registered to Judge Sudbury, an' it's never been reported stolen. Say, what do you remember about him?"

"Why, he was always nice to everybody when he come to his shootin' shack," Jennie said. "He liked to shoot."

"Just so, an' he was the whale of a good shot," Asey said. "In fact, it was the Judge who stopped a buck with one shot from a gun just like this. You

seen him walkin' his dogs, an' I seen him only just
now, walkin' them dogs again. When you think it
over, a scorchin' day like this ain't ideal weather for
so much dog-walkin', is it? But, if you wanted to
roam around an' keep your eye on things without
attractin' suspicion, there's no nicer way than walkin'
dogs. What else can you remember? I need you to
check up on what I been recallin'."

"Well, he was always lookin' up ancestors in the
town records, makin' out family trees an' talkin'
about family," Jennie said. "He was so proud of
bein' descended from a Bay Colony governor, but he
lost interest in his precious family awful quick when
he found out two of his ancestors was such scala-
wags they was hanged, and some others got booted
out of the Colony. Not long afterwards the Judge
left the Cape, and it was common gossip he felt so
worked up about his ancestors turnin' out so bad
he couldn't stand the place any more."

Asey nodded. "That all come back to me, too. An'
the Judge's a relation of the Lathrops. He just said
so. I wonder, now, if he got sore seein' his relative
Liss Lathrop rompin' around underwear ads, an'
posin' with a dead-pan dummy that was her twin.
Huh! We'll go call on him, but first I'll see how big
a check Peg Whitin' wrote for herself."

"Was it a lot?" Jennie asked a minute later as he stared at the checkbook.

"Only twenty-five dollars. Seems modest enough." Asey returned the checkbook to the drawer and looked thoughtfully around the studio. "Jennie, somethin' in here ain't the way it was when I was here before!"

"How could it be, with her lyin' there, poor thing?"

"I don't mean her. I mean somethin's wrong in all this truck." He indicated the litter of disjointed arms and legs and plaster heads. "Let's see. There's the dummy that Peg called Bella, an' there's the fat-man dummy with the hat. An' the chairs an' tables an' bric-a-brac—"

Jennie sniffed. "Findin' what was different in this mess would be a hundred times worse than findin' a needle in a haystack! Why didn't someone hear the shot that killed her?"

"In the city, a loud bang's a car backfirin'. P'raps people who heard it thought it was the cops makin' more din in here," Asey said. "Or else someone bangin' away makin' scenery in one of the other studios in the buildin'. Golly, I'm usually good about rememberin' things an' how they're laid out, but there's a few million too many items here. I'm stumped."

"What you wigglin' your nose like that for?" Jennie wanted to know. "Smell something?"

"I noticed it here before," Asey said, "while I was tryin' to open that consarned window, an' it's somethin' else that's stumpin' me. It ain't exactly a perfume smell—not Liss Lathrop's kind, anyway. I spent enough time in her closet to know hers by heart. An' d' you know who this reminds me of? Old Cap'n Porter. Oh, well; come on! We'll go chat with the Judge— Oho!" He stopped on the threshold and crossed the studio to the window.

"What *now?*" Jennie demanded.

"I sort of hankered to see just what'd jammed that window before," Asey said. "It's a piece of old wedge. I can see the end of it. Huh. I s'pose Poor just happened to shove it the right way from outside. Well, that's that. Now, let's get goin'!"

Once outside the building, Asey marched along Arlington Street at a rapid pace, ignoring Jennie's breathlessly bitter comments about possible heat prostration, and did he think he was Paul Revere, rushing like that? When he abruptly stopped, Jennie's indignation mounted even higher.

"Why *are* you gapin' like a sight-seer from the country at that statue, as if you never saw it before? George Washington's been up on that horse all your life— Oh, for land's sakes!"

She broke off as Asey turned into the Public Garden and walked quickly past the little potted palm trees to the base of the Washington statue, where a boy with a homemade sling in his hand stood looking disconsolately up toward Washington's horse.

"Asey!" Jennie hurried after him. "Sometimes you provoke me so! What's the matter with you?"

He grinned and pointed up. "This youngster's lost his parachute trooper up on the general's epaulette. See the little lead soldier danglin' from the cloth 'chute up there?"

"I'm sure it's too bad he lost it," Jennie returned, "but there's nothin' much can be done. . . . Asey, you mustn't climb that statue! You'll be arrested!"

Practically before the words were out of her mouth, Asey had swung himself up the statue's base to the pedestal, rescued the soldier, swung down, and presented the toy to its small owner, who looked dazed by the whole proceedings.

"Gee, thanks!"

"Thank *you*," Asey said. "Come on, Jennie!"

"I think the heat's got you," Jennie told him as

she followed him back to Arlington Street. "One minute you rush me to death, and the next minute you got so much time on your hands, you stop to play Good Samaritan to a dirty-faced boy! What's got into you? What you got that cat-that's-swallowed-a-canary look on your face for? You remembered what was wrong at the studio?"

"Nope, not yet."

"You think," Jennie suggested derisively, "maybe a parachute trooper landed that gun at the girl's feet? You decided that gun dropped out of a Nazi plane?"

"Nope. Shush up, Jennie, I'm thinkin'."

The note of finality in his voice caused Jennie to refrain from further comment as she trotted along beside him. When Asey used that tone she gave up.

On the sidewalk opposite Judge Sudbury's Beacon Street house, Asey came to a sudden halt and took her arm. "Look over there, goin' up his front steps! There's the Judge with his dogs, an' Mrs. Lathrop, an' Chub, an' Peg, an' Poor! Going to hold a council of war, I bet! Oh, if I could turn into a fly on the wall an' listen to 'em, I'd find out what I want to know, in one swoop! I wonder— Come over to this bench an' sit down an' get your wind while I figger!"

"Why? You know it was the Judge's gun, and you know he was in the Garden this mornin'," Jennie said. "Why don't you just march in and confront him?"

"What we got," Asey said, "is a lot of suspicious-soundin' odds an' ends. Not proof. If I tried any confrontin' act, the Judge'd hand me over to the cops—an' remember they're already dragnettin' for me!"

"I think you've got proof enough!"

"We know the gun belongs to him, that he's a good shot, an' that he was doin' a powerful lot of wanderin' around, yes. We can guess that, in his mind, Liss might've been tarnishin' the family's good name by posin' for ads an' such. But that ain't near enough," Asey said. "An', if you think, you'll find the Judge ain't the only one with a suspicious aura floatin' around his head."

"But it's *his* gun!" Jennie protested. "And you said the cops hadn't any report of its bein' stolen!"

"P'raps," Asey returned, "he don't know it *has* been stolen. Mrs. Lathrop an' Chub have access to his house. They might've swiped it without his knowledge. P'raps Poor did, or Peg. Now, I sort of gathered that Chub supported his stepmother an' half-sister largely from a sense of duty. Once Liss

was married to Poor, you could reasonably assume
he wouldn't have to support 'em any longer. P'raps
then he could get married, himself—"

"To that dark-haired Whitin' girl, I bet!" Jennie interrupted. "When I saw her lookin' at him
over in the Garden, and again comin' into the
buildin' there, I guessed she was in love with him!
That's where I was figurin' out a triangle; see? Her,
and the blond girl, and the rumple-haired boy.
That's why I was disappointed when you said he was
Liss's brother. I bet he wants to marry Peg Whitin'!"

"Maybe. Anyway, s'pose Rudi Brandt was hornin'
in on Poor. Chub sees the rich tycoon bein' eased
out of the picture. I can see how Chub might have a
motive for shootin' Brandt."

Jennie frowned. "But why'd he kill Liss, then?"

"You got me there!" Asey said. "But it gives him
one motive, anyway. Take Peg. It's possible she was
good an' sore with Brandt for givin' her modelin' job
to Liss, an' jealous of Liss for bein' the one to oust
her. Maybe she was in her apartment when Chub
phoned, an' maybe she wasn't. 'Course," he added
thoughtfully, "killin' both of 'em leaves her without any job at all, but there you are."

"I still say," Jennie insisted stubbornly, "that gun
belongs to the Judge!"

"Um." Asey didn't seem to hear her. "Maybe Poor thought Rudi was a rival. Maybe he thought that Liss's continuin' to pose for Rudi when she promised she wouldn't meant that she was in love with him. But, doggone, he certainly wouldn't have shot the girl, too! Now, Mrs. Lathrop likes money, an' wants Liss to marry Poor. She wouldn't like Brandt's cuttin' in. An' she was in the Garden. An' later, Liss strikes her. No love pat, either! You know, Jennie, that phone call about the odd-soundin' reporter was awful fishy! But she sure got rid of me in a hurry. P'raps she wanted me to go to the studio an' find Liss's body. P'raps she'd just come back from shootin' her. An' she'd been talkin' with the Judge on the phone. Let's see, now; how can I do it? I might get into a Cape Cod house pretendin' to be a brush sales-man or somethin', but that'd never work on Beacon Street. Give me your pocketbook, Jennie. I seen a badge in there. I'll be an inspector."

"That's my Woman's Defense Corps badge!" Jen-nie said as he removed it. "And my Defense Corps certificate!"

"Uh-huh. I know. An' with them an' a notebook an' pencil," Asey said, "I'll be a Defense Inspector makin' a survey."

"You got a touch of sun?" Jennie inquired.

Asey chuckled. "Whenever I visited the Porters in Boston, I always remarked on the pile of inspectors prowlin' around that everybody took for granted. Now the Judge an' the others'll be too busy to be bothered by an inspector, an' I think I can convince the help. Nobody ever reads credentials, but, if they ask for some, your badge an' certificate are awful impressive. When I get to the back door, I'll put on my yachtin' cap. It'll make a queer uniform, but it won't be any queerer than some defense outfits I seen. Golly, here's a tape measure, too! Just what I need. Stay here, now, till I come back!" . . .

Fifteen minutes later, Asey was in Judge Sudbury's hall outside the living-room door, measuring the floor with his tape measure, and listening as hard as he could to the conversation inside. Two perspiring maids, whipping up what appeared to be a spur-of-the-moment buffet lunch, had let him into the kitchen at once and without question, only commenting that he was the third inspector they'd had in a month.

"Mayo is unquestionably on her trail." The Judge's anxious voice came to him clearly. "We must find her! She can't be at the studio if the phone's not answered. Are you sure, Monica, that Liss intended going there?"

Asey nodded to himself as Mrs. Lathrop assured the Judge that the studio was the girl's destination. As he'd hoped, no one had as yet found Liss or told this group of her death.

"If Liss shot Rudi," the Judge continued, "Mayo will find out! He's uncanny! He always stumbles on things!"

At the moment, Asey thought, he was stumbling on more than he'd dared anticipate.

"He certainly bowled me over, popping up in the studio!" Peg said. "My eyes nearly popped out!"

"When *I* saw him in Liss's room"—Mrs. Lathrop's voice was nervous and twittery—"I was stunned! It was just after I'd phoned you, Thatcher, when you'd warned me about your seeing him. I tried to find out what he knew! I insinuated Liss had called him in—and, really, he somehow made *me* believe she really had!"

"He can make people believe anything," the Judge said. "The instant I saw him rushing across to the Garden, I felt in my bones he knew about Rudi! And when I watched him from the window here, through the binoculars, and saw him make for the landing, I knew the family was in for it!"

"Why didn't you report the gun, Uncle That?" Chub's broad "a" wasn't nearly so broad as it had been when he talked with the cops earlier, Asey noticed.

"My dear boy, when I saw that Smith & Wesson Magnum on the swan-boat seat, I recognized what it was, but I never suspected it was mine! You see, I'd caught a glimpse of Liss and Rudi running along Arlington Street, and wondered what they were up to at that hour, but I lost track of them before I could round up the dogs to follow. Then, later, I heard the shot, although I thought then that it was only a car backfiring. When, still later, I strolled past the landing and saw Rudi lying there and the camera and the dummy, frankly I was appalled!"

"Was that when you tipped over the case of plate-holders?" Poor asked.

"Yes." Out in the hall, Asey found himself blinking. "It was obvious that Liss had broken her promise to you about posing, but I was determined that if Rudi'd actually taken pictures of her, no one should know it, or know she was there. When I returned to the house I saw Mayo, and I give you

my word, I felt as guilty as if I'd shot Rudi myself!
I scuttled up the steps out of his sight, and rushed
for the binoculars. I don't know what impelled me
afterward to go to the library and see if my Smith
& Wesson was all right. And I found it was gone!"

Mrs. Lathrop broke the ensuing silence: "But who
stole it? I still can't understand what happened!"

"It took some unwinding," the Judge said. "You
see, both Susie and Jane were out last night. I dined
at the club and went on to a concert. Only old Annie
was here—"

"She's *so* feeble! Why do you keep her?" Mrs.
Lathrop said.

"My dear Monica, you can't discard someone who
served your family faithfully for fifty years! Old Annie has nowhere else to live! Anyway, the bell rang
about nine last night, and old Annie went to
the door, to find a policeman standing there. He
told her the police wanted some gun of mine for
some kind of test. She couldn't remember what kind,
but when I suggested ballistics, she thought that
might be it. So old Annie told the fellow to come in
and get the gun he wished, and he did!"

"And walked off with it! That's incredible!" Poor
said. "D'you believe her? *Was* it a cop? How could
she have done such a thing!"

"I was furious at first," the Judge said, "but you know policemen often do come here on business; I'm on their Fund board. Annie's seen them come and go. And, as she tearfully said, she thought it was always all right to let in a cop, and, besides, the dogs liked him. Their approval clinched the matter."

"But wouldn't she know him again?" Chub asked. "Can't she describe him?"

Asey heard the Judge's sigh. "To quote her, a cop is a cop and looks like any other cop. Her description of him would fit any male in Boston. Unquestionably he was a fake. I found out that, before he came, Annie had answered the phone three times—a call for each of the maids as well as one for me, so it seems that the man first found out who was home here."

"Well, *he* took the gun!" Mrs. Lathrop said. "So Liss *couldn't* have had it! That settles everything, doesn't it?"

"Yes," the Judge said hesitantly. "Yes, except that old Annie's story is so shaky! I tremble to think what might happen if she were cross-examined in court. She could so easily be confused into admitting that the person masquerading as a policeman might have been a man, *or* a woman! Of course, it's fantastic to think for a moment that one of us would murder anybody, but Liss is so impetuous! Monica, why were you hunting her this morning? I thought you intended to stay in Portsmouth with Mary all week!"

"I did, but she had to rush to New York on the earliest train, so she drove in and dropped me at the house about five this morning; neither of us had had the time to change, because we got Bob's telegram when we got back from the club. And the first thing I saw was a note on the hall table, a message for Liss from Rudi. Of course, I didn't want any more fuss with Liss and Jack about posing, after those underwear ads! I did *so* hope I might catch up with her and stop her, because I truly didn't think I could stand that bickering again!"

"My reaction exactly!" Chub said. "Oh, if Mayo gets onto us! Your gun, Uncle That, and Monica there, and you there, and me there, and Liss there! Anyway, Peg, you and Jack are safe! And, by the way, Peg, what was the idea behind all this early-morning picture taking? I never got that."

"Yesterday, while I was out, Rudi got a call from *Fashion-Allure* for a patriotic cover, so—"

"How in hell"—Chub echoed Asey's own thoughts—"could Brenda and Liss on a swan boat be called patriotic?"

"Old historic Boston, the swan boats, and red, white, and blue costumes," Peg said. "It's no crazier than those two lions with a head of lettuce we did —that was Aid to Britain, did you know? Anyway, they offered Rudi such a fabulous price that I wanted to call back and check on it when he told me."

Out in the hallway, Asey's eyes narrowed, and a frown gathered on his forehead.

"The problem," Peg continued, "was that they wanted the picture today. Rudi couldn't work yesterday, with those afternoon thunderstorms, so the only time left was early this morning. If the weather'd been bad, Rudi would have been licked, but there was too much money at stake not to take the chance, so we whipped up some costumes. I suppose that after I went home Rudi decided to use Liss and Brenda instead of the two dummies. Judge, someone else must have been in the Garden! Didn't you notice anyone?"

"I passed a charwoman with a bag." Asey grinned at the Judge's description of Jennie. "And I noticed a gas-station man. Didn't you say you saw a milkman, Chub?"

Stifling the sudden exclamation that came to his lips, Asey pocketed the tape measure, hurried downstairs, thanked the maids, and departed.

He found Jennie on the settee where he had left her, eating an ice-cream cone and fanning herself with a handkerchief.

"Why do people live in this hot, muggy place! Asey, I can tell by your face you found out a lot!"

"Some. Look; you got to help me keep that bunch there at the Judge's— Don't look suspicious. I mean it. I want you to take this watch"—he drew an old silver repeater from his pocket—"an' go ask to see the Judge. If the maids say he's busy, you tell 'em you got a bequest for him."

"What?"

"It's always best to string along with as much of the truth as you can," Asey said. "So you tell him you been to Cousin Ed's funeral in Chicago. Then give him the watch an' say Cousin Ed left it to him as a remembrance of the days they went duck-huntin' together. That won't seem too odd, because Ed was his handyman for years. Then you settle yourself down an' ask if the Judge minds your waitin' there for me, because somehow you've missed connections with me, an' we planned I'd pick you up at the Judge's if anything slipped up. Bein' as how you was kind enough to bring him the watch, he can't very well refuse you, an', considerin' the worried mood that bunch is in, I think they'll be only too willin' to wait an' see what I been up to. Now, hop along!"

Jennie hesitated. "Then what'll I talk about?"

"To the best of my knowledge," Asey told her, with a grin, "you never been at a loss for words in your life. Just don't mention what's gone on here today. Talk about the Cape. It's always a good, safe topic. Sooner or later, I'll get back there."

"Where you goin' now? What you goin' to do?"

"I'm goin' to make some phone calls an' do some plain an' fancy house-breakin'," Asey said.

"I know! You've remembered what was wrong at the studio! Tell me, what was it?"

Asey smiled. "Took me a long time," he said, "but I finally got there. The fat-man dummy didn't have on a green top hat, an' the smell was Honeywell's Dressing."

Jennie looked at him. "An' on the basis of that you think you're goin' to find a murderer?"

"Wa-el," Asey drawled, "I'll throw in a vote of thanks to George Washington, too. So long!"

The atmosphere in the Judge's living-room had been tense enough at two o'clock. By three, Jennie was as uncomfortable as she had ever been in her life, but she went on doggedly talking about Cape Cod. Occasionally Judge Sudbury helped her keep the conversational ball rolling with a politely dutiful query about the health of some former neighbor, and once, when Jennie paused to relieve her parched throat with some iced tea, Peg Whiting roused herself and related several nervous and pointless little anecdotes about her life at the Meweesit Camp. Mrs. Lathrop wiggled in her chair, alternately craning her neck to look at the door and twisting her head to read the thermometer. Chub adjusted and readjusted the swing of the electric fan, while Poor sat and traced the carpet pattern with the toe of his shoe, until Jennie wanted to scream at the pair of them to stop their futile, monotonous motions. Instead, she serenely described her method of making bayberry candles, and her grandmother's recipe for beach-plum jelly.

When the mantel clock tinkled at quarter past three, Poor interrupted her in the middle of a sentence: "Stop gabbling about Cape Cod! Where's this cousin of yours? Where's Mayo?"

"I'm—" Jennie caught herself just in time to keep from telling him hotly that she was tired of the Cape, too, and wanted Asey more than he did. "I suppose," she amended in the pleasantest voice she could muster, "he's trying on a new suit, as he planned. Does that thermometer say ninety-*two?*"

"Ninety-*four,*" Mrs. Lathrop told her. "The humidity is ninety. . . . *Is* that the doorbell at last?` Is it Liss?"

The Judge rose, but before he could cross the room a maid ushered Asey in. He looked incredibly cool. But, as he smiled a greeting, he took from his pocket a blue bandana handkerchief Jennie had never seen before and mopped his face with it.

"I'm sorry I'm late. I got delayed." Asey twisted the bandana into a roll, held both ends in the fingers of his right hand, and sat down at a mahogany table opposite Poor and Peg Whiting.

Jennie experienced a sharp, let-down sensation. She expected fireworks, maybe even a fight, and here was Asey sitting back, gently swinging his rolled-up handkerchief as if he were rocking a cradle!

"Have you seen Liss?" Mrs. Lathrop asked eagerly. "Did you find her?"

"Yes, I have— Huh, that looks familiar!" Reaching out, Asey took his old silver watch from the table, balanced it in the loop of the handkerchief, whose ends he continued to hold in the fingers of his right hand, and swung it back and forth.

"You'll drop that!" Jennie warned him sharply.

"Where *is* Liss?" Peg asked anxiously. "We've been so worried. We've phoned everywhere, and we can't locate her. Where is she?"

"In Brandt's studio." Asey continued to swing the handkerchief with the watch balanced in its fold, and everyone in the room followed the motion as if fascinated by it. "In the Arts Buildin'."

Jennie pricked up her ears at the purring note in his voice and realized suddenly that, for all his calm expression, Asey was somehow set to spring. He was setting a stage for something, leading up to something.

"Mayo, what's the idea? What are you driving at?" Poor demanded impatiently. "We've stood enough of your drawling, homespun nonsense! We know that Liss isn't at the studio! We've phoned there. We—"

"Look *out* for that watch!" Jennie interrupted.

"I said she was at the studio." Asey paused, and then added more gently, "An' I'm awful sorry to say that she's been shot."

Mrs. Lathrop's scream pierced Jennie's eardrums. Chub turned from the electric fan and stared at Asey as if he were talking some strange foreign language, and for an instant the Judge's face seemed as white as his hair.

"Shot? You don't mean—" Peg's voice broke.

"I'm sorry, but I'm afraid I do," Asey told her.

"Asey." The Judge swallowed. "Asey, has Liss— has she been killed? Asey, do you know who did it?"

"I came here," Asey said, "to get him, Judge!"

The watch dropped suddenly from the loop of the bandana, and even Jennie, with a perfectly clear conscience, found herself at first terrified and confused by the sound. She half jumped from her chair, and then sat back and stared at the group in amazement. They were like a tableau, she thought. Mrs. Lathrop looked like a marble statue; Peg's face was a mixture of fear and confusion; the Judge was gripping the arm of a Chippendale chair till his knuckles seemed almost to drive through the back of his hands. Chub was dazed and bewildered, and his fingers still hovered over the adjustment screw of the electric fan. Asey, grim-eyed and immobile, still sat at the table, still waiting, still set to spring.

"You'll never get me!" Poor's hoarse cry put an end to the little tableau. "Never!"

Jennie's jaw dropped at the sight of the short-barreled revolver that had appeared in his hand. Automatically she turned to see what Asey would do.

"Now, that"—Asey casually took an end of the

handkerchief in either hand and smiled coolly at
Poor—"is just what I been waitin' for! I felt sure
you had on you the gun you potted at Jennie with,
an' I kind of didn't feel like rushin' you till you'd
pulled your spare—"

"You'll never rush me! You'll never—"

In a motion so quick that Jennie couldn't follow
it, Asey's left wrist jerked, and the end of the bandana he had been holding in his right hand seemed
to whip across the mahogany table toward Poor's
face.

"Oh, my eye!" Poor cried out. "My eye!"

His right hand, still holding the revolver, involuntarily went to his eye, and before he knew what
was happening Asey had wrenched the gun from
him.

"There!" Asey said. "That's that! Chub, give me
your belt to tie him up with— That's right. Now
fish in his coat pocket an' see if that piece of twine's
still there. Is it? Good! Judge, you s'pose you could
fix things up so that the cops'd be willin' to exchange a batch of parkin' tickets an' an assault charge
for a double murderer?" . . .

Half an hour later, the Judge turned from his
front window and joined Peg Whiting on the sofa
over by the electric fan. "I'm glad you didn't watch

Poor's departure!" he said. "The police had to carry him out. He's just gone to pieces. I've seen that sort of thing happen before. His kind wilts very easily—"

He broke off as Asey and Chub entered the room. "Ah, Asey, I'm glad you've come. There's much I want explained. And I've already called my friend, Judge Mason. Thoroughly improper, of course, but I can assure you that Poor will be very effectively thwarted if, when he pulls himself together, he attempts to use his wealth or his position or his lawyers to grasp at any possible loopholes in the law. Chub, how is Monica?"

"Jennie and the maids are looking after her, Uncle That." Chub, Asey thought, still had the look of a halfback who'd been hit over the head but who nevertheless intended to play through the last minute of the fourth quarter. "She's stopped crying, and she's getting hold of herself. By the way, Asey, don't let her find out what I did to Poor, will you?"

"What *did* you do?" Peg demanded.

"Nothin'," Asey told her, "that the cops wouldn't have done to him sooner or later if he tried any of that mad-dog snarlin' on them. It was a good, solid right to the jaw, an' it sort of quieted him right down. I don't think he'd ever had a tooth knocked out before."

"Tell me," the Judge said; "what *did* you do when you flipped that handkerchief at him?"

"It's an old gambler's trick," Asey said. "If you'll look, you'll find I tied a lead sinker in the corner I held in my right hand—I got it from my pail of tackle in the car. I wondered if I couldn't harry him some by danglin' a sling in front of him, what with him bein' hot an' anxious, an', so's I wouldn't be entirely unarmed, I added the sinker; see?"

"No," Peg said, "I don't."

"You hold an end of the handkerchief in either hand; see?" Asey demonstrated. "An' then you let go with the weighted end, flip the other wrist, an' someone gets the lead smack in the face. Poor got hoist with some of his own petard."

"Asey, why *did* he kill them?" the Judge asked.

"He thought Brandt was cuttin' him out with Liss, an' he wanted to get Brandt out of the way for good," Asey said.

"He admitted it, Uncle That!" Chub added, as the Judge shook his head in disbelief. "He couldn't see any other reason why Liss continued to pose for Rudi against his wishes. It never occurred to him that she might want money!"

"D'you mean"—the Judge sounded incredulous—"that Poor was really that jealous of Rudi?"

Chub nodded. "Apparently Rudi had always goaded him, all along, ever since he got engaged to Liss. All that fuss he made about Liss's posing, and all his bickering and his pettishness, and his ranting about her running around in underwear ads— all those things that we just put down to his vanity were serious business with him. He was insanely jealous."

"I suppose," the Judge said slowly, "that there are people like that. Yes, I think I see how he might have been goaded by Rudi's casual air of sophistication. The fellow did have a certain charm—though I'm sure Poor never would have understood it."

"I don't get the rest, Asey," Chub said. "Poor was in such a gabbling state, I couldn't make head nor tail of it."

"It was sort of a variation on the old dime-novel stunt of a villain makin' a horse run away so's he could rescue the heroine," Asey said. "Poor intended to kill Rudi, implicate Liss, an' then heroically get her out of trouble. Oh, I should've got suspicious when he was so quick about suggestin' he get his lawyer to help get Liss out of possible trouble! Then, see, because he'd be the one to save her, she'd have to do what he wanted—like no more posin'— out of gratitude. That was his plan."

"How horrible!" Peg said.

"Uh-huh. But he got stung. Jennie begun gum-min' his plan up when she chased Liss away from the scene. An' Liss heard Jennie an' me talkin' in the alley of Nineteen an' a Half, an' it frightened her so much, I guess she decided to sit tight an' say nothin' at all. She didn't pour out the story to Poor an' ask for help. She only asked him to get her dress. After thinkin' things over, she went out on her own to find the murderer; but, in the meantime, the Judge ruined those plates, so there wasn't any pic-tures for the cops to find her by."

"I can't believe he meant to involve her!" the Judge said.

"He did. He just confessed it. Liss was a good shot, she was impulsive, she was on the scene. That'd be enough to start the cops questionin' her. When it came to a final showdown, Poor knew she'd get off all right, with his lawyers an' Annie's story. An' Poor thought things was workin' out fine. He was sure of it when he heard Peg tell her story in the studio. But, just before the cops bust in on us, I mentioned that someone had seen the whole busi-ness, an' after the hurly-burly of gettin' down the fire escape, Poor was a changed man. He wanted to find out who saw things, an' how much; see? I left him to go after Liss without realizin' that his panic when the cops come was real."

He paused and turned toward the door as Jennie and Mrs. Lathrop came into the living-room. Mrs. Lathrop looked years older than when he had first seen her at No. 19½, Asey thought. She was still white and shaken, but she had calmed down to a state of cold, bitter fury not unlike Chub's when he'd smacked that vicious right to Poor's jaw.

"Jennie didn't want me to get up," Mrs. Lathrop said, "but I've got to understand things. Why did he shoot Liss? *Why?*"

"That's what I want to know, too," the Judge said, as he helped her to a chair. "Why, Asey, if Poor shot Rudi to be sure of Liss, why in the world did he shoot *her?*"

"Because this mornin', after I left him, he went to his apartment," Asey said, "an' got his mornin' mail. An' in it was a letter from Liss, breakin' off their engagement."

"No!" Mrs. Lathrop said. "No!"

"Uh-huh— Look, Mrs. Lathrop; don't you want to go back an' lie down? I mean—"

"I'm perfectly all right!" Mrs. Lathrop said. "It's

better that I know about things instead of wondering about them. Why did Liss break it off? Did she get that Hollywood offer she was hoping for?"

"She did," Asey said. "You know, I kept wonderin' why she hadn't told Poor more about the jam she was in. Then I remembered the litter on the desk in her bedroom. All the sheets of stationery crumpled up an' discarded, like she'd had a hard time writin' somethin' the way she wanted it. I wondered if maybe she might have busted things off with Poor. So I broke into your house a while ago, an' those crumpled sheets was the first drafts of her letter to Poor. She'd come to the conclusion that her career was goin' to be more fun than him. Then, when I busted into Poor's apartment, I found the original he got this mornin'— Golly, that reminds me, I got to tell the cops his man's tied up there, an' they better send someone to undo him. Call 'em, will you, Chub? The feller said Poor went wild readin' his mail. An' why shouldn't he? There he'd gone an' shot his supposed rival, an' his girl had jilted him anyway!"

"Was it Poor who phoned in that funny voice?" Mrs. Lathrop sat upright.

"Yes. You were home, which he probably hadn't expected, an' he disguised his voice so's you wouldn't recognize him—" Asey stopped short and mentally kicked himself for bringing up an angle he hadn't intended to mention in front of Mrs. Lathrop.

"Then— Oh, *I* told him where she was! Oh!" Mrs. Lathrop said in anguish. "Oh, it was my fault!"

"I hope you won't reproach yourself about that," Asey said gently, "because I'm sure Poor would have killed her, no matter where he found her. Where she was wouldn't have made any difference. But, you see, you talked quick an' said somethin' to the effect that the cops would know about him. You meant you'd tell them if he didn't stop botherin' you with calls, but Poor heard you wrong. He thought you said that Liss went to the studio, an' the police would know. He thought you was insinuatin' that Liss knew who killed Rudi, an' was goin' to tell the cops; see?"

"I never seen Poor come to the studio buildin'!" Jennie said.

"You wasn't watchin' for him," Asey returned. "Nor did he see you; mercifully, he didn't recognize you in a blue dress any more'n I did. But he saw Peg an' Chub, an' hid till they left. An', when Liss come, he followed her in, an' I gather from what he said that she taunted him into a fury, an' he shot her."

"What I want to know," Jennie said, "is how he got that gun off the swan boat!"

"Chub says that he an' Peg an' Poor went back to the Garden just as the boats was startin' up," Asey said. "You seen 'em then, yourself, Jennie. Chub remembers a boatman warnin' Poor to get out of the way as they hooked a boat up to the landin'. Poor caught his heel, an' slipped, an' fell over the boat— That right, Chub?"

"Yes. It seemed a genuine fall, but that must have been when he spotted the gun and took it."

"I guess," Asey said, "he was realizin' then how haywire his plans had gone, what with the cops not mentionin' Liss, at all, but only worryin' about a bag-snatcher an' her pal."

Jennie sniffed. "Fools!" she said. "Asey, why'd he take that gun if he already had another?"

"Wa-el, by that time, he'd read Liss's letter an' probably was determined to kill her; an' when he spotted that Smith an' Wesson on the swan boat, he was smart enough to grab the opportunity of sneakin' it away. You see, he could use the Smith an' Wesson on Liss, an' leave it behind, an' it'd only be traced back to Judge Sudbury. Probably he figgered that would be a lot smarter an' safer than usin' his own spare gun, that some expert might be able to trace back to him. It ain't easy to pick up guns these days. That's why he had to make such an elaborate plan for swipin' the Judge's."

"Why'd he carry the spare gun anyway?" Jennie interrupted.

Asey shrugged. "Wa-el, he also wore both suspenders an' a belt, if you know what I mean. He planned all along to get rid of the Judge's gun, so I s'pose he wanted to have his own, too, in case he might need it."

"What about that dummy," Jennie demanded, "and Honeywell's Dressing?"

"Honeywell's Dressin' is a hair pomade that old Cap'n Porter used to use," Asey said. "Young Bill Porter sometimes uses it now, unless his wife stops him. It's made by an old barber at the Atlantic Club, an' he loves to sell it. I s'pose Poor figured it give him an air of old Boston. Anyway, when I remembered the smell an' finally placed it, I remembered Chub's tousled hair an' the Judge's flyin' locks, an' how Poor's hair was slicked back, an' how he always wore a hat. He was the only one who'd have used the stuff."

"But the fat-man dummy!" Jennie said.

"Oh, when I seen him first, he wore a green hat, but what was wrong later was that he had a visored

cap on—get it? In hot weather, anyone in dark
pants, like Poor had on, an' a white shirt an' a black
tie an' a visored cap, they're a cop. At least, they
are to you, Jennie. To Chub, they're milkmen, an'
to the Judge, they're gas-station attendants. An'—"

"And to old Annie," the Judge interrupted,
"they're cops, too! I see!"

"Just so. That visored cap was made of cardboard,
an' it folds up. Poor left it on the dummy, havin' no
further use for it, an' assumin' that people would
take it for a studio prop if they noticed it at all. It
wasn't anythin' anybody could trace to him, an' even
if anyone took the trouble to smell, there wasn't
any reason for 'em to trace the smell back to the jar
of Honeywell's on Poor's bureau!"

"How," Peg asked, "did you ever start suspecting
him?"

"Wa-el, he had the best motive for killin' Brandt.
I worried about the Judge for a while"—he grinned
at the Judge's look of indignation—"but when I
seen him outside the Lathrop's house he didn't act
much like a murderer, an' murderers don't usually
take their dogs along. Then there was the pomade.
An' I knew the feller that got the gun from Annie
knew the house layout here, an' the maid arrange-
ments, an', as Annie said, the dogs accepted him,

which is more'n they did to me! They knew he wasn't a stranger. It all run together—that cop, Jennie's cop, Chub's milkman, the Judge's gas-station man—all somebody with a visored cap."

"Hm!" Jennie said. "Now tell me, smarty, how *did* Liss pick up the gun if she didn't drop it an' no one we could see threw it?"

" 'Member the boy with the David an' Goliath sling at the Washington statue?"

"What's that?" Peg asked. "You mean a forked sling with an elastic?"

"David," Asey told her gently, "didn't have no elastic to toy with in them days. What they call a David an' Goliath sling is two pieces of string with a loop at the end of one, an' a knot at the other, attached to a pouch. The kid we saw hurled his lead soldier an' parachute up into the air by slingin' em from a pouch."

"An' that's what Poor used?" Jennie demanded.

"Nope, he used the twine we took from his coat pocket. To think," Asey said, "I *seen* that fall out on the studio floor, when he mopped his face with a handkerchief, back when he was huntin' Liss's dress! But it's the same principle, Jennie. He threaded his twine through the trigger guard of the Smith an' Wesson, put both ends of the string in his hand,

swung his arm sort of like a pitcher windin' up—
only underhand—an' then let go. An' the gun
landed just where he meant it to, at her feet, probably fifty-sixty yards away."

"But how could he aim it so it landed at her
feet?" Peg demanded.

"With a little practice you can sling pretty accurate," Asey said. "The fellers who used to heave
an' haul for bass on North Beach could sling their
leaded cod lines out an' hit a chip of driftwood on
the nose more'n two hundred feet from shore. I've
done it myself. Anyway, Poor shot Brandt—he'd
been standin' there waitin' for Brandt to make a
good target—an' then he hurled the gun at Liss's
feet an' run out to the Garden entrance an' put on
his visored cap."

"Why?" Chub asked.

"He was clever enough not to run where folks'd
see him runnin'," Asey said. "Standin' there, he was
anyone you think of when you see what seems to be
a man in uniform. You see, he expected the combination of Brandt's bein' shot an' the gun landin'
at her feet would be enough to throw Liss into a
panic. He thought she'd run out of the Garden
screamin' for the police, or for help—"

"Then why'd he stay there?" Jennie interrupted.

"If she'd run screamin' to him, she'd have recognized him right away!"

"Because he naturally expected she'd run toward Boylston Street, the short way out of the Garden, an' not all the way over to Beacon Street; see? Even if she'd taken it into her head to rush home without howlin' for the cops, she'd have cut over toward Arlington Street. You gummed up that part, Jennie. You just plumb chased her out the one entrance Poor never expected her to take. When he seen you larrupin' after her, he fired a shot—he told me he done it on impulse—to scare you off. 'Member I figgered it was somethin' like that? Anyway, then he whipped back to his apartment an' waited for Liss to yell to him for help. If anyone seen him shoot, why it would seem all right, because he was a cop, to all appearances; see?"

"Where'd you go," Jennie asked curiously, "besides the Lathrops', an' Poor's, an' the studio? Where was you the rest of the afternoon?"

"Wa-el," Asey smiled, "I got the red diary Peg took from Rudi's desk."

"*My* diary?" Peg's cheeks flamed. "Did you—you *didn't* read it! You didn't break the lock and read it!"

"Uh-huh. It was very enlightenin'," Asey said,

"an' Chub's a very lucky feller. An' maybe it'll be some small consolation to Mrs. Lathrop to know she's goin' to acquire a daughter-in-law—"

"Oh, I am glad!" Mrs. Lathrop brightened. "I'm so glad, Peg dear! Because Liss and I were so worried that Chub would take forever getting around to asking you! He's so conservative about things!"

"Then what else did you do?" Jennie demanded.

"Then," Asey said, "I went an' found out about the really interestin' part of all this. I give Poor credit for that angle. That was good."

"What're you talkin' about?" Jennie demanded.

"Wa-el, all the time everyone kept callin' Poor a tycoon, an' I got to wonderin'," Asey said, "what he was a tycoon of. I found out he owns magazines. Includin' *Fashion-Allure*. But there's no record in the *Fashion-Allure* office of any order for any cover like Rudi got that call for yesterday."

"What!" Peg said.

"That was Poor who called. Honest, that was clever of him! Because you'd assume that the editors of *Fashion-Allure* would read about Rudi's death in the papers, an' you wouldn't do anythin' more about that swan-boat cover, would you? I thought not," Asey said as Peg shook her head. "An' you wouldn't think it was funny if you didn't hear from them. In short, no one would do any checkin' up on it. See?"

"No," Peg said. "Frankly, no!"

"Poor called Rudi late yesterday; he knew about the thunderstorms as well as you. He knew the only time Rudi could possibly take any such pictures, in order to get 'em done this afternoon, would be this mornin'; see? So Poor knew that at daybreak today Rudi'd be out there on the landin' by the swan boats in a nice, empty Garden."

"D'you mean that order for that cover was a *fake?*"

"I mean that the cover an' the picture was only the means to the end of placin' Rudi where Poor wanted him. An' Liss, too. Poor admitted that he specified that Liss must be in the picture. That's why he offered such a big price—to make sure Rudi'd do it. Poor told me before they took him away that Rudi first hesitated at the order, an' then said okay. I s'pose Rudi misled you, Peg, knowin' you'd try to talk him out of usin' Liss, like Chub an' Mrs. Lathrop wanted to talk her out of it. Really, it was a smart plot. If it rained, he could call an' set another dead line for the picture. . . . Is that my roadster that cop's drivin' up to the door? Honest," Asey said, "when I went to get that sinker out of my pail, I never seen so many parkin' tags an' tire chalk marks!" Casually, he picked up the silver repeater. "Come on, Jennie. We got to get your bags at the station first."

"You're not going to rush off!" the Judge protested. "The police will need you—"

"They won't need me, Judge," Asey said. "Poor give 'em what amounted to a full confession before they took him off, an' he'll clear up any odds an' ends for 'em, all right! You see, tomorrow the Porter factory gets goin' on new big tanks, an' I got to be there. But I promised myself one last fishin' trip before I go, an', with luck, I can make the tide."

"Land's sakes, my cleanin'!" Jennie said. "I forgot my cleanin'! Well, if you're goin' to make the tide, I guess I can still get my curtains washed on time! Where's my hat?"

"And why," the Judge said, "are you walking off with my watch, Asey?"

Asey grinned. "Sorry," he said. "That was only a passin' contribution to the Swan-Boat Plot. So long!"